BLOODY DISCOVERY

Denise opened the door to the linen closet and slid the towels onto the top shelf, which was empty: bath sheets on the left, large towels on the right, hand towels and facecloths in the middle. It was very satisfying to see that shelf filled.

She checked the time. Four o'clock. Lots of time for a bath before going out to dinner.

She reached for the interior knob of the linen closet door, glancing casually in that direction as she did so . . . and somehow she knew immediately that she should not have done this. She tried to shout, No! in an effort to distract herself, to cause her head to turn quickly in another direction—

But it was too late. She had seen it.

She hissed, and clapped her hand over her mouth.

Denise couldn't scream, couldn't run, could only stand there, paralyzed, unable to look away from the bloody handprint that shrieked at her from the inside of her linen closet door. . . .

Also by L. R. Wright

———

Mother Love

A Touch of Panic

Neighbors

The Suspect

Sleep While I Sing

Love in the Temperate Zone

A Chill Rain in January

Fall From Grace

Prized Possessions

Strangers Among Us

ACTS OF MURDER

L. R. Wright

SEAL BOOKS

This edition contains the complete text
of the original hardcover edition.
NOT ONE WORD HAS BEEN OMITTED.

ACTS OF MURDER
Seal Books, a division of Random House of Canada of Limited.
Published by arrangement with Doubleday Canada

PUBLISHING HISTORY
Doubleday Canada hardcover edition published 1997
Seal Books edition published October 1998

CIP: C97-930714-7
All rights reserved.
Copyright © 1997 by L. R. Wright.
Cover art copyright © 1997 by Doug Martin.

For information address:
Doubleday Canada, a division of
Random House of Canada Limited
105 Bond Street, Toronto, Ontario M5B 1Y3

Seal Books and colophon are trademarks of
Random House of Canada Limited.

ISBN 0-7704-2782-0

This book is a work of fiction. Names, characters, places, and
incidents either are products of the author's imagination or are used
fictitiously. Any resemblance to actual events or locales or persons, living or
dead, is entirely coincidental.

Printed and bound in Canada

UNI 10 9 8 7 6 5 4

ACKNOWLEDGMENTS

The author wishes to acknowledge the information and assistance provided during the writing of this book by Brian Appleby, Elaine Ferbey, Kate Jarvis, Murray F. Macham, Renee Patterson, Kim Reilly, Warren D. Turner and, as always, by John Wright; any inaccuracies are her own.

This book is for John . . .

What we call the beginning is often the end
And to make an end is to make a beginning.
The end is where we start from.

T.S. Eliot
"Little Gidding"

AUTHOR'S NOTE

There is a Sunshine Coast, and its towns and villages are called by the names used in this book. But all the rest is fiction. The events and the characters are products of the author's imagination, and geographical and other liberties have been taken in the depiction of the town of Sechelt.

May 1985
Abbotsford, B.C.

———

Mrs. O'Hara, driving to work, reached a certain point on the road that crossed the floor of the Fraser Valley and pulled over, because from here was available one of the finest sights she knew, especially on such a day as this: it encompassed Mount Baker and its atten-dant peaks; and bumpy, low-slung green hills; and a row of poplar trees that had been there as long as she could remember, languidly sweeping the springtime sky in concert with the breeze; and herds of cattle, too. The sky was an unusually deep, radiant blue that morn-ing, royal blue, it was, a pulsating concentration of blue.

This was the second most important thing that happened to Mrs. O'Hara that day, savoring the sight of the mountains and the poplars and the sky, and the sweet scents of spring that drifted in through the car window. . . .

It was late evening and almost dark when she got home. As she pulled up in front of the house she was immediately enveloped by a stillness that was deep, fragrant, and significant. The porch light was on, spilling bright light upon the rickety staircase. Above her, stars pierced the darkness that wasn't black, but navy.

She could see no lights on inside the house, which stood tall and narrow and melancholy. Mrs. O'Hara felt an odd compassion for it at that moment and into her head came strange notions like buying it new curtains or painting its exterior, all the while knowing that camouflage wasn't the answer.

She got out of the car and closed the door—quietly, respectful of the hush of twilight—and headed across the yard. In her right hand she carried her purse and a plastic bag that contained her waitressing shoes. She was aware, as she approached the house, of the extraordinary, tender warmth of the evening.

She started up the steps, gripping the railing with her left hand, and the tiny diamond in her wedding ring glinted in the harsh light from the porch. She looked down at the steps and saw her feet, uncomfortable in dark brown pumps. She was more than halfway up the staircase when the door at the top was abruptly opened.

Mrs. O'Hara had heard nothing, had thought her husband, Tom, was out. She looked up quickly, stumbling in her shock, and her hand flew from the railing as she lost her balance. Tom was standing directly beneath the light so that from her vantage point his nose, his chin, his cheekbones flung small darting shadows upward, distorting his face, and where the light struck his pupils, she saw a glint of astonishment.

Behind him, slightly shorter than he, huddled against his back like a shadow, was a white specter with long pale hair.

Mrs. O'Hara's shoebag and her purse went flying as she grabbed wildly for the railing. Her hands brushed it, missed it, and she felt herself falling backward down the steps. She wondered if the fall might kill her, and hoped it would not hurt.

It didn't kill her, but it knocked her out. Not for long, but long enough for the specter to vanish.

**1995
SECHELT, B.C.**

ONE

—

Mrs. O'Hara nudged her old VW van along the road that led to her first house of the day, a residence several miles inland from Sechelt, out of sight of the sea. The wipers shuddered weakly across the windshield and back again and Mrs. O'Hara fiddled impatiently and unsuccessfully with the heater controls. She had wakened in a bad humor, depressed and dissatisfied, and had been tempted to grant herself a mental health day. She was a disciplined woman, however, and hadn't considered this possibility for long.

She had begun, four years earlier, when she turned sixty, to pace herself, to take on just as much work as she needed, no more, no less. She could afford to do this because her wants were few. She didn't smoke, she didn't drink. She hadn't had to give up either of these habits—she had never found them particularly interesting. The only vice that had seriously tempted her was marijuana. But Mrs. O'Hara considered extremely dangerous anything that robbed her of comprehension and control, and had firmly triumphed over her urge to smoke pot. She needed food, and books, and money with which to maintain her house and her vehicle, and an occasional amount for clothes, and that was about it. No, Mrs. O'Hara didn't worry about not having enough money to support herself.

Especially since she had only eighteen months left to

live. She would die, she knew, on or around her sixty-fifth birthday. Both her parents had done so. Mrs. O'Hara had no siblings, but if she had had a brother or a sister or two she knew that they, too, would have died when they were sixty-five. She didn't know why.

Until recently this fact had not bothered her much. It had certainly relieved her of worry about the concerns associated with growing old. Some of those concerns, however, were visiting her already—she was afflicted with arthritis, for example—and this was distressing.

As she turned off the main road onto a narrower one, pressed upon by woods that dripped rain in what Mrs. O'Hara perceived to be an excessively mournful fashion, she fretted again about the task that had to be completed in the next year and a half, despite her arthritis and her declining vigor.

Mrs. O'Hara was a tall woman, large, with long, thick gray hair and dark eyes, pouched. Her throat was wattled and her face was deeply lined, but she paid no attention to these things. She kept herself clean and presentable, and her clothes were unpretentious. Mrs. O'Hara thought herself humble, and called her pride by other names, called it self-reliance and conviction.

The rain had stopped, at least temporarily, by the time she reached the Grangers' house. She was about to pull into their driveway when she saw that Mrs. Granger's car was there. So she drove past the house and parked at the side of the road. She climbed out of her van and hauled back the side door to unload her supplies. And heard the dog barking. She had a certain amount of trepidation about this dog. She had never been an animal lover and found people who flaunted friendly, anthropomorphic relationships with dogs embarrassing.

Mrs. O'Hara stopped what she was doing and gazed thoughtfully across the top of the van at the woods on the other side of the road. It had just occurred to her that ten years ago she wouldn't have known that word, anthropomorphic, and now here it came spilling into her head, calmly and surely. She had made good use of these years, the final decade of her life. She had created a brand new existence, one that was centered, admittedly, around service to others, but one that had also tended to the critically important cleansing and refinement of her own character. She straightened, pulling her rib cage up and her shoulders back, grateful for the strength and suppleness she still possessed, and swung closed the van's side door. She picked up the pails containing her cleaning supplies and strode across the grass toward the Grangers' porch.

The dog was bounding excitedly back and forth on the cement driveway in front of Mrs. Granger's car, which was parked a few feet away from the closed door of the garage. It was barking and barking, and Mrs. O'Hara didn't know if it was barking at her or not. She didn't greet it, but threw an uneasy glance in its direction. Before she reached the porch, the door was flung open and the Grangers' teenage daughter barreled through.

"Hi, Mrs. O'Hara," she said, and turned to shout into the house. "Mom! Mrs. O'Hara's here!" She rushed past Mrs. O'Hara toward her mother's car and the dog followed, loping, continuing to bark. Mrs. O'Hara decided that it was only excited, and not potentially dangerous.

She knocked on the half-open door and while she waited she watched the two of them, the ungainly girl and the rambunctious dog. The girl was speaking loudly to the animal, as if it were deaf. Well, of course, maybe it was. But Mrs. O'Hara doubted that. Suddenly the girl raised her arm, as if to clout the dog on the side of the head. The dog flinched and reflexively sat, eyeing the girl uneasily. Perhaps the Grangers' daughter felt Mrs. O'Hara's disapproval, for she turned, then, and caught Mrs. O'Hara's eye.

"He's trained," said the girl defensively. "He just likes to pretend he isn't."

Mrs. O'Hara raised an unfriendly eyebrow. She glanced impatiently inside the house and heard a distant call: "I'll be right there!" She set down her pails with a sigh.

"Watch this," said the girl.

Mrs. O'Hara folded her arms as the girl wrestled the dog into a sitting position, his back end almost nudging the closed door of the garage.

"Stay!" she said loudly, sounding surprisingly stern, and delivered a sharp-edged gesture that Mrs. O'Hara assumed was a hand signal. The girl then turned her back on the dog, marched briskly around the car, climbed in, and fired up the engine. The dog watched, his head cocked. He waited, panting, but not barking, apparently content; Mrs. O'Hara saw no impatient quivering in him. The girl revved the motor with heartless fervor, and Mrs. O'Hara winced.

"I'm sorry to keep you waiting, Mrs. O'Hara," said Mrs. Granger, slightly breathless, appearing in the doorway.

The dog turned his head at the sound of her voice, and his tail swept congenially across the cement. Mrs. O'Hara would always remember that single languid sweep before Mrs. Granger's daughter slammed her foot down on the accelerator, flooring it.

"Jesus God!" said Mrs. Granger, her voice rising and becoming a scream, piercing the air like a swarm of mosquitoes. But she didn't move, and neither could Mrs. O'Hara, and neither did the astonished German shepherd, as Mrs. Granger's daughter Rebecca shot the car down the driveway in reverse gear, slamming the dog into the garage door.

In the next days, Mrs. O'Hara felt she had been plunged into an abattoir. Everywhere she turned, she encountered examples of man's inhumanity to animals: an upended truck on the television news, crates of chickens smashed, chicken blood running crazily along the highway, cracking thin red splits in the asphalt. A small, casual story in a magazine recounted the pilgrimage of a confused and panic-stricken deer trying to get through traffic: "Two cars were banged up when they hit the animal and three others, including a police car"—Mrs. O'Hara could hear the smile in the story— "smashed into each other during the incident. There were no human injuries. The deer's condition is not known."

The night she read this, Mrs. O'Hara sat upright in her bed trying to erase from her mind the unwelcome images that had lodged there: the deer's terrified eyes, the thumps heard as the cars struck it, the crumpling of its internal organs, their collapse, their bleeding, as the deer staggered off the highway and into the woods.

She also read about a dog-grooming establishment that was fined $500 after two dogs died there: they had been confined to a cage with an industrial blow-dryer running on a summer day when the outside temperature stood at thirty-two degrees centigrade. The veterinarian who testified at the long-delayed trial said that one of the dead dogs was still hot to the touch forty-five minutes after it had died. What would they have felt, those dogs? Mrs. O'Hara imagined herself in the hottest desert, deprived of shade and water. She felt her skin begin to crack; breathing created inconceivable pain in her lungs; every drop of moisture in her body was quickly evaporating, leaving her an agonized husk.

Mrs. O'Hara pored over newspapers, she found an abundance of horrifying television documentaries, and she wept . . . for dogs and cats abandoned on country roads; for cattle squashed together in trucks and transported for fifty-two hours without food, water, exercise, or consideration of weather, kicking and screaming in pain and terror until the trucks' steel trailers rocked; for poultry whose limbs were ripped off when they froze, alive, to tarpaulins in winter; for pigs who fell and broke their necks while being herded into trucks.

These were not matters that had engaged her attention in the past, and eventually, after several days, she emerged with considerable relief from her distressing preoccupation.

Then Mrs. O'Hara had a dream. She dreamed that she was in a familiar house. It was dusk. She prowled through the rooms, turning on no lights, looking for something, or someone, tiptoeing, moving cautiously, so as not to be discovered. But discovered by whom? The house, she knew, was empty. She moved up a staircase and along a hall and into a bedroom that, unlike the other rooms in the house, was furnished: there was a large, canopied, four-poster bed, its covers thrown back and rumpled. A stuffed chair, worn on the arms and the headrest. A faded carpet on the scuffed wooden floor. And a desk, with many drawers. Although this room was not familiar to her, Mrs. O'Hara went straight to the desk. There was light, from somewhere, and it shone directly into the widest, shallowest drawer as she slowly pulled it open.

Only one thing in the world terrified Mrs. O'Hara: snakes. She thought the bravest thing she had ever done in her life was to *not run* but to stand still on the steps of the post office in Abbotsford, as a ten-year-old girl, while a grinning boy waggled a live snake in her face, holding it by its tail as it whipped hopelessly in the air.

In the drawer was an orange and white snake. It was curled up, but as she opened the drawer it lifted its head and the first several inches of its body, gazing at her, and Mrs. O'Hara knew that it had been waiting for her.

Mrs. O'Hara found herself standing, awake, beside her bed.

When she felt calm enough, she stripped the bed, shook out the sheets and the blankets, and made it up again.

She had never dreamed about snakes before. She knew, therefore, that this was serious.

And the more she thought about her dream the clearer it became that the snake had intended her no harm, but had been of a tender, compassionate nature, and had wanted to convey to her an urgent message, which was twofold: in the contrivance of the important matters within her purview, age was not a consideration; nor was species.

TWO

Tuesday, February 14

———

Rebecca Granger studied her mirror self, seeking the sunny, optimistic sixteen-year-old she was when daydreaming, the person for whom good things waited just around the corner. She wished she could lapse into a daydream whenever she needed to. But it didn't seem to work that way—it was the daydream that snared Rebecca, not the other way around. This wasn't fair, but then hardly anything was, in Rebecca's opinion. A person just flailed away at life, not knowing what else to do, and she ended up creating confusion and disorder—and sometimes pain and grief—where she desperately wanted only calm and purpose.

In the mirror, her face looked blank and hopeless.

She also saw zits there. "Shit," she said, leaning closer.

Paula Granger tapped on her daughter's door and peeked in. "Ready for breakfast?"

"I'm not hungry," said Rebecca, turning quickly from the mirror. "But I'll have some coffee." And she followed her mother to the kitchen.

Halfway through breakfast, Rebecca's ten-year-old brother Timothy, looking up from his comic book, asked, "Can we get another dog yet?"

"No we can't," said his father wearily. "Not yet."

"Not yet. Not yet," said Simon, who was six, kicking the table leg. There was raspberry jam all over his face.

"That's what you always say, Dad. When can we, then? Huh?"

"Eat your breakfast," said his father sharply.

Paula, buttering toast, saw that Rebecca's face had become blotchy and miserable. Paula wanted to comfort her, but knew she mustn't. She offered a sympathetic smile, though, which Rebecca chose to ignore.

She was a big girl, tall and broad, with a brooding presence that Paula found occasionally stifling and always unsettling. It was perhaps as much because of this as because of the recent family tragedy that she had lately been allowed, in her father's words, "to get away with too much." This had exasperated Paula, for he had said it to her—to Paula—and not to his daughter, for whom he had a spot so soft it had turned squishy and begun to decay.

Yet she agreed. They *had* let Rebecca get away with too much. And so on this mild February no-school morning, a day so sweet with spring and sun that it had made her giddy and given her courage, she said to her daughter, "I'm afraid you can't have my car today. You'll have to walk into town. Your father will give you a ride home."

Paula braced herself . . . and as she did so, she felt a reassuring pang of empathy for the child, so thoroughly hostage to the seething of her emotions, and for the thousandth time reminded herself that Rebecca's roiling passion was strictly hormonal.

This, too, shall pass, she told herself, as Rebecca exploded with rage, erupted from the breakfast table, and stalked out of the house.

Simon watched her go, then fell on the floor in a fit of laughter.

Timothy continued to eat his cereal and read his comic book, oblivious to the commotion.

It was the last time any of them ever saw her.

•   •   •

Half an hour of walking diminished Rebecca's anger. It wasn't entirely gone, but at least it wasn't biting at her heart anymore. She began to enjoy the day, which was a lot warmer than she'd expected. And this was a good thing, since she had rushed out of the house without a jacket. It was lucky she had at least thought to grab her bum bag.

She strode along with the sun warm on her back, squinting a little—maybe she'd buy sunglasses at her lunch break; she couldn't remember what she'd done with her old ones.

There was some traffic on the highway, but not a lot. Mostly she was able to walk on the pavement itself instead of on the gravel shoulder.

She figured it would take her about an hour to get to the village, to the stationery store where she had a part-time job as a clerk. She would probably arrive early enough to have a coffee and some toast at Earl's before the shop opened. Her stomach was rumbling because her mother, the cow, had been so keen to deliver the bad news that she hadn't had the decency to wait until after breakfast. She'd forgotten, as usual, that it took a while for Rebecca to get hungry in the morning.

But never mind, she told herself. The walk would be good for her, she had to admit it. She ought to walk more, get herself in shape. And once she had the exact body she wanted, she and her best friend Holly were going to take the ferry over to Vancouver and get themselves tattooed. Rebecca thought she'd have some native art—a huge raven, maybe—tattooed on her back.

A car whizzed by very fast, over the limit by a whole lot. It came so close to her that the slice it carved out of the air fell right on top of her. Rebecca felt a tiny nibble of repentance. That's why she hadn't been allowed to have her mother's car today. She'd received three speeding tickets in the last month, and hadn't had the money to pay them, so her mother had had to, since it was her car, plus her insurance was probably going to go up.

"Shit," said Rebecca to the blue spring morning.

This particular acknowledgment of guilt caused her to remember that other thing, so much more important, so much more awful, for which she had also been responsible.

"Shit," said Rebecca again, wrapping her arms around herself, struggling not to cry.

Her mother had told her to put it behind her. "It was a dreadful thing for which you were entirely responsible," her mother had said. "This is true." She had reached toward Rebecca then and Rebecca had flinched, for some reason. She hated to think of that now. Her mother had just wanted to brush some hair out of her eyes, that was all. "And the whole family has seen how much you've suffered," her mother had said. "You mustn't keep on torturing yourself, Rebecca. It's time to put it behind you."

And she was right, too. Rebecca would start life over again, once more. This very minute.

She stopped and stretched her arms heavenward, then shoved her bum bag to the side and bent over at the waist to touch her toes. And then she resumed walking, with a lighter heart.

Rebecca walked along the edge of the highway, heading southeast, toward Sechelt. Forest huddled at the edges of the road, and beyond the trees to Rebecca's right was the ocean, sometimes visible, sometimes hidden. She walked with long, confident strides, swinging her arms, her brown hair cascading down her back in soft shiny waves. She had broad shoulders, large firm breasts, and more flesh than she wanted on her thighs and buttocks. Today she wore sneakers, tight jeans, and wide red suspenders over a long-sleeved white shirt. And she'd tied a red ribbon in her hair, to keep it from falling in her face as she stocked the shelves at work.

In her bum bag were cigarettes and a throwaway lighter;

a change purse containing a ten dollar bill, two loonies, three quarters, and four pennies; her nearly new driver's license; a few crumpled tissues; a ballpoint pen; and a hairbrush.

She was about fifteen minutes from town when a familiar vehicle passed her, slowed, and pulled up on the shoulder about fifty yards ahead.

Rebecca stopped, hesitated, then walked toward it.

THREE

When Cassandra Mitchell awakened, she felt that she really hadn't slept at all. She knew she had, though, because that was daylight out there, squeezing itself into the bedroom through the cracks between the narrow slats of the vertical blind, and the last time she'd looked, it had been night.

She heard sounds from the kitchen, and smelled coffee.

At the end of the bed the senior cat stirred and swiveled her head to glance at Cassandra. She did a long, slow, painful stretch, sat up and looked toward the doorway, back at Cassandra, toward the doorway again, and then slid off the bed and walked stiffly out of sight. Cassandra looked at the clock on her bedside table and saw that Karl had switched off the alarm. She turned on her side, hands under her cheek.

But then she sat up, plumped the pillow and leaned against it, running her hands through her short wavy hair, which was dark, but generously streaked with gray. She was wearing a T-shirt. Should she put on something different, something special, when they went to bed tonight? "Hell's bells," she said out loud. She'd lived with the man for years. She was over fifty, for heaven's sake. There was no call for black lace.

Still . . .

Alberg came in with a tray that held coffee and toast and a jar of strawberry jam. He handed it to her and climbed into bed next to her. He was wearing a bathrobe she'd given him for Christmas, made of wool, in a muted green tartan. He hardly ever put it on, preferring the white terry cloth one that was almost worn through at the elbows and in the back, where he'd been sitting on it for almost fifteen years.

"What's the occasion?" she asked him, indicating the bathrobe.

"I thought I might get married today," he said, helping himself to toast.

"I wish we'd managed to find a house first," said Cassandra gloomily.

"We will," he said.

"With closets," said Cassandra. They were making do with two gigantic wardrobes that were too big to fit into the bedroom. One stood awkwardly against a wall in the living room. The other lived out on the sunporch, where the dampness had caused its doors to swell so that they no longer closed properly. "And a couple of extra rooms," she added.

"We'll find something. And if we don't," said Alberg, "we'll find somebody to build us one. Something little. But big enough."

"Huh," said Cassandra thoughtfully. "Now there's an idea."

"So," he said, "it's happening at seven, right?"

"Right."

"We should leave then at what, six-thirty?"

"I think maybe we should get there a bit early, Karl. Let's leave at six."

"Okay. And it'll take me half an hour to shower, shave, and dress. So I'll be back here at five-thirty."

"Back here from where?"

"From work. Where do you think?"

She slammed her mug onto the tray, spilling coffee. "You're going to *work*? On your *wedding day*?"

But he was laughing. He took the tray, put it down on the floor next to the bed, and grabbed her in a hug.

"I don't mind telling you, it's a big disappointment to me," Sid Sokolowski said to Isabella. He was at his desk, which sat against the wall behind the reception counter, and he was looking gloomily down the hall toward Karl Alberg's empty office. "He should be doing this thing properly. We should be doing the red serge, the whole number."

"It's not him, though, is it?" said Isabella, peering awkwardly through half-glasses at her computer screen. "It's not his style. Subtle, that's Karl."

"Subtle. Huh." Sokolowski lifted himself out of his chair and resettled in it, causing it to creak. He had recently appropriated this chair, which was made of wood. It had arms, and this was important for a person as large as Sokolowski. It also had wheels. He liked to use it to propel himself—lugubriously, as he did most things—across the room. He did this now, pushing himself backward with his heels, heading for the coffee machine.

"Besides," said Isabella, "the dress uniform probably doesn't fit him anymore."

"There're tailors," said the sergeant stubbornly, "who could alter it. Or he could have got a new one."

"Yeah. Well, dream on," said Isabella, over the clacking of her computer keyboard.

The door opened and a stocky man of about sixty entered.

"Richard!" Isabella stood up. "No! Go away!"

"Oh jeez," Sokolowski moaned into his hands.

Richard Harbud was Isabella's recently retired husband. He had fallen into the habit of spending most of his time at the detachment, sitting on the bench in the reception area, reading the paper—not bothering anybody.

Or so he had thought. His presence bothered Sokolowski greatly. "Maybe that'll be me out there, in a few months," the sergeant had said to Alberg in dismay.

"Haunting the place." He had finally decided to leave the job at the end of the year.

"Not to worry," Alberg had told him cheerfully. "If that happens, I'll have you carted off. To a psychiatric wing. Over on the mainland somewhere."

But Sokolowski knew he'd be more likely to haunt the place in Vancouver where his wife Elsie now lived. He was going to try not to do that, though.

Isabella leaned over the counter. "We had an agreement, Richard. Tuesdays and Thursdays, an hour in the morning and an hour in the afternoon. Today is Wednesday. You are not welcome here." She touched her hair, as if still not quite used to her chic new cut, and the gold streaks that had replaced the gray.

"I was just passing by," said Richard calmly. He was wearing good pants, a sports jacket, a white shirt, and a tie. "I thought you might like to know that I've got a job."

Isabella examined him intently. "Is that a joke?" she asked finally.

"No joke," said Richard.

Sokolowski looked out, hopefully, between his fingers.

"I'm going into real estate."

Isabella sat down.

Sokolowski launched himself, one-handed, back to his desk, carefully, his eyes on the coffee mug he was carrying. He put down the coffee and stood up. "Now this is none of my business," he said to Richard, "but outta curiosity, why don't you just change your mind about retiring and go back to being a chiropractor?"

"I'm sick of being a chiropractor," said Richard, shaking his head. "I've been sick of it for years."

"Really?" said Isabella incredulously.

"Really," said her husband, looking amused.

"Why didn't you tell me?"

"What could you have done about it?" Richard sat down on the bench, pinching the creases in his pant legs between thumb and forefinger. "I have to take a course," he continued. "To get my license."

"When do you start this course?" asked Sokolowski.

"On Monday morning."

"Monday. So you're kinda at loose ends 'til then," said the sergeant, nodding. "Isabella, why don't you put the guy to work?"

"That's a distasteful idea," said Isabella, giving her hair a shake and smiling slightly.

"No, really. He can get people organized. For tonight." One enormous hand dropped to her desktop and picked up a notepad and a pen. "Make a list. Tin cans. Confetti. Whatever. And let Richard here take care of it."

"You should have let me make you an appointment with my hairdresser," said Helen Mitchell. "This is ridiculous." She was standing in the doorway to the bathroom, where Cassandra was washing her hair for the third time.

"Go iron the suit, Mom," said Cassandra. "Make yourself useful."

Alberg was on the sunporch peering at the sky, which had clouded over, and from which rain had begun to fall. Cassandra had said it was the rain that was causing her hair to go frizzy. He looked harder at the sky, although he didn't care whether it rained or not, and couldn't see that Cassandra's hair looked any wavier today than on other days.

He was thinking, now and then, about his first wedding, a formal, glittering, red serge affair. They had been so young, he and Maura. . . .

She and the accountant had sent a card, and a gift. That

was nice. It was good that she was still fond of him. And he of her.

His daughters were here: this was also good. Diana, the younger one, was staying in a local bed and breakfast. Janey and the musician had taken a room in a seaside motel.

But listening to the companionable bickering between Cassandra and Helen, Alberg suddenly missed his mother desperately, remembering her at his first wedding, standing proudly in the receiving line next to his tall, lanky father.

But that was long ago. Now his parents lay in side-by-side graves thousands of miles away.

Would he and Cassandra be buried side by side, he wondered? And where would this happen? And when? And who would be there to mourn them?

Alberg gazed out at the rain, buffeted and melancholy.

FOUR

Mrs. O'Hara, hands tight on the wheel, urged her van northward along the highway toward Pender Harbour. She realized that she shouldn't be driving, not yet.

A spasm of shuddering shook her body. She was as helpless against it as against an assault by a tornado, or an earthquake. Mrs. O'Hara felt her bones knocking within their sheaths of muscle, gripped and shaken by something inexorable, implacable.

She was in shock. This was to be expected, she told herself. But oh god. . . .

She should have been traveling in the opposite direction, toward Sechelt, and the Dyakowskis' house, but she had to go home first, clean herself—there'd been no blood, but oh god! She needed to gather herself. She knew what it meant, now—to pull oneself together. For she had come apart. Bones were at odds with muscles, brain was alienated from body. She had to bring everything back together again, recreate the natural biological harmony that made her a functioning human being.

The weather had changed dramatically: Mrs. O'Hara was hurrying through a downpour. The wipers trembled and squealed against the windshield, the heater created racket in lieu of heat, and the van shuddered in protest as she pushed the speedometer up to eight kilometers an hour.

. . . She had taken responsibility for just a tiny portion of the world: only a tiny portion. She had a recurrent image of herself flourishing a large broom, sweeping vigorously. Sometimes she saw herself in a barn. Light flooded through the expansive doorway and it was littered with the dust and hay that flew up from the floor as Mrs. O'Hara swept, with brisk, robust strokes. She swept hard and fast, coughing, her eyes watering, and she never stopped, never even slowed down. A presence that was probably the sunlight observed her activities with tranquillity and a certain amount of amusement; she detected no particular sympathy in this presence. Mrs. O'Hara swept and swept, sweating, coughing, resolute to the point of obsession, convinced that eventually the barn floor would be clean, the air in the barn pure, the sunlight immaculate. . . .

Finally the Volkswagen van reached the turnoff. There wasn't another vehicle in sight, but Mrs. O'Hara put on the turn indicator anyway before propelling the van around the corner.

For several miles she followed a rough, narrow road that led through the bush to a small lake, then pulled off under a shelter constructed of four two-by-fours and turned off the motor. The rain sounded like gunfire as it struck the shelter's tin roof.

Mrs. O'Hara climbed out of the van, leaning heavily for a moment on the door, taking a few deep breaths. She left the keys in the ignition. She wasn't worried about thieves. This was a remote part of the coast, and besides, her van wasn't much of a temptation—its body was falling apart. She kept it in excellent mechanical condition but didn't concern herself with its appearance. The mechanic who tended it fretted a lot about this. He was always wanting her to do something about the body, or the interior, but Mrs. O'Hara ignored him.

. . . Sometimes in her fantasy she saw her broom-wielding self sweeping a green meadow that was surrounded by trees, sweeping up bugs and worms and bits and pieces of grass and ferns and weeds and wildflowers. It was a ridiculous sight, and she knew that it signified Mrs. O'Hara jeering at herself: she was well aware of her own doubts and misgivings. But she had to keep the faith. She had to maintain her trust in decisions made a decade ago. . . .

She turned wearily to a path that wound steeply upward from the road, pushing through ferns and undergrowth and the lower branches of cedar trees, and she grabbed hold of this sturdy greenery, pulling on it for assistance as she made her way. Then a small structure appeared, quite suddenly, as if created by the imagination.

The exterior had been constructed of various kinds and colors of used timber. Here and there faint lettering was visible: "IM'S C" in one place, "SOLI" in another. In some places it was green, in others, orange, but most of it was brown, and all of it was faded by sun and wind and rain.

There were two tiny windows in the front, one on either side of an oversize door, thick and strong, from which two wooden steps led down to the ground. The cabin sat on four large concrete bricks, about two feet above the earth. The path led up to the door and also encircled the house, pushing through trees and bushes—mainly salal—that crowded close. Mrs. O'Hara went around to the back. The rain stroked her face and crackled in the greenery.

Behind the cabin were several small clearings, mainly outcroppings of exposed rock, but also places where undergrowth had been uprooted. In some of these clearings Mrs. O'Hara planted things each year: peas here, lettuce there, sunflowers near the house, a couple of tomato plants. In or near each clearing there was a seat of some kind. On the rockiest one, from which she could glimpse the lake, she had placed a faded, tattered deck chair, and liked to imagine, while sitting on it, the famous people who might have lounged upon it when it had perhaps graced the deck of the *Queen E*. Near another clearing she had hung a hammock between two yellow cedars: from this she would have a good view of the sunflowers when they bloomed.

The tall trees that stretched high above her little cabin moved restlessly in the high winds. When she heard them lamenting she wondered if they felt pain, tossed cruelly about by the blustering winds.

. . . They were like tempered steel, those long-ago decisions. Or rather, Mrs. O'Hara had felt like tempered steel when she made them. It was not possible to keep the planet clean, or the country. She would mark out a small piece of territory, then, and sweep. That's what she had done. That's what she was still doing. She had cheated a bit in coming to the Sunshine Coast, where the community was sheltered and small. But it was of a size that matched her quota. She had been confident, then, of meeting her quota—after all, she would have ten years. . . .

Reaching for the doorknob, she glimpsed the face of her wristwatch: yes, she would be late at the Dyakowskis, but it couldn't be helped.

Inside her small cabin, Mrs. O'Hara went directly to the bathroom. She stripped, dropped her overalls and underwear on the floor, bathed, and put on clean clothes. Then she put her soiled things in the tub and filled it with cold water.

A few minutes later she was sitting in her massive recliner, holding a mug of herbal tea in her hands, breathing deeply. She had stopped shaking. The various parts of her body were apparently working together again, compatible and cooperative.

Ten sweeps in a decade. She had thought this would be plenty of time. But now here she was only eighteen months away from the deadline and she was still three short.

A cold paleness stole across her skin. How on earth could she do it three more times in only a year and a half?

How could she find three more deserving people, in just eighteen months?

Lukewarm tea slopped from the mug onto her hand, and into her lap.

Mrs. O'Hara took the mug into the kitchen, wiped up the mess and left the cabin, heading wearily down the hillside to her van, her head full of clutter and uncertainty.

When Denise Dyakowski got home shortly after five-thirty, Mrs. O'Hara ought to have come and gone, having used the key that was snuggled onto the kitchen window ledge. But she hadn't. That is, she had come, but had not yet gone.

Denise and Ivan hadn't been invited to the wedding ceremony itself, just to the reception, which was to begin at seven-thirty. Since it was now not quite five-thirty, Denise should have had plenty of time to get ready, but she hadn't counted on Mrs. O'Hara still being there.

She pulled cautiously into the backyard, following a muddy, rutted pseudo-driveway that led between a large gap in the falling-down fence and a shed whose swaybacked roof threatened to fall in on the rusty garden implements that had been abandoned there by previous occupants. Denise's elderly Toyota bumped and bounced slowly along the track as she wondered why the hell she always insisted on parking there instead of on the street. There was no shelter for the damn car there and she had to pick her way to the back door through sticky, gloopy mud, getting her shoes more dirty than necessary. Inside the house, thanks mainly to Mrs. O'Hara, Denise's small world was clean, orderly, tranquil. But outside, it was a mess. Denise stood in the rain, hands on her hips, surveying the backyard with exasperation. But even as she looked, she was calmed.

The house was on a street off the road that led to Porpoise Bay. It was yellow, with blue shutters, and Denise thought it looked quaint, like a fairy-tale cottage. The extensive accumulation of vegetation that surrounded it enhanced this impression: laurel, broom, blackberries, and trees: several pine trees, a willow, and an arbutus whose trunk made a ninety-degree turn and grew horizontally for a foot or so before changing its mind and aiming upward again. Grass grew shaggily in the back and front yards. The brush that filled in the spaces among the trees and shrubs was today newly, shrilly green, and snowdrops, violets, and crocuses had struggled up through the long grass at the edges of the yard and next to the house. The rain fell softly on Denise and pattered tenderly in the greenery as she looked around and pronounced much of her surroundings pleasing. Sometimes enchanting.

But the mud wasn't enchanting, nor the falling-down shed, nor the rusting garden equipment. They really must prop up the shed roof, and oil the damn garden tools, and do something about the fence.

She was reminded by Mrs. O'Hara's van, parked next to the fence, of the cleaning woman's continued presence inside. She'd send her home, Denise decided, heading across the spongy grass to the front door, whether she'd finished or not, because Denise wanted to get in and out of the shower before Ivan got there. He would be late, as usual, and distracted, as usual, and in a flurry of ill-planned activity.

The smells of furniture polish and a strong cleaning agent appeased Denise and she called out cheerfully to Mrs. O'Hara, who called back to acknowledge Denise's arrival. Denise, shedding shoes and coat, heard water running in the bathtub and the flushing of the toilet. She padded into the bedroom in her stockinged feet and dropped her handbag on the bed.

"I'll be out of here in a minute," said Mrs. O'Hara.

Denise heard the squeaking of a cleaning rag on porcelain and stuck her head around the bathroom door, smiling.

She saw Mrs. O'Hara squatting next to the bathtub, slowly polishing, and was about to speak when Mrs. O'Hara suddenly sank back on her heels, gripped the edge of the tub, and lowered her head until it was resting on her hands. Anguish was sketched in the slump of her shoulders, the curve of her back, the crook of her elbows. Denise, frozen in the doorway, was appalled. She was instantly transported back in time to a day in her childhood when her grandmother had died. Her mother had received the news over the telephone, and she had slumped, just like Mrs. O'Hara, and her body had curved, just like Mrs. O'Hara's, in an instinctive but unsuccessful attempt to shield itself from pain.

Denise stepped back, out of sight. And there was silence in the house, Mrs. O'Hara motionless in the bathroom, and Denise thinking, What to do? What to do?

Then Denise moved swiftly back into the bathroom and, before Mrs. O'Hara could react, she knelt next to her and put an arm around her shoulders—broad shoulders, fleshy shoulders; they were warm, and probably sweaty, and brought to Denise's mind large roasts of beef.

"What is it, Mrs. O'Hara? What's wrong?"

Mrs. O'Hara gave her head a shake and blinked several times. Denise wondered if she wore contact lenses, or if she possessed eyesight exceptionally fine for a woman her age.

"Oh, well," said Mrs. O'Hara, in a voice so heavy with weariness that Denise doubted for a moment whether she'd ever be able to rise to her feet again. "Oh, well," she said again. "It's been a long day."

"Did you get some bad news?" said Denise, tentatively rubbing Mrs. O'Hara's back, uncertain whether this was more likely to soothe or to irritate.

Mrs. O'Hara choked out a small laugh. Denise took this as concurrence.

"I'm very tired," said Mrs. O'Hara, speaking slowly, as

if she had to push each word through a mouth filled with dust, or ashes.

Denise stood up, aware of feeling fit and slim, and took Mrs. O'Hara's elbows in her hands. "It's time you went home," she said firmly.

Mrs. O'Hara pretended for barely an instant that she wanted to protest. She pushed on the edge of the bathtub while Denise pulled gently on her elbows, and soon she was standing. She tucked some squiggles of iron gray hair back into her bun and wiped her eyes with the backs of her hands, a gesture that clutched at Denise's heart. Adjusted her denim overalls. Tugged at the wristbands of her denim shirt.

"I'll be going, then," she said. "And I owe you two hours," she added, gathering her cleaning tools, assembling her supplies.

Denise watched from the front door as Mrs. O'Hara, laden, moved across the grass and through the mud to her van. She heaved back the side door and thrust her equipment inside, closed the door, and trudged around the van. Denise couldn't see her any longer, but she waited anyway, shivering, until the motor started and the van moved off down the street.

Half an hour later she had had her shower and was standing on the bathmat, drying herself. She had opened the window slightly, to let the steam out. She noticed a crack in the paint on the bathroom wall and, frowning, reaching out to pick at it with her fingernail, flaking off white paint, revealing lime green beneath.

Denise knew only vaguely where Mrs. O'Hara lived, somewhere up the coast, near Pender Harbour, she thought. This was a long drive from Sechelt when one was exhausted. Denise wondered, what was the bad news she'd gotten this day?

She pulled her shoulders back and examined her profile, cupping her breasts with her hands, then running her palms down her sides to her waist. She was still slim but she'd definitely put on weight there, around her waist, enough to make some of her clothes uncomfortable. Exercise had been on her list of things to do for months now. No, she admitted silently, not months—years. Three years. Ever since she'd hit thirty.

She didn't know much about Mrs. O'Hara, who had been cleaning house for the Dyakowskis for the last two years or so. Well it was no wonder, she thought now, since she hardly ever saw the woman, usually only once a month when Mrs. O'Hara stayed late so Denise could pay her.

Denise, absentmindedly stroking her body and thinking about Mrs. O'Hara—she had been absolutely gray with exhaustion, her eyes black pits in a face swollen, maybe, with weeping—didn't hear Ivan's car pull up outside. But she did hear the front door open and close.

"Denise? It's me," he called out, and Denise smiled.

"I'm in here," she said, "just out of the shower."

"Okay. Me next," said Ivan. He rapped lightly on the bathroom door as he passed.

Denise looked down at her smooth belly, slightly rounded. Ivan liked to press his face against it before putting his tongue in her navel and starting to lick his way down, down. . . .

She fingered herself, and considered calling out to him. But she knew they didn't have much time. It'll keep, she thought.

And this was a moment that her brain decided to save. It plucked it free of the strands of minutiae that made up her everyday routine, strands that would have ordinarily choked this moment, inconsequential as it seemed, into oblivion. Her brain snatched this instant from the mainstream—rescued it from life's momentum—and stored it in a memory cupboard. Later, the red light above this cupboard would start flashing, and Denise, rummaging around in there, would wonder if things might have been different, if she could have altered the course of her own personal history, if she had not decided, *It'll keep*. . . .

Denise rubbed her wet hair vigorously, streaked the towel across the foggy mirror and turned on the blow dryer, fluffing her hair with her fingers as it dried, pleased with her new perm, which had given body and a certain amount of panache to her unremarkable sandy hair. She dropped the towel into the blue laundry hamper and went into the bedroom.

"Hi," she said to Ivan's back.

"Hi, hon," he replied, turning to smile at her over his shoulder as he tossed his shirt onto the bed and stepped out of his shoes.

Denise was feeling very horny. It was hard to keep her hands off Ivan, who was bent over, wearing only jockey shorts by now, selecting clean socks from the bottom drawer of his dresser. She wanted to press her crotch against his ass and slip her hands inside the front of his underwear, where he would be warm and damp and muskily fragrant.

She let him be, though, contenting herself with sideways glances filched while she burrowed in her closet for her yellow dress.

Ivan was a restless individual. Sometimes Denise saw him tremble. He might not actually physically tremble, but she saw this in him—a shuddering reaction to life, like ripples in water, or the sudden swelling of sunlight.

She relished the delicacy of his narrow waist, savored his flat stomach, craved his hairy genitals, admired his wide shoulders, and the blunt brutal thickness of his neck. She wished she could persuade him to let his hair grow longer, thick and black, so she could entwine her fingers in it. This had always been one of her fantasies: to wrap her fingers in his hair, both hands, and bring his face close, to kiss it. She could do this now, taking his head in her hands, but believed it not to be the same as gripping his hair would be.

Ivan had brown eyes and thick eyebrows, and a nose that was too small for his face. His lips were rather thin, and there was a space between his front teeth.

The only thing she didn't like about him was his table manners.

He taught school in Sechelt. Denise worked in a bank in Gibsons, fifteen miles south, doing word processing and reception. She was perfectly contented with her job, over-qualified though she was—she had left her university degrees off her résumé when she had applied for the position—and disregarded Ivan's frequent nagging that she ought to look for something more challenging, more rewarding.

With the yellow dress Denise wore a gold necklace and earrings, thigh-highs, and tan pumps, and she would carry a small tan clutch bag.

She watched the TV news while she waited for Ivan. During the commercials she glanced around the house, getting up from time to time to straighten the sisal mat in front of the door, clean some smudges from the glass-topped coffee table, wash and dry and put away a glass that stood on the counter next to the kitchen sink.

She imagined Mrs. O'Hara, tall and dense with flesh and muscle, filling the glass, draining it, refilling it, draining it again. Had someone in her family died? Surely not. Surely she would not have come to work at all, if that had been the case.

Denise and Ivan's living room contained a high-backed rocking chair with spindles and a slip seat covered with ivory silk. A love seat, wheat-colored, with several cushions, some brown, some rust. The coffee table was far too big—Denise was forever banging herself against one of its edges. A tall bookcase stood against one wall. And there was a halogen lamp, so slim and black and angular that it resembled a giant insect, hibernating in the corner. Denise, waiting, amused herself with a fantasy about the halogen lamp awakening, now that it was spring, pulling itself free of the electrical outlet, and prowling about the house.

"Hurry up, Ivan. We'll be late."

He said something Denise couldn't quite hear. She moved to the kitchen where she rested her head against the window sash and closed her eyes. Soon Ivan came around the corner, rushing, tying his tie.

"Ready, hon? Where's the gift?" he asked, looking around. But he was the one who had bought the gift, and wrapped it, so really he was talking to himself.

Denise waited, leaning against the window sash, until he'd found the present, which was on the bed, under the clothes he'd flung there.

Mrs. O'Hara would be home by now. Would she be on the phone to family or friends, sharing grief, deriving comfort?

"Okay," said Ivan. "Let's go."

Denise picked up her purse from the coffee table, and followed him out to the car.

FIVE

The tiny white church had its back to the woods, and trees grew so close to the building that they pressed against its windows. It was as if they were looking inside, curious about what went on there.

Several cars were parked on the street in front and in the clearing next to the building. To the accompaniment of organ music drifting outside, Richard Harbud and two RCMP constables were hard at work tying strings of tin cans and bunting onto a white 1994 Oldsmobile.

Inside, Alberg stood next to Cassandra, facing the minister, acutely aware of the small crowd that breathed and stirred and murmured behind him. He had insisted that only relatives and close friends be invited to the ceremony itself: Diana and Janey and the musician; Cassandra's mother; Elsie Sokolowski; Isabella and Richard Harbud; some friends and colleagues of Cassandra's. In such a small gathering Alberg had thought that he would feel his mother's absence keenly, painfully; and maybe Maura's, too, although he knew it was probably inappropriate to wish for his ex-wife's presence at his wedding—he hadn't actually invited her, of course. And now he was feeling nobody's absence, not his mother's, not Maura's, as it turned out, because the small church was crammed full of people who had come uninvited. He had thought he ought to feel indignant about this. Cassandra wasn't indignant, though—a church was a public place, she had reminded him, and they had every right to be here, especially since they had come to wish the two of them well.

Alberg took a quick glance over his shoulder and was relieved to see his daughters in the front pew. They made him think of flowers sitting there, smiling at him, dressed in flowerlike colors, moving with the grace of blossoms stirred by a summer breeze. And then Diana blew him a kiss, put a tissue up to her face and dabbed at her eyes, and Alberg turned, hurriedly, looked wonderingly at the minister. He felt Cassandra's hand brushing against his and took hold of it, tightly, not daring to look at her, trying to master the hugeness of his joy.

Helen Mitchell had been put in charge of decorating the hall for the reception, and there wasn't a streamer in sight, Alberg was relieved to note half an hour later.

The place was crowded with people. He hoped there would be enough food. But he put that worry instantly from his mind: it wasn't his problem. The only thing he and Cassandra had to do was—Jesus, the receiving line thing. Okay, he thought, as he made his way with Cassandra to the front of the hall, in response to Helen's imperious beckoning—okay, meet everybody in the receiving line, then wander around for a while, and then they could leave.

There were flowers everywhere. He hoped nobody on the invitation list suffered from allergies. There were vases of flowers on each of the tables set for dinner, on the gifts table, at the coat check—and there were banks of them where he and Cassandra were now gathered with Sid Sokolowski, his best man, and Phyllis Dempter, the matron of honor. It was ironic, Alberg observed, that both of the latter had not long ago separated from their spouses. What kind of a recommendation is that? he asked himself. What kind of support is that, for god's sake?

"Come along, now," said Helen Mitchell briskly, moving Cassandra into place, and then Alberg. His new mother-in-law's silver hair shone, her skin glowed pink, her bright eyes were shrewd but happy, today, behind her glasses. "You stand here, Phyllis. And Sid—over there. Janey? Diana? Come on, children—you're here."

"How do you know these things, Mother?" said Cassandra, sounding exasperated. "How do you know where everybody's supposed to stand?"

"I got books, dear, from your library."

Alberg nudged Sid. "So what kind of a day was it?" He had to speak loudly to be heard above the talk and laughter, and the music being played by a trio in the corner.

Sid looked at him reproachfully. "You aren't supposed to be thinking about work on your wedding day."

Alberg spotted Sid's wife Elsie in the crowd, talking animatedly to someone. Jesus, he thought, alarmed, I hope she hasn't brought a date.

"Not much happened," Sid was saying. "Drunk driver, in the middle of the damn day. Vandals broke into the drugstore and tore the place up. And we got a missing person who's probably a runaway."

People were starting to make their way down the receiving line now. Cassandra leaned close to Alberg. "Ready?"

"I resolve to be both courteous and attentive," said Alberg, smiling at her. "You smell wonderful. What is that, anyway?" But he no longer had Cassandra's attention, so he turned back to Sokolowski. "What missing person?"

"A sixteen-year-old girl," said the sergeant. "Jeez, they can be trouble. Big fight with her mom, and boom."

Alberg arranged his face in a smile and prepared to

extend his hand to a woman he'd never seen before in his life. "Do her parents know where she might have gone?"

"Everything's in hand," said Sid patiently. "Come on, Karl. Enjoy your party."

Alberg shook hands, and smiled, and accepted congratulations, and eventually he had met everyone there was to meet. Cassandra slipped her arm through his and he leaned over to kiss her, and heard a chorus of laughter and applause. Startled, he looked around him, at the smiling faces of family, friends, and co-workers, and thought how pleasant it was that they'd gotten all dressed up for this occasion.

Denise and Ivan deposited their package on the gifts table and turned to face the crowd.

This was always a bad moment for Denise. She and Ivan had gone to London for their honeymoon, at Christmastime, and one day, in an ordinary square, they were suddenly enveloped and separated by a crushing crowd of people. Denise thought there had been some kind of emergency and that everybody was panicking, but they weren't, they were just crowding each other, and there were no expressions on their faces. Denise had thought she was going to be squashed to death and her body trampled by those blank-faced Christmas shoppers, who hadn't even seen her. She couldn't breathe. She couldn't remember in which direction she and Ivan had been trying to go, and soon she stopped trying to go anywhere and concentrated on remaining upright. Eventually she was washed up against a building. She had leaned against it for a long time, breathing heavily, terrified, before Ivan finally found her.

Now she tried to take hold of his hand, but he was barreling forward to the receiving line. She took hold of the back of his jacket instead and let herself be towed.

Later, sitting at one of the tables, Denise rested her head

on his shoulder, and Ivan put an arm around her. "I don't know anybody here," she said to him. Ivan and Karl Alberg had been brought together by Alberg's occasional talks at the school, and also because their boats were moored next to each other at the marina.

He nodded and smiled at someone. "That's because you work in Gibsons," he said, giving her a squeeze. Denise cradled her hand on the back of his neck. Gently, he took it away.

She whispered in his ear, "I'm not wearing any panties."

His eyes flickered over the crowd.

She turned slightly and pressed her breasts against him. She whispered, "Let's go outside and find a place to fuck."

"Denise," said Ivan, "this is not your party." He stood up and made his way off through the crowd.

They pulled up in front of Alberg's house at the head of a parade of cars, horns honking. The neighbors next door and across the street emerged onto their porches and stood with hands on their hips, or leaned against the railing, their weight on one foot—Cassandra saw one woman drying her hands on her apron as she watched. Cassandra couldn't see their faces clearly, but she thought they were smiling.

"Christ," said Alberg, waving halfheartedly as the parade departed, still honking.

When they'd disappeared, he got out of the car and hurried around to open the door for Cassandra, before she could do it herself.

"Look at the loot!" she said, gloating at the piles of presents in the backseat.

Alberg nodded to the neighbors and began to remove the strings of tin cans, which clattered as he did so. "Christ," he muttered again.

Cassandra disappeared into the house with an armful of presents.

He got the first string off, then the second, and had started working on the bunting when Cassandra emerged. She came over to the car and stood beside him. "Karl."

"Yeah? What?" She put a hand on his sleeve. He thought her very beautiful. Light from the streetlamp allowed him to admire her wavy, mostly gray hair, her wide-set hazel eyes, and her skin like cream—yes, just like Devonshire cream. He laid a soft kiss on the corner of her mouth. "You've got great legs," he said. She was wearing a suit that had a long jacket and a very short skirt, pearls that were a wedding gift from her mother, with earrings to match, and shoes with heels high enough to make her legs look even better.

"Did I ever tell you about my Uncle Barry?" she asked.

Alberg considered this. "Is he the one who lives in New York?"

She nodded.

"Yeah. Your father's brother, right?"

She nodded again.

"What about him?"

"He died," said Cassandra. "There's a message on the machine."

"What, today?" said Alberg.

"A few days ago. But they read the will today. Karl." She leaned close to him. "He left me some money." She stood back and clasped her hands in front of her. There was a quizzical expression on her face. "*A lot* of money."

———

Mrs. O'Hara was flat on her back in the dirt when she began regaining consciousness. She struggled to fumble her way out of a gray and blurry state of mind that she found not frightening, but thoroughly bewildering. She began trying to move before she knew anything about her physical condition, which she later thought was odd: she would have expected herself to lie still and gather her wits before attempting to budge, for who knows what dangers budging might have incurred—but no, there she was flexing her limbs, urging her body upright before she was even completely conscious. She had gotten halfway into a sitting position and was leaning on her left elbow when she became fully aware of Tom, kneeling next to her.

A moaning sound burbled from his lips. He was on his knees with his hands clasped and his eyes closed, as if he was praying. And this gave Mrs. O'Hara a terrible start. For an instant she wondered if she had actually been dead for a while—then if perhaps she still was.

And that was when the pain began. A huge hurt thundered in her head, agony jabbed at her right elbow, and there was a sharp, vicious stinging in her backside. "Jesus Mary Mother of God," breathed Mrs. O'Hara.

Tom stopped his moaning, drew in a quick shudder of air and threw himself upon her, his skinny arms flailing at her shoulders. "Oh god, you're okay! Thank god you're okay!"

"I'm not okay," said Mrs. O'Hara, who had put a hand to her face to brush aside the hair that was obscuring her vision and discovered that it wasn't hair, but sticky blood. "Go get some cold cloths, Tom," she said, cautiously touching the back of her head, which seemed to be the source of the bleeding. She must have landed on her stomach, or rolled onto it, and the gash had dripped blood into her eye until Tom had turned her onto her back; now it was soaking the earth beneath her head. "Go on, Tom. Quick."

While he scrambled up the stairs and disappeared inside the house, Mrs. O'Hara finished pushing herself upright. Her hands stung, too, she noticed, and tried to examine the palms, but the light was too dim. She pressed her hands against her ears, as if to compress her head and the size of the pain in it, but to no avail.

Tom rushed down the stairs, carrying a dripping tea towel. "Where is it, where are you hurt, hon?" Then he spotted the blood flowing from her scalp. "Oh Jesus," he whimpered, and thrust the cloth at her.

"You'll have to take me to the hospital, I think," said Mrs. O'Hara. "I'm pretty sure I need some stitches."

Tom helped her stand, helped her to the car, helped her inside.

"I'm bleeding all over the damn car," said Mrs. O'Hara faintly.

Tom leapt into the driver's seat. "I'll get those steps fixed, I swear it. I'm gonna get them fixed first thing tomorrow," he said, as the car lurched out of the yard and onto the road.

"Who was there with you, Tom?" said Mrs. O'Hara, clutching the cloth to the site of her injury.

She was looking down when she said this and didn't see his face, only knew that his head took a sharp turn in her direction, briefly; then he was looking out the windshield again.

"Who was who?" he said, in a voice scratchy like on an old record.

"Whoever was with you in the house. I saw somebody standing behind you, in the doorway."

"I think you got your brain jangled a bit, hon," said Tom.

"There wasn't anybody else there. Only me. And the cat. But even the cat wasn't there, as it happens." He attempted a hearty laugh.

"You're such a terrible liar, Tom," said Mrs. O'Hara. But she was too weak to argue with him.

She rested her bleeding head against the car seat and closed her eyes, comforted by the rhythm of the car purring along the highway and by the memory of the earthy warmth on which she had awakened, the fragrances of which she had been only subconsciously aware. She was comforted by the realization of her own strength, and by the knowledge that spring lived and was present in the world again.

In the hospital, Tom sat in the waiting room while they shaved part of Mrs. O'Hara's head, cleaned her wound, and stitched it up.

He sprang to his feet as she emerged from the treatment area. Mrs. O'Hara regarded him wonderingly. He was extremely pale, although that could have been a trick of the harsh hospital lighting. His thinning hair was askew. His eyelids fluttered rapidly in a kind of an ocular stutter as he glanced at her, and away again. He was slightly hunched, and he didn't hurry over to her but stood where he was, thrusting his hands in his pockets. Mrs. O'Hara felt embarrassed, as if she were seeing him with a clarity so intimate as to be shocking to them both.

Trauma and injury, she decided, had added something to her. She didn't know what, didn't know if this something had weight, or significance, or was just a momentary thing like a shiver or a tremble or the cold prickling of gooseflesh. But she felt it as a distinct addition to her total, unknowable self.

Would things be different now, she wondered, if they had had children?

If Tom had owned a hat he would have been turning it in his hands now, she thought, watching him; he'd be turning it by the brim, around and around, he was that nervous.

What she needed, of course, was a big hug, and maybe some crying time. Tears were about the best healer Mrs. O'Hara knew of.

But she hadn't enough trust to cry in front of Tom, and his scrawny arms couldn't provide enough of a hug to comfort her.

She felt like patting him on the back. There there, she'd say to him. There there, Tom—it wasn't your fault.

And it wasn't, she thought, walking slowly, heavily toward him, cupping her right elbow protectively in her left hand, aware of the chalky bulk of the bandage on her head. She was prepared to put the whole business aside—the fall, the cut, her scraped backside, and all the bruises that had, even now, begun to stir and flower in her flesh—all this she was ready to put aside, to file away as the unfortunate accident she knew it had been.

But Tom was, in fact, a very bad liar. You had to be an extremely able liar to get away with the things Tom had tried to get away with during their years together, and it was a skill he had never acquired. And Mrs. O'Hara knew that he had lied to her tonight.

"Let's go home, Tom," she said, taking his arm.

"Did they give you pain pills?"

"They gave me a prescription."

"We can stop on the way home and get it filled. Watch your step now, hon," he said solicitously, steering her through the door and outside into the spring night.

In the car half an hour later, the drugstore bag in her lap, Mrs. O'Hara was aware of pain kept at bay by the shot she'd been given at the hospital. Take things easy for a few days, they had told her. But if she were to ask for time off from work, she would find herself scheduled for a lot fewer hours when she went back. And she couldn't afford that.

She was a big, strong woman, she told herself. She'd be okay. But what about the bandage? Maybe she could wind a scarf around her head. Pretend she'd done it in the name of fashion. Were they fashionable again, scarves?

"Who was it, Tom?" She spoke thickly, because of her tiredness.

This time he didn't even look at her. "You're crazy, hon. I told you. There was nobody there but me."

"If it was that Ron Farber, Tom, I'm gonna hang you up by your ears and starve you to death."

"I ain't seen Ron for weeks," said Tom sullenly. "Months, maybe."

They drove on, along the highway that led to the U.S. border, and the high-riding moon silvered the rows of poplars whose branches were moving restlessly in the night. Tom turned left, onto their road, and they traveled parallel to the poplars for a while. Mrs. O'Hara watched them intently. She thought they looked like gray silk, and imagined she could hear the whispering of their leaves.

"Who, then?" she asked. "What grungy scheme are you working on now, and who's in on it with you, if it isn't Ron?" She felt unutterably weary. This was obviously explained by what had happened to her. A fall—losing consciousness, however briefly—this was going to totally deplete a person, of course it was, and cause her to feel teary, too.

But she couldn't leave it alone, because she knew that she could not go through it again, could not suffer another of Tom's crazy schemes, all of them teetering on a thin line between legal and illegal, all doomed to failure and ignominy.

They drove on in silence. Mrs. O'Hara wanted to open her window, but she was starting to feel more pain in her elbow and was reluctant to encourage it with even the slightest movement. She watched Tom's profile, wielding upon it an imaginary magic crayon, creating for him a forthright chin and a sturdy nose. She considered adding, while she was at it, long sweeping lashes and a proud forehead and maybe some dark curly hair. But that would be too ridiculous. She sighed and turned away. She'd made her bed, after all. Etcetera, etcetera, etcetera.

"I'm hurt, hon," said Tom, with a quiver in his voice. "That you would think such a thing. I told you, no more funny business. And I've kept my word."

As he spoke, Mrs. O'Hara heard the disquieting ring of truth, *and was for a moment doubtful of her memory. She cast her mind back. . . .*

There she was, climbing the stairs. Her lower back ached, her feet hurt, and she badly wanted some hot tea. She had pulled at the railing with her left hand, climbed another step, let go of the railing, was about to take hold of it again when—the door opened. Suddenly. She had looked up. Stumbled. And fallen.

And just before she saw herself fall, she saw Tom, looking astonished. And alarmed, too, she thought. She saw his right arm move swiftly behind him, pressing at something, or making an attempt to conceal. And she saw, flattened against his back, the specter, the white specter, the shape that could have been Tom's shadow if it hadn't been white.

"Maybe not Ron, then, but somebody," she said, with conviction. "Somebody was there, Tom. I saw." She threw him a swift glance and winced at the swell of pain this created in her head. "Either you're up to your old damn tricks or you've got yourself another woman, Tom O'Hara. Huh," she snorted.

And then she closed her mouth on whatever she'd been about to say next and looked blankly out through the windshield. With infinite care, she retrieved the memory once again. Saw the white shape draped against Tom's back. . . .

She turned and looked at him, incredulous. "Tom?"

He peered out through the windshield. "Almost there," he muttered. "Almost home."

"Tom?"

He drove on.

SIX

Saturday, August 19

―――

"Of course it's hard, it's very hard, it's damn near impossible, sometimes," said Paula Granger to the reporter.

She was sitting on the edge of the sofa, her feet together, her hands twisting in her lap. She blinked frequently, in an exaggerated fashion and it looked to the reporter deliberately, as if she were deciding to blink and then doing it. The reporter, whose name was Cindi Webster, thought this must be distracting for her, if not actually painful.

"But you go on. You do the things you have to do," said Paula, "you make meals and do the laundry and vacuum the rugs and have baths. . . ." The reporter was nodding sympathetically but she wasn't writing anything down. There was a stenographer's notebook in her lap and a ballpoint pen in her hand, but she wasn't writing anything down. Sometimes she tucked her hair behind her ears and when she lifted her hand Paula would think, now she's going to take a note. But she never did, she just listened, and nodded. Paula didn't understand this. Was nothing she was saying worth writing down? What was the girl doing here, if not to put Paula's pain in her notebook?

"You have other children," said Cindi. "Where are they this afternoon?"

Paula frowned. "Why do you ask me that?"

Cindi blushed. A wave of redness crept up from her

cleavage to claim her throat, chin, cheeks, and then forehead. Paula watched this, pleased. Then she relented.

"The boys are out with their father," she said.

"I'd like to talk to them, too, if—"

"No no. No. They don't want to talk to you. Neither does my husband."

"But they must miss her—"

"Of course they miss her. That doesn't mean they want to talk about her all the time. Only I want to talk about her all the time. It's only me who's afraid—" She felt tears spilling from her eyes, and, boy, she thought, it's a marvel, the way the body cannot use them all up, just keeps on making more and more tears. She blamed her body for the state she was in. If it would just stop making the damn tears, Paula would stop crying. And then what? she thought. Would Rebecca come home, if Paula stopped crying for her?

"Excuse me," she said, and left the room, went into the bathroom to rinse her face, blow her nose, and take a couple of good, big breaths.

When she returned to the living room, Cindi was looking at photographs hanging on the wall. "This is so nice," she said, pointing. In the picture, Rebecca sat on a tree stump in the Grangers' backyard, laughing, her arm flung around a German shepherd who was sitting next to her and who also seemed to be laughing. "He must miss her, too," said Cindi. "The dog."

"He's dead," said Paula flatly. She looked more closely at the photograph, reaching out with her index finger to touch the glass. "Poor Hannibal."

"I'm sorry," murmured the reporter.

"It was an accident," said Paula. She put her hand over her mouth and shook her head, still looking at the photo. "She put the car in the wrong gear." She turned to Cindi, her eyes so bright with tears she looked demented, and Cindi felt a sudden flush of fear. "He didn't move. And when he did move, it was too late." Tears spilled again, glistening on her cheeks. "It's time for you to go now," she said abruptly.

"I'm sorry," Cindi said again, awkward and miserable.

"This wasn't a good idea." Paula opened the front door. She watched the girl try to argue with her, but didn't hear anything she said; she just waited. I'm good at that, she said to herself, I've gotten good at waiting.

Cindi looked bewildered. Paula knew she had thought she had a fine story here, a nice little feature, a six-month update, with maybe some pictures to complement the one of Rebecca the paper had on file. Paula had made her leave her camera in her car, though. The girl walked slowly toward the door, then outside onto the front steps.

She stretched out her hand. It was strong and unlined, the fingernails manicured but not polished. Paula took it. "I'm very sorry," said Cindi. "I hope very much that you hear from her soon."

Paula heard a cry. It might have come from a small animal caught in a trap. But it had come from her.

Cindi put her arms around her. "I'm so sorry."

Paula let herself be held. She permitted herself for those seconds to let go of something, and realized when she did so the extent of her exhaustion.

She withdrew from the young woman's embrace, her head averted, and saw crimson petals from the dahlias disappearing on the wind.

Paula went into the house and closed the door.

An hour later, Larry came home with the boys, who turned on the television and flopped down on the living room floor.

In the kitchen Larry saw the birthday cake sitting on the counter. He knew there were gifts, too, in Rebecca's room, on the bed. He wondered if things would be easier once this day, Rebecca's seventeenth birthday, was over. But no.

There'd be Thanksgiving in a couple of months, and then Christmas, and then, god help them, Valentine's Day.

He wanted to embrace his wife, but knew that she would be rigid in his arms. He didn't want to feel that again, not today. He had to be strong indeed to embrace Paula now, strong enough to accept her rejection of him.

He went down the hall into their bedroom and lay on the bed. His pain had become part of him, it had saturated his blood and his marrow—he thought of it as a kind of cancer that was killing him, and Paula, too. He knew about the five stages of coping with death. Paula was still in the first stage: denial. Larry was in the fourth stage: depression. Did this mean that he loved Rebecca less?

"We've done all we can," he'd shouted at Paula last night, holding her tightly by the arms, forcing her to look at him, or at least to see him. . . .

The bedroom door opened, and Paula was standing there. Larry took one look at her face and he was on his feet. "What?"

She said, hoarsely, "There's a police car."

Larry put his arm around her, gripping her shoulder.

They went into the living room and faced the front door.

The boys glanced over their shoulders at their parents, then scrambled up. Timothy looked out the window, then quickly at his mother and father.

"What's the matter?" said Simon, in a small, timorous voice.

With his arm still around Paula's shoulders, Larry went to the door and opened it. He searched Sid Sokolowski's face, wanting to know, to learn, without hearing it.

The sergeant took off his cap and put it under his arm. "I am very sorry to inform you," he said, "that we have found what we believe to be the body of your daughter."

Larry Granger crumpled against the edge of the door. "No," he said. "No. No."

The boys began to cry.

"I'm afraid," said Sokolowski miserably to Paula, "that we'll need you to identify some objects."

Paula looked beyond him at the brown grass, the cedar trees that encircled the house, the hot blue sky. Objects. Red suspenders? The narrow red ribbon from her hair?

"I knew it," she said dully to Sid Sokolowski, "when I saw the dahlia petals. Flying."

1996
SECHELT, B.C.

SEVEN

Sunday, March 24

It was as warm as a summer day. Cassandra picked up her mother at Shady Acres in the late morning and brought her to the house, where the three of them were to spend the afternoon packing.

Cassandra kept a sharp eye on Helen, who tired quickly these days, and they hadn't been working long when she said to her, "Let's get a glass of fizzy water and sit outside for a while."

Helen put down the book she'd been about to add to a box that was almost full. "Put some lemon in mine, please."

At Cassandra's insistence Helen took the chaise, even though she complained that she had to struggle to get out of it. She fished prescription sunglasses and a package of pocket Kleenex from her handbag, and put the tissues next to her glass, on the white plastic table that sat between the chaise and Cassandra's deck chair.

The warmth of the day was deep and strange. To Cassandra, fanning herself with her hand, it suggested bougainvillaea and hibiscus, instead of the daffodils that were sunning themselves against the fence. She was wearing shorts and a T-shirt hastily dragged from a carton marked "SUMMER CLOTHES" and the whiteness of her bare legs was blinding.

Cassandra's mind wandered frequently to her inheritance.

It had provided her with a new and unexpected confidence. But what did this say about her, that it had taken money to bolster her confidence? She tried not to dwell on it.

But the will hadn't explained why her uncle had made her his beneficiary, and until Cassandra had figured this out, she thought she probably wouldn't be able to bring herself to actually spend any of the money anyway.

"I barely remember him," she had said to her mother, when she got the news.

"I guess he remembered you," her mother had replied dryly.

"Uncle Barry reminded me of Fred Astaire," she said to Helen now. She recalled him as a man constructed of angles. In her mind he stood with arms lifted at the elbows, and legs bent sideways at the knees, his head lolling to one side: she remembered him as a puppet, slack at one moment, springing jerkily to life at the next.

"Ridiculous," said Helen. Cassandra noticed that she flushed as she scoffed.

"Well, you tell me, then," she said. "Tell me how you remember him."

Helen hunted in her handbag until she found a small black and white photo, which she handed to Cassandra.

He was looking directly at the camera with an air of tolerance. Much younger than Cassandra had ever known him. Wearing a shirt with the top button undone. Short dark hair, ears that stuck out, a funny little smile. "Hmmm," said Cassandra.

"I took that," said her mother. "In 1937."

Cassandra heard this, idly, like she heard the car passing along the street in front of the house, and the breeze that rustled in the leaves of the lilac . . . but then she focused on it. "Before you were married," she said.

"Of course," said her mother. "We were neighbors. His

family lived down the street from us. You knew this, Cassandra. I'd known them both, Barry and your father, for years."

"I always thought he was gay," said Cassandra, gazing at the photo.

Her mother looked shocked. Then she laughed.

"Well?" said Cassandra.

"Well what?" Helen turned her sunglasses toward her daughter. "No," she said finally. "He wasn't gay."

"But he never got married."

"I think he was married, once. For a while. Not for long."

"Mother. Do I sense a certain smugness in your tone?"

"I certainly hope not."

Cassandra felt light dawning. "Mother. Was my Uncle Barry in love with you?"

Helen sipped her mineral water. "That, my dear, is none of your business."

Cassandra put down the photo and sat back in the deck chair, studying her mother cautiously. "Mom, is there something you ought to be telling me?"

"If there were," said Helen, sliding the photograph back into her purse, "I would. If there is," she said quickly, cutting into Cassandra's protest, "if there is," she repeated, leaning slightly closer to her daughter, "I will."

Cassandra nodded, slowly.

"Now," said Helen briskly. "Tell me what you're going to do with your newfound riches."

Cassandra sighed and picked up her glass. "Oh. I haven't made up my mind yet." She took a long drink and looked at what was left in the glass, wanting more, but not wanting to get up to go get it.

"You've had the money for six months now," said her mother. "What are you waiting for?"

"Oh, it's complicated," said Cassandra halfheartedly. "Very complicated. It feels complicated, anyway."

"Hey," said Alberg, from the sunporch. "Have you two packed it in for the day, or what?"

"Come on out here, Karl," said Helen. "Tell me what Cassandra's going to do with her money."

He reached behind him for the can of beer he'd just opened and went outside, letting the screen door bang shut behind him. He sat on an ancient lawn chair that squeaked a protest. "I don't know what she's going to do with it." He glanced at Cassandra, sprawled in her chair. "She says maybe she'll quit the library and start a business."

Cassandra felt like smiling every time she looked at him. It really did make a difference, being legitimately wedded to a person. She wanted to smooth his slightly rumpled fair hair, touch the planes of his face, and close his eyelids with her fingertips. He'd lost weight, she noticed with ridiculous pride, and she loved the way he moved, with a lumbering assurance.

"I'm not going to start one," said Cassandra. "I'm thinking about buying one that's already started." And she giggled.

"Earl's, maybe," said Alberg to Helen. "Earl's threatening to sell."

"Earl's," Helen repeated, with aversion. Then, "At least if Cassandra ran that place," she said, "it would be clean."

"Or else the bookstore," said Alberg. "She's heard that the Olivettis want to retire."

"The bookstore," said Helen. "Of course. Excellent." She looked approvingly at Alberg, as if it had been his idea.

Cassandra giggled again. Her mother shot her an irritated look. "It's because I'm nervous," Cassandra explained. She sat up. "It's a big responsibility," she said solemnly, "having all that money."

"Give me a break," said Alberg, drinking his beer.

EIGHT

Monday, March 25

The following morning Alberg gazed across his desk at Sid Sokolowski's replacement. He had been short-handed for three months. Yet it was with mixed feelings that he regarded his new sergeant, who had an open, friendly smile and was apparently relaxed, sitting there with legs crossed, looking around his office with unconcealed interest now that they'd gone through the preliminaries: Alberg had described the community and the detachment; outlined the duties of his second-in-command; and brought the sergeant up to date on current cases.

"You found a place to live, did you?" he asked pleasantly. His office window was pushed open as far as it would go, and he heard birds outside. It seemed an incongruous sound.

"Yes, thank you, Staff. Came up a month or so ago and looked at houses, and got moved in last weekend."

She was called Edwina Henderson. The joker at the Puzzle Palace who had first brought up her name referred to her as Eddie, and talked his way carefully through their conversation, so as never to have to use a pronoun. Then her sheet arrived. Six feet one inch tall, one hundred and fifty pounds, thirteen years on the force, unmarried, female. The joker would have enjoyed this moment, Alberg had thought, experiencing the shock the joker had anticipated.

He had nothing against female sergeants. He just hadn't expected to get one. He had nothing against female staff sergeants, for that matter. Inspectors. Superintendents. Whatever. He appreciated fully the unique attributes of members like Norah Gibbons. Constable Gibbons would make a good sergeant someday, he thought, eyeing Eddie Henderson.

She had wide blue eyes, prominent cheekbones, a generous mouth, and a single thick braid of yellow hair that fell to the collar of her shirt.

Alberg felt slightly muddled. He looked down at her file. An excellent record, including two commendations. She came to Sechelt from Burnaby, which was an urban posting, part of the Greater Vancouver Regional District. It was a promotion. Next thing—eventually—she'd probably have her own detachment. Unless she wanted a GIS posting somewhere—the detective side of things. How old was she? Thirty-five.

Jesus, thought Alberg. I've been around too long . . . but it wasn't a thought, really. More like a nostalgic feeling that drifted, unbidden, into his head as he looked at this woman, bright, gorgeous. He'd bet that she possessed a great deal of completely realizable ambition.

"You were going to tell me about open cases," she reminded him.

"There's really only one," said Alberg. "There are some we haven't closed, but we know who we're after. But there's this homicide. We haven't made a goddamn bit of headway. And it's a year old now."

Alberg felt that he shouldn't have left town, once Rebecca Granger's parents had reported her missing. At the time, she had been considered more truant than missing. But she hadn't turned up for work that morning, and this was uncharacteristic. And Alberg couldn't help but reflect that if he'd stayed on the job instead of buggering off on his honeymoon, things might have turned out differently. Which he knew was not only arrogant, but illogical.

"Rebecca Granger," he said dispassionately to his new sergeant. "That was the victim's name. She was sixteen years old. She left her house at 8:30 on the morning of Tuesday, February 14, last year. And that was it."

He had been over and over the investigation undertaken at the time and could find no fault with the way Sid Sokolowski had handled it: the search was meticulous, the interviews as thorough as Alberg could have wished. He knew he couldn't have done any better.

"Her body was found six months later," he said. "Buried in a clearing north of here. Between the highway and the sea."

Still, it rankled. It continued to rankle. It was the only homicide still on the books, and it bugged the hell out of him.

"Do you mind if I take a look at the file?" asked Eddie.

"Mind? I expect you to take a look at it, of course. And every other file in the place as well." He looked across the desk at her and smiled. "Let's go introduce you to the troops."

They stood up, and yeah, he thought, she was six one, all right. When he looked at her he looked straight across, not a whisker of an inch down.

He preceded her down the hall to the reception area, where Isabella was peering over her half-glasses at the computer screen. Draped over her shoulders was a thick gray and white sweater that sported a pattern of Canada geese in full flight. Beneath it, Isabella wore black slacks and an orange silk T-shirt.

"Isabella."

"Yo," she said, looking up, which caused her gold and brown hair to swish, gently.

"Have you met Sergeant Henderson?"

Eddie stretched out her hand, smiling. "Hello." Her hand was large and square, with short nails. She wore no rings.

"Hi," said Isabella, giving Eddie an appraising glance. "Welcome."

"Thanks."

"Okay, over here, now," said Alberg, leading the way behind the counter to the table against the wall that had been Sid Sokolowski's turf. "There's office space down the hall, between me and the exit to the parking lot, or you can take this here. It's up to you. And this is Constable Mondini. Ralph, come and meet your new sergeant."

Alberg felt falsely hearty, and imagined that Ralph and Isabella were glancing at him with curiosity and amusement; and god only knew what was going through the new sergeant's head.

"Come on, Mondini, get the hell over here," he said, gesturing fiercely. The constable got up so fast he tripped, and had to grab the edge of the reception desk to prevent himself from falling. "This is Sergeant Henderson," said Alberg, reaching out to steady him.

"Hi," said Eddie, grasping his hand and giving him a brilliant smile.

What the hell had Mondini done to deserve that kind of a smile? Alberg wondered irritably.

"When you finish the tour," said Isabella, stretching, "get Ralph here to take you over to Earl's for coffee. It's a good place to observe the civilians."

Alberg looked at her coldly. He had planned to do that himself. "Come on, Sergeant," he said. "Let's go take a look at what passes for the locker room."

As he strode down the hall with Eddie Henderson at his heels she called out, "I think I'll take the desk behind Isabella's. I like to be in the middle of things."

Alberg nursed his mood of incivility and complaint but

it was too weak, and he soon succumbed. He decided that he liked the fact that she was tall and strong. He decided that she had a friendly, ingenuous quality that could be perceived as pleasant. He expected that she would also turn out to be smart, and decided that he could live with this.

He walked her through the detachment, watching her shake hands, smile, and file away first and last names with rank. He observed that she ignored Cornie Friesen's blank, judgmental stare with as much aplomb as she disregarded the covertly lascivious inspection of Constable Joey Lattimer. And welcomed with her wide, confident smile greetings of genuine friendliness from Norah Gibbons and Frank Turner. And kept her body relaxed and her mind alert through the ordeal of being a newcomer.

Alberg, who was familiar with the difficulties often faced by female officers, wondered what experiences Eddie Henderson had had; what moments of embarrassment, rejection and unpleasantness might have littered her thirteen years on the Force. Had she ever lain awake at night, struggling against an urge to give up, to resign? How important a role had pride and image played in her decision to tough it out?

He was pretty sure he'd never ask her.

Susan Atkinson had wakened that morning slowly, easily—early. She reached over to turn on the radio, tucked her hands under her head, and smiled at the ceiling. A few minutes later she stretched under the covers, pointing her toes, reaching high with wide-apart fingers. She was thoroughly savoring spring break, and the end of the longest stretch of the teaching year.

She had decided for once not to program her days off. She was keeping them unstructured, uncluttered, so that she could spend time at a moment's notice with her lover. But even so, she had mentally composed a list of things she wished to accomplish during her precious days off. Lying in bed, she reminded herself that she must order hanging baskets from the nursery for her balcony; give the apartment a thorough cleaning; return that pile of books to the library; and make a dental appointment, too. And do some preliminary looking around for a new car. And replace her portable telephone, which was broken.

Consequently, her mind was pleasantly, purposefully cluttered as she glanced at the clock and threw back the bedclothes, but she knew that she would drop any plan, set aside any good intention, if her lover had a better idea.

She went into the kitchen and opened the fridge. And as she stood there, examining its meager contents, Susan had a thought that was completely alien to her. It sprang into her head uninvited, and unwelcome.

She let the fridge door close, lowered herself onto a kitchen chair, and experienced an extremely sobering moment. She considered, within it, a myriad of choices, including quitting her job and moving away, instantly, that very day: this was for a while quite the most appealing alternative that presented itself.

She got up, crossed to the sliding door, and let herself out onto the balcony, which faced west. She pulled her robe tightly around her and leaned out, looking down at the gravel shore. A man with a cane and white hair to his shoulders walked slowly along, accompanied by a blond shorthaired dog that was somewhat overweight; otherwise, the beach was empty. Susan rested her forearms on the balcony railing and gazed across Trail Bay, its winkled surface glinting in the early morning sun.

She had not believed that this would happen. She had assured her lover that it wouldn't, confidently telling him: "I'm only interested in your body, sweets," laughing, pressing him close to her. And she had meant it. But looking into her fridge, at the almost empty shelves there, she had felt an instant of impatience: she had thought, When is he going to leave her, for god's sake?

It was the kind of unguarded, utterly revealing moment from which there was no retreat. She could pretend it hadn't happened, but that would become increasingly painful, because she was a person who tried to live honestly.

He would have an advantage over her now, she realized, even though he wouldn't know it. She would be vulnerable to all kinds of crap, now that she had exposed herself as having serious intentions toward him.

Susan shivered and went back inside. She had absolutely no interest in breakfast now.

She was already thinking about him differently. Instead of wondering *when* he would call, she was wondering *if* he would call. Instead of figuring out what would be the best way for her to get in touch with him if he *didn't* call, she had already decided that she couldn't possibly *get* in touch with him—this would be indicative of infatuation, and she didn't want him to think of her as infatuated.

Damn! Why had she had to open the damn fridge door?

She didn't even feel like drinking coffee now.

In the bathroom she showered and dressed. She had for the moment even lost confidence in her body, in its ability to lure him, seduce him, satisfy him. She observed with dissatisfaction her broad shoulders and muscular thighs, the width of her hips, her stout neck, her strong capable hands. Her hair was wet and sleek from the shower and she thought she looked like a sea creature, robust and sturdy, an excellent swimmer, which in fact she was.

It wasn't as if she wanted to be married to him herself. She was almost certain that she didn't. She just all of a sudden didn't want him to be married to anybody else. She considered this as she stepped into a pair of cotton underpants. She was confused. She attempted to apply logic, meticulously, as she pulled on pantyhose, buttoned her shirt, stepped into a skirt and flat shoes. She dragged a comb through her short, damp hair, fluffing it with her fingers. It would fall into soft waves as it dried. Her hair was Susan's best feature and she was grateful for it, but wished that her eyes were a darker blue, and larger, and thought she would probably have plastic surgery someday to reduce the size of her nose.

But this was ridiculous, she told herself crossly. She had a perfectly serviceable face, a strong, trustworthy body, and a healthily libidinous nature that gave her much pleasure. Also, a job that she enjoyed and that was actually worth doing. And if she had a biological clock, at thirty-five she hadn't yet become aware of it.

She went back into the living room and looked out through the glass doors at the unruffled sea. No, she definitely didn't want to marry him. She didn't even want to live with him. Much as she loved being with him, she was always glad when he left, always turned back contentedly to the comfort of her apartment, her books, her balcony.

What, then, did this signify, this flash of impatience, her treacherous ego making this mean little display—"When is he going to leave her?" As if he had ever said he would. As if Susan had ever wanted him to. But apparently she did want him to, now.

Susan looked at the telephone, wondering how she would feel when next he called, allowing herself to imagine for a moment that his voice would wipe all this extraneous shit from her mind; that at the sound of Ivan Dyakowski's voice she would laugh with relief and be right back where she was yesterday, or first thing today, or just before she opened the damn fridge.

•   •   •

It was five o'clock in the afternoon when Janet Maine locked the door of the lawyer's office where she worked as a secretary and set off up the street. She wore a plaid skirt, a red sweater, and a navy blazer, with thick cotton socks over her pantyhose and sneakers on her feet—gray, with purple stripes along the sides. Her shoulder bag was slung across her body and she carried a plastic bag containing a pair of navy pumps. She was on her way home, to a townhouse in a complex that had recently been carved out of the forest that blanketed the hillside outside the village.

She lived there with her husband Andrew, who was twenty-five. Andrew worked in a men's clothing store. They had only one car, and although there was a bus system in place on the Sunshine Coast the service was not frequent, so that when Andrew had to work late at the store, which happened several times a week, Janet sometimes stayed at the office, getting caught up; or had dinner with Clara Mulholland, who worked for the doctor in the office next door; or, if she had remembered to bring the proper shoes and socks to work in the morning, she might walk home. It wasn't far—only a couple of miles.

Janet wasn't in the mood to do extra work tonight. In fact, she had left work early, which was fine with her boss, because of the days she voluntarily stayed late.

She would heat up some soup, she decided, walking quickly through town, and make some whole wheat toast, and eat her dinner while mulling over the situation with Andrew. Maybe she'd call her mother—talk about it with somebody sympathetic.

She strode along the edge of the highway, glimpsing the sea from time to time, through trees and underbrush already thick with new growth.

It was old news she had given Andrew, after all, events from the first year of their marriage. Old news and not relevant. Yet she must have decided that it was relevant, for she had decided she had to tell him, hadn't she? What a big mistake that had been. There were definitely times when confession was not good for the soul, neither the confessee's nor the confessor's.

He had tried at first to pretend that it didn't bother him. But she could see the untruth of this in his face, of course. Andrew's face always revealed absolutely everything that was going on inside his head.

"I'm just telling you, Andrew," she had said—last Friday morning, it had been—"so as to get it out of the way, because I think it's time now that we had a baby." And she had reached across the breakfast table to give his unresponsive hand a squeeze.

Now, days later, he was still unresponsive. Andrew needed time to absorb important things. This was obviously considerably more important to him than Janet had anticipated.

She glanced left and right, crossed the highway, and headed uphill on a newly paved road with forest on both sides.

Andrew was the happy one, the optimistic one. She depended on him for this, and was being made increasingly uneasy by his uncharacteristic gloom.

And impatient, too. Janet wanted to have two children, one right after another, getting all the childbearing stuff over with as quickly as possible, and she was ready to start now. At twenty-eight, she still had lots of time—but she had decided to go back to school to become a lawyer, and knew that if she put off motherhood until that had been accomplished, it might never happen at all.

She hadn't told Andrew about law school yet. But she was confident that he would be thrilled, and proud of her, as usual.

She stopped and gave a quick sigh, looking across the tops of the trees to the moving sea, softly blue and gray.

She should have told him about it at the time. He was right, it had been his decision, too. Not as much his as hers (although they disagreed profoundly about that), but certainly he had deserved to know. And she had deliberately withheld it from him.

The sunlight was filtered through wispy layers of clouds and Janet couldn't see the horizon, only the sea, and occasional winkings of sun on the water. She turned and resumed walking.

The only problem with her becoming a lawyer was that it might accentuate their differences, and maybe create a chasm between them. She was a lot smarter—intellectually—than Andrew. They both knew this. Andrew was good-natured about it and Janet tried hard not to let it bother her, and most of the time it didn't. She had never met anyone, before Andrew, who was genuinely, consistently happy, and his happiness was more seductive than she could have imagined. Although the sex between them was pretty good, too.

Janet reached the top of the hill and the end of this stretch of forest. Here the land had been cleared for more development. She could continue walking along the road, or cut across the newly cleared area. She stopped to consider, poking her toe into the earth to see how wet it was. It wasn't very wet at all, so she struck out across the clearing, which was about the size of a square city block, keeping her eye on the ground so as not to stumble over rocks or branches or the ruts left by bulldozers.

The only thing that bothered her about Andrew's limited intellectual powers was whether this might be passed on to their children. But surely it was just as likely that they would inherit his ability to find life joyful, she thought, glancing up from the ground to check her bearings: once she reached the other side of the clearing, she'd have about half a mile to go, up an old logging road that paralleled the clear-

ing and then zigzagged up the hillside behind the complex
where she lived.

Before there could be children, though, or law school,
Janet had to coax Andrew out of his depression. She had to
persuade him to trust her again.

She stopped walking. She heard an engine in the distance. She looked up at the sky, aware of the absence of
birdsong, and saw that the clouds were thickening. But she
had lots of time to get home before it started to rain.

She missed Andrew's cheerfulness, the frequent affectionate manifestations of his love: evening baths drawn for
her and perfumed; morning coffee brought to her in bed;
phone calls at work just to tell her that he missed her; flowers. . . .

She had tried wheedling, persuasion, seduction—he had
rebuffed her every time, kindly, patiently, but firmly.

"I have to think, Janet," was all he'd said. "I need to
think about this thing."

It was possible, she thought, that she might not be able
to bring him around. It was possible that Andrew would not
trust her ever again. And what then? she wondered, sudden
panic clotting her chest. What then?

She heard the motor again, and in her peripheral vision
saw a vehicle disappear up the logging road that would take
her home.

NINE

Alberg stood in front of his house, trying to see it through the eyes of a prospective buyer. Small, but neat. Freshly painted. Looking good. Eavestroughs only a couple of years old. The front porch was new, too, and the fences, front and back. And the sunporch had been repaired. There was a little brick patio now, and a raised bed in the southwest corner of the yard where Cassandra planted vegetables.

It had been on the market for only a few days and Alberg was hoping for a quick sale: the house they were building was almost finished. He was determined not to drop the price below fair market value, however, even though they didn't need to get as much for it now because of Cassandra's windfall.

Alberg liked to walk around the place, feeling proprietory, but he wasn't about to do this today because Peter's truck was there. Alberg didn't pay much attention to the things that grew in his yard—he never had, except when greenery of various kinds had threatened to invade the house. Cassandra took care of the garden. With Peter's help. Alberg often came home to find this dreamy, rotund person standing in his yard, leaning on a rake. Alberg didn't know his last name. He thought Peter was perhaps besotted with Cassandra, who assured Alberg that Peter did good work at a reasonable rate of pay. He had made her acquaintance while looking in the library for books about needlework.

He was there today, raking the lawn. Alberg gave him a brief but courteous greeting and hurried inside.

They had almost finished packing, which Alberg found encouraging. But every time he looked at the colossal wardrobes he became more claustrophobic.

Their new house wasn't on the water. It was on a hill. Maybe he would drive over there after dinner and walk the site, something he did rather frequently. He was a little worried, though, because he thought he surveyed the new house with less enthusiasm these days, and he hadn't figured out why.

He looked in the fridge: he'd make dinner, eventually. Thaw some ground beef, make one of his special meat loafs, and some mashed potatoes. There were green beans in the freezer. And he'd open a bottle of red wine.

He looked at his watch. Six o'clock. Cassandra ought to be home by now. He called her at the library.

"My new sergeant," he told her, "she's as tall as I am."

"She?"

"Didn't I tell you? I must have told you. You don't listen to me these days, Cassandra," he said. "Are you coming home for dinner?"

"Of course I am."

"When?"

"Oh—soon."

"How soon?"

"Give me an hour?"

"Sure."

He walked restlessly from room to room, edging past the wardrobe, stepping over packing boxes—and was suddenly reminded of Sid Sokolowski's retirement party, back in December. He hadn't realized how many personal possessions Sid had kept secreted away in various detachment cupboards until he'd watched the sergeant retrieve them and pack them in boxes: photographs of Elsie and their five daughters, of course, several coffee mugs, a few books, but also a collection of paperweights, some fishing tackle, a cushion with a knitted cover, a couple of flower vases—Alberg was amazed.

They had helped him load the boxes into his vehicle, then everyone not on duty had trooped to Alberg's house in Gibsons for food and drink. And at an appropriate moment, late in the party, Norah Gibbons had wheeled out of the sunporch Sid's wooden armchair. Alberg remembered how it had squeaked and squealed, and the bewildered look on Sid Sokolowski's face, which was by then flushed and damp, as he recognized the sound.

"Here, Sarge," Norah had said, grinning at him, "Staff says you can take it with you."

And Sid had stroked its back tenderly, making helpless croaking noises, waving his beer in the air. Alberg had been terribly afraid he was going to weep as he lowered himself into the chair and scooted across the living room floor.

Alberg, looking out the window, was reluctant to admit that months had passed since Sid had sent him his new address and phone number, on a postcard: Alberg hadn't once called him. He thought Cassandra had sent a Christmas card, from the two of them, but he wasn't sure.

He didn't want to talk to Sid. He didn't want to know how unhappy Sid was, retired.

Of course, maybe he wasn't unhappy.

Alberg thought about his IN basket, crammed with paperwork, overflowing with it. He imagined what his IN basket would look like a week from now, a month from now, a year hence, if he were to just leave it alone to collect more paper, to begin gathering dust. Paperwork would spill onto his desk, submerge his desk, eventually, cover the floor, pile up on the floor until the room was stuffed full of paper, until it would no longer be possible to open the door.

"To hell with it," Alberg muttered, pulling on his jacket. He'd go down to his boat for a while.

It was about nine-thirty when Andrew got home. He sat in the car for a moment, hating it that he wasn't happy to be home these days, hating it that he had nothing to say to Janet.

He had never before so resented not being smart. A smart man would know what to think, what to do, what to say to his wife. But Andrew just kept going over and over it in his mind—the fact that there had been a baby, and Janet had killed it.

No no, he told himself, shutting his eyes, vigorously shaking his head. She hadn't killed it. It wasn't a baby yet, when it died. Andrew knew all this stuff. He understood it. He knew about it being Janet's body, and she had a right— he knew all that.

But his heart was bruised and aching as he climbed wearily out of the car and walked toward his house, because he also knew that what had been inside Janet's body was as much his as hers: and more than hers, more than his, it had been its *own*, its own potential person. And Janet had snuffed it out like a candle flame before it had had a chance to—

Here he was doing it again, he thought unhappily, going up the front steps. He needed somebody to talk to, that was for sure. He'd talked a little bit to someone at work, but that hadn't been very satisfactory. Maybe he should try again.

Andrew stood by the door, reluctant to open it. There was this huge canyon between them now, and Andrew, watching Janet get smaller and smaller on the other side of it, had no idea how to cross over to her.

He reached for the knob, glancing at the living room window—and noticed for the first time that there were no lights on inside.

And his first reaction—he didn't admit this, later; he never admitted it—was relief: maybe he could go quickly to bed, he thought, and fall asleep, and not have to talk to Janet, or listen to her. And maybe tomorrow he could sneak out of the house before she awakened and find somebody to talk to who could help him with this mess.

His next thought was that it still would have been daylight when Janet got home, and that maybe she'd fallen asleep in front of the TV.

But the door was locked.

He told them later that that was when he got the first bad feeling. Janet wouldn't have locked up unless she was going out somewhere. And if she was going out, she would have phoned to tell him.

Okay, so she went out on the spur of the moment, he thought, as he let himself in. He didn't even bother to call out, he told them later, because he could feel that there was nobody home.

He went around turning on lights and looking for a note, because maybe his feelings were all screwed up and he was getting the wrong message. But there wasn't any note.

Andrew told them later that he'd never felt this way in his whole life before: terrified, and not knowing why. And guilty, too, although he didn't tell them that.

He phoned Janet's boss, Mr. Alexander.

"We shut up shop early today, Andrew. I left about four-thirty and I'm pretty sure Janet was going home almost right away."

"Did she take the bus?"

"I don't think so—she was putting on her running shoes when I left. Don't worry, Andrew. I'm sure there's a perfectly reasonable explanation. She's probably gone off somewhere with a friend."

He called Clara next.

"I saw her leave," she told him. "She knocked on the window when she passed and waved at me."

"What time was this?" said Andrew, holding tight to the phone, frowning at the beige wall-to-wall carpeting that covered every room in the townhouse except the kitchen and the bathroom.

"I'm not sure," said Clara. "Before five-thirty, though, because that's when I took off myself. Why? What's the matter?"

"Oh, she hasn't come home yet, that's all. And I'm worried." He leaned back on the sofa and then sat straight again, looking at the window, seeing his distorted reflection there.

But Clara just said the same thing Mr. Alexander had said. "Oh, Andrew, Janet's probably just gone out for a hamburger with somebody."

Clara reminded him of several more of Janet's friends, and he called them all, but nobody had seen her.

Andrew then got in the car and drove slowly along the rainslick streets of his neighborhood, retracing what he thought Janet's steps most likely would have been. In the dark, wet night this was a hopeless task, and he knew it, but he didn't know what to do instead.

He went home, eventually, but he couldn't sit still there. He had a petrifying sense of urgency. He found himself looking in drawers and closets—for what, he couldn't have said. Finally, he hurried back out to the car.

The new sergeant was sitting at Sokolowski's old table in the reception area, familiarizing herself with the casework, when

Andrew burst through the door. The duty officer started to get up.

"I'll take care of it," said Eddie. "What can I do for you?" she asked, approaching the counter.

She saw a man slightly shorter than she was, wearing a gray suit, a white shirt, and a tie. His dark blond hair curled almost to his shoulders. He had blue eyes, a triangular face with a wide forehead and a narrow chin, unusually full lips, and a prominent Adam's apple.

He leaned heavily on the counter with both hands and looked searchingly at Eddie. "Are you a cop?"

Eddie looked down at her uniform. "I guess I am."

"My wife—I don't know where she is." He was pale and shaky.

Eddie walked around the counter. "What's your name?"

"Andrew."

"Sit on the bench there, Andrew," said the sergeant, and she sat down next to him. "What's your wife's name?"

"Janet. My wife is called Janet Maine."

"Janet. That's a pretty name. Okay, Andrew. Tell me."

He concentrated, staring at the floor. "I called people. And this is what I know. She left work between four-thirty and five-thirty. She walked home, but she never got there." He clasped his hands tightly between his knees. "She didn't phone me. She didn't write me a note. She wouldn't go off anywhere without phoning or leaving me a note." His shoulders hunched, as if he had pain somewhere. "I drove around," he said, "looking for her. I don't know where she is. I don't know where she went. I'm very afraid for her. That something's happened to her." He continued to talk, haltingly, stopping sometimes to suck in air through clenched teeth.

Eddie listened intently. When Andrew finished, he lifted his gaze from the floor and looked into her face. She felt the weight of his distress, which she knew he hoped to transfer to her. But even if she were to accept it—which she would not—this wouldn't rid him of it, but only double it.

Besides, Eddie knew that if his wife *had* disappeared, Andrew Maine was the person most likely to be responsible.

"We can't do anything until morning, Mr. Maine," she said.

"Oh my god," said Andrew, who couldn't begin to imagine how to get through the night.

"I want you to phone somebody, your boss, a friend, a relative—I want you to do it from here."

"Oh god," said Andrew, shaking, his hands pulling at his hair.

"And you go on home with this person," said the sergeant, gently removing his hands from his hair. "And tomorrow we'll look for your wife."

A person wasn't officially missing until he or she had been gone for twenty-four hours. But Eddie Henderson thought they ought to start looking for Janet Maine as soon as it was light.

"I'm sorry to bother you at home, Staff, but I thought you'd want to know."

"You're probably right, Sergeant," said Alberg, on the kitchen phone. He and Cassandra were packing dishes they hardly ever used. "What is it that I want to know?"

"A guy came in to report his wife missing. And I've been reading the files, and—"

"Rebecca Granger," said Alberg. Cassandra turned to look at him, newspaper in one hand, a large serving platter in the other. Alberg sat down at the table. "Right?"

"Right."

"Okay. Tell me about it."

He listened. Cassandra sat down, too. He took one of

her hands and became apparently engrossed in the lines in her palm. "Okay. . . . Yeah. . . . No, we don't have to wait. First light."

When he'd hung up, Cassandra said, "What is it?"

"Probably nothing," said Alberg. "Somebody didn't come home when she was expected." He got up and went into the living room, where he stood with his hands in his pockets, looking at his wingback chair. It was pretty old. Probably time to replace it. He found himself jingling the coins that were in his pockets. This had been a habit of his father. Alberg realized that he hadn't thought about his father for a long time.

He wanted to get into his Olds and drive out of Gibsons toward Sechelt, to the place where Rebecca Granger's body had been found seven months earlier; to the clearing a couple of miles from Sergeant Bay.

He heard rain falling outside and imagined it falling in the clearing, clattering on salal and blackberries, pattering on the carpet of pine needles. He imagined a freshly dug grave. But the breeze would smell of spring.

Cassandra came up behind him and slipped her arms around his waist. "Are you okay?"

He'd feel like an idiot, pushing through the forest, branches snapping in his face, showering him with their collections of raindrops while more fell on him from the sky.

"Yeah, I'm fine," he said to Cassandra. He turned around. "Let's pack some more dishes."

But tomorrow, he thought. It wouldn't hurt to go take a look tomorrow. In the morning. As soon as he'd emptied his IN basket.

It was three o'clock. The middle of the night.

A mid-sized four-door sedan, metallic blue in color, proceeded rapidly through Sechelt along pavement that was shiny from a rain shower. The only light to be seen burned in an apartment above the hardware store.

The car glided quickly through the town, then swerved abruptly, turning right onto a road that hadn't existed a year earlier. It passed a collection of houses clustered along the hillside, advancing more slowly now, and gleaming, occasionally, as it proceeded through the light from widely spaced streetlamps. In the headlights a fine mist began to form—the start of another nighttime shower.

The car reached the top of the hill, where the street ended. It stopped and remained there for several seconds, motor running, exhaust trailing into the air, headlights illuminating a bank of undergrowth that had spread among the fir and cedar trees. Then it turned left.

This road—a lane, really—was not paved. There were ruts in it, and large stones. Denise Dyakowski drove slowly, her hands clenched on the steering wheel, lurching the car through puddles and mud. In the headlights she watched the trail become narrower, the trees moving closer, until eventually the underbrush spilled out from the forest and scraped against the car, making small grating noises.

The lane now forged a ninety-degree angle and headed downhill. Its surface became still more rough. Denise drove so slowly that the speedometer was barely moving, but still the car bounced and rattled.

In the headlights she could no longer see the track, only the thickening brush that leaned across the lane, that looked impenetrable, but she kept going, the car kept going, pushing through the dense foliage, battling a foot at a time, until it could proceed no farther. Denise revved the motor, but it was no use.

She turned the motor off, and the headlights, and scrambled quickly out of the car. Bushes and saplings thrust themselves toward the open door, but she pushed them aside and got it closed.

Denise leaned against the car, blinking. She could see practically nothing. She thought she heard the forest breathing.

The car's motor made a pinging sound as it began to cool. There was a soft slow pattering of rain on leaves, on trees, on the earth, on the car. There was no light anywhere, only the deep cool darkness of night.

With hands outstretched, Denise pushed through the thicket that had wrapped itself around the car and struggled along the lane, back the way she'd come, uphill, stumbling from time to time, having caught the edge of her shoe in a rut or stepped on a slippery stone. The bushes rustled as she pressed through them, and sometimes blackberry brambles caught at her sweater.

After a while she began to see better. The darkness seemed less dense, and she could make out shapes: tall trees, a huge boulder, and ubiquitous blackberry canes waving high in the air.

The rain was a gentle shower, cooling her skin, soothing her skin as she pushed aside salal and broom. The rain had coaxed fragrances from the forest. Denise stopped to breathe them in.

Suddenly she turned and shouldered her way into the woods and started blindly taking hold of branches, breaking them off. Most didn't want to be broken—she had to tear at them, and sometimes gnaw them with her teeth. She tried to avoid the blackberries but there were other kinds of thorns in the woods, too, and she got several scratches. She backed out of the woods with an armful of branches, looked up the lane, and thought she saw the glint of a streetlight beyond the next curve. Denise set off through the dark wet night for home.

When she got there she was exhausted, but she put the branches in a tall vase and filled it with water.

A black plastic garbage bag, full and tied securely closed,

sat in the middle of the kitchen floor. Denise walked around it several times while tending to the branches. Then she washed her hands at the kitchen sink—gently, because they were sore from tearing the branches free and had been pricked by brambles. She dried them, and reached to turn out the light. Saw the garbage bag. Leaned against the counter and studied it, frowning. Then she lifted it, tentatively, testing its weight.

Before she went to bed, she took it outside and put it in the shed with the others.

———

Mrs. O'Hara thought about the bed she shared with Tom: the mattress had such a pronounced hollow in the middle that the two of them inevitably became tangled together in sleep, and then in sex. A bed designed to incite procreation, one would have thought.

They could have adopted, though.

Whenever she looked at him in daylight it was as if she was observing another person entirely.

In fifteen years of marriage it had never, ever occurred to her that another woman would find him attractive.

When they reached the house, the sky was darker than it had been when Mrs. O'Hara arrived home from work, and the stars were brighter, and now there was the moon, as well, flooding the yard with light.

What happens now? she wondered.

Tom turned off the motor, pocketing the keys, and went around to Mrs. O'Hara's side of the car to open the door for her. She allowed him to help her out. The touch of his hands was strange, conveying an alien firmness . . . but she knew she was making this up. Was it really true, then, that you don't appreciate what you've got until you don't have it anymore? Or, in this case, until somebody else has it as well?

She leaned on his arm, crossing the yard, and was tempted to deliver her entire weight upon his shoulder, to make him collapse, or at least stagger.

She clung to the railing as she made her way slowly and painfully up the stairs, with Tom behind her, and she thought maybe she ought to plunge backward down the steps again, deliberately, now that Tom was there to break her fall: maybe she could manage to land on his face and crush him to death.

This was the first time killing entered her mind. It was a casual, insincere notion, proposed as an early attempt at self-defence, a slow, almost dreamy concept held aloft by a narcotic.

"I'm going to bed," she said when they were in the house. She turned on the kitchen light and struggled out of her jacket, hanging it clumsily on one of the wooden hooks on the wall by the door.

"Sure, hon," said Tom. "Can I get you something first? Juice? Cocoa?"

Mrs. O'Hara was filling a glass with tap water. She fumbled the vial of pills out of the drugstore bag, checked the directions, and swallowed two of them. "I don't think I can get up another flight of stairs," she said. "I'm gonna sleep on the couch."

"I'll get you a blanket," said Tom, and he scampered upstairs.

When he came back, Mrs. O'Hara was sitting on the couch taking off her pumps. She curled up with her head on a throw cushion and Tom tucked the blanket around her.

"You have a good sleep there, hon," he said. "And tomorrow we'll talk."

Mrs. O'Hara closed her eyes and was almost instantly asleep. Was there a way to go here on demand? she wondered as she drifted off. It was such a blessed destination—sleep.

In the morning, pain awakened her: a throbbing head, an elbow in agony. She pushed back the blanket and sat on the edge of the couch, ineffectually tugging at her skirt, and she stayed there until the dizziness had subsided.

She found Tom at the kitchen table with the radio on low, digging into a plate of scrambled eggs and toast. He looked at her in astonishment; Mrs. O'Hara wondered if he had expected her to vanish in the night.

"Hiya, hon." He looked down at his plate. "Can I get you some eggs?"

The smell of his breakfast was making Mrs. O'Hara nauseous. Clinging to the edge of the counter, she swallowed repeatedly: throwing up was one of the things in life she found most disagreeable. "No," she gasped, finally. "Nothing." She took a couple of pills with some water and left the kitchen.

Tom got up from the table and followed her to the bottom of the stairs. Mrs. O'Hara felt his eyes on her as she plodded upward, and was mortified.

In the bathroom, she stripped, laboriously washed herself, and dressed in clean clothes—slacks, a short-sleeved blouse, and sandals. Then, leaning heavily on the sink, she inspected herself grimly in the mirror. Jesus god. No way could she make it in to work today, not looking the way she looked. And she was relieved to have made this decision, because her whole body had been just slightly atremble ever since she stood up from the couch. She had been ignoring this, but she knew that ignoring it was unwise: she had, after all, lost a lot of blood. She peered more closely at her image in the mirror. Her face was pale, her eyes looked as if they'd shrunk, and her hair, combed straight down around the edges of the bandage, appeared dank and lifeless. Her task for the day would be to find a scarf and practice wrapping it around her head.

Mrs. O'Hara went back downstairs. Tom was washing his dishes in the kitchen sink and said to her over his shoulder, "I'm gonna get at those steps first thing."

Mrs. O'Hara picked up the phone and called in sick for work. "Yeah, maybe tomorrow," she said. "I don't know. I'll call you in the morning. Thanks, I will." When she showed up with her head wrapped, everyone would know that she'd been more than just sick. But what the hell, she thought. So what?

Her heart was beating unusually fast. Mrs. O'Hara sat at the table watching Tom dry the pan in which he had scrambled his eggs. "Okay, Tom. I've gotta know what's going on."

He turned so quickly that she knew he'd been preparing

himself. "It's Raylene from the diner," he said. "She had a flat tire one day and I was passing by and I stopped to help her with it and—and one thing led to another."

Mrs. O'Hara felt as if she had been dropped from a great height. There was too much information here to absorb all at once. "Raylene from the diner," she said, seeking guidance. Tom's ears were red at the tips, where they splayed out like mushroom caps.

"Yeah," he said, turning the dishcloth in his hands. It was dripping soapy water down the front of his jeans and onto his cowboy boots and the floor. He was a small, slight man but he had a wiry strength that Mrs. O'Hara had always enjoyed in bed.

There was, however, nothing much else to recommend him, she reminded herself.

"She'd just split up with Dean," said Tom, "and she felt kinda miserable about it."

Mrs. O'Hara knew these people, Raylene and Dean. She considered them now in a daze, unwilling to believe that they could have ripped her life apart.

She asked Tom when, and for how long, and then she said, "And what do you want to do now?"

"We want to get married, Raylene and me," said Tom. He tossed the dishcloth into the sink and sat down opposite Mrs. O'Hara. "I'm sorry, hon. But you know how much I want to have kids."

He talked on for quite a while. Mrs. O'Hara didn't hear much of what he said but she watched his face intently and saw several things there: regret, compassion, sorrow—and a sly, mean triumph that sealed his fate.

When he finished speaking, she asked him to leave.

"But hon," he protested, throwing out his hands, palms up. "I want to fix the steps for you. And—and—"

"Tom," said Mrs. O'Hara. "You just told me you want to marry somebody else."

"Yeah, but not right away," he said, very seriously.

Mrs. O'Hara felt like laughing: hysteria, that's what it was.

"It's my house," she reminded him, almost kindly. *"And I want you to leave. Now. Today."*

While he packed, she remained at the kitchen table with her mind in neutral.

"I can't carry it all at once. I'll have to come back another day," he said to her from the door.

Mrs. O'Hara nodded, fixing her gaze elsewhere.

Why hadn't they adopted?

"Do you want my key?" he asked.

But perhaps it was just as well.

"When you come back," she said.

She heard the door open, and close. She heard Tom trot down the outside staircase, and listened for the car. When he had driven away she switched off the radio and sat at the table in silence. She was still shaking, slightly, whether from last night's physical injuries or the trauma suffered by her ego she wasn't sure.

Mrs. O'Hara lowered her forehead to the table and let grief engulf her.

If she had known the full extent of its power, she would have at least tried to resist.

TEN

Tuesday, March 26

———

When she awakened that morning, Denise knew instantly that the weather had changed again, that the clouds and rain had been swept away. She was not usually a person greatly affected by weather but the thought of sun, and a sky that was blue again, instead of slate gray, filled her with joy.

She got out of bed, smoothed the duvet, plumped the pillows, hers and Ivan's, too, and wrapped herself in a robe. She hurried into the kitchen to put on a pot of coffee and then opened the front door to look at the gilding sunshine. She discovered that not only was it a bright day, it was another astonishingly warm one.

She turned on the radio that sat on the kitchen counter, though, and waited for the next weather forecast, because she didn't yet trust the sun shining on her front door. It couldn't really be as warm as it felt—maybe she had a fever. She would wait, not get dressed immediately, for if it really was that warm she had better wear shorts instead of her habitual weekend jeans.

She realized that she had decided not to go to work today. She would probably pretend to have the flu.

She was on her way to the bathroom when she saw the big vase of tall branches sitting on the bookcase.

For a few seconds Denise felt as if she was in a dream—in someone else's dream.

It was a good thing she had turned the radio on: its drone provided the real world as a reassuring wash in the background while Denise, frozen, stared at the vase filled with branches.

She didn't even know what most of them were. There were several different kinds. A plume of yellow broom. A branch with large leaves, loosely furled along its thick stem. Another kind was slender and white, with thorns and tiny pink flowers.

Denise rushed forward and touched one of the thorns. She opened her hands, spreading them, and saw flesh that was pricked, flesh that was bruised. She looked at her hands . . . and her flesh remembered, and sent the memory rocketing to her brain.

Denise sat down slowly on the love seat.

She looked at the branches, concentrated hard, and— and she remembered—yes, she remembered thrusting into the woods, breaking off those branches.

She shook her head disapprovingly as she recalled chewing at them when they were too supple to break. Like a beaver, she thought, shocked. Chewing away like a little beaver. Only instead of building a dam with her branches she had brought them home, a piece of the natural, living, flowering world to live and flower for a while in her living room.

But what a thing to do in darkness! And in rain . . .

She remembered the coolness of the rain, the sounds it had made. The woods had been alive with the sounds of the rain. And with the smells of the earth and the trees and the layers of rotting leaves dropped to the ground by seasons past. And the rain itself had a smell, too, a pungent metallic odor. . . .

Why had she been out there, in the woods, in the rain, in the black night?

The phone rang, returning her to daylight and sunshine.

"Hello?" said Denise eagerly. "Oh hi, Penny. . . . No no, I thought it might be Ivan, that's all. He's in Penticton. At some kind of conference . . . All week," she said. "Yeah, poor me . . . No no, I'll be fine. We're busy at work, and I've got lots to do around here, too. . . . Tonight?"

Denise hesitated, glancing at the branches in the vase, trying to remember if there was something else she was supposed to do tonight—trying rather frantically to remember.

Suddenly she thought, Screw it, if it's not right there ready to be remembered, it can't be that important.

"Sure, yeah," she said. "I'd love to come. What time?" She hung up the phone.

Instead of going into the bathroom, she tied her robe more tightly around her waist and stepped outside into the backyard. She shut the door and leaned against it, letting the sun bathe her.

Her mind felt empty. She rather liked having no thoughts rattling around in there—no important thoughts, anyway.

Denise stood in the sun, the hot seductive sun, listening to bird-song and traffic and seaplanes, offering herself to the sun, and soon sweat dampened her forehead, and gold-encircled coals were glowing behind her closed eyelids.

Mrs. O'Hara had set her alarm for six o'clock as usual that morning, but as soon as it went off she knew she wouldn't be getting out of bed any time soon. She had overestimated her strength again, stubbornly insisting that her aging body was more resilient, more recuperative than it actually was. The last three had been too hard on her. It was stupid not to concede that, physically, she was in serious decline.

She turned on the radio and reached, wincing, for the second pillow on her bed, tucking it under her head. And she lay there cautiously assessing her aches and twinges. Maybe she wouldn't get up at all today. Maybe she'd stay right where she was, listening to the radio, reading, watching television. She had done this several times recently, and sometimes worried about it. What if it were to happen two days in a row? And then three? What if she ended up never getting out of bed again, except to go to the bathroom?

Soon it wouldn't matter, because her sixty-fifth birthday was approaching swiftly, hand in hand with death.

First, though, she had to finish what she'd started ten years ago: with five months remaining before her deadline, she still had one sweep to go.

She would let the weather decide her day, she thought. If the morning was mild and pleasant and the sun was shining, she would get up. In order to determine the weather, though, she would have to get out of bed and hobble over to the door, because the glass in the small windows of the cabin was opaque, and the walls and roof emitted a constant colloquy of groans, moans, and lamentations that although hushed and, Mrs. O'Hara believed, even deferential, and not at all unpleasant to her ear, did prevent her from determining whether rain was part of their orchestrations.

She had to get up to pee, anyway.

She massaged her left shoulder, without effect, and threw back the covers. She padded to the back door, which was smaller than the front door but equally thick and strong, undid its several locks, and pulled it partway open, blinking at the sudden onslaught of sunshine. She closed it immediately. That was that, then.

No rest for the wicked.

But after she had peed she climbed back into bed, just for a while, just until the seven o'clock news was over.

She took some aspirin before settling herself in bed, half-sitting against her pillows, and lay quietly, listening to the radio, soothed in the embrace of her small cabin.

It had wooden floors, waxed and polished, and wood-paneled walls—except for the bathroom and the small kitchen area, which were tiled in a shade of peach that was Mrs. O'Hara's favorite color. The kitchen contained a small electric range and refrigerator, a double sink and several countertop appliances: toaster, blender, toaster oven, micro-wave oven. The bathroom had several cupboards and a tub, but no shower.

A selection of Robert Bateman prints hung on the walls, realistic representations of Canadian wildlife, land-scape, and seascape.

Mrs. O'Hara had a massive leather recliner, a large tele-vision set and a whole wall of books. She had no tapes, no CDs—music unsettled her. In one corner was her bed, with a lamp next to it, and there was a closet and a chest of drawers for her clothes.

And, almost in the center of the cabin, there was a black, full-bellied, wood-burning stove to keep her warm in winter.

After the news report, Mrs. O'Hara got up. She made her bed, wincing at the pain—her arthritis was getting stead-ily worse; she had to swallow a lot of aspirin every day.

Then she dressed in clean overalls, a T-shirt, a sweat-shirt, heavy socks, and work boots.

No rest for the wicked. . . .

But she had brought it on herself. The first had been accomplished so smoothly, so efficiently, that she knew she'd uncovered a hidden talent.

And then she had felt fate enfolding her, coldly, relent-lessly, and had imagined it as the twin black wings of an enormous bat.

She had resisted fate, strenuously, at first. It was as if all the juices had been sucked from her bones. She had trem-bled, continually, like a willow leaf in the wind. Her misery was a fever; her body hurt when she touched it; when she dressed it, cleansed it, when her fingers accidentally brushed against it. Her skin even anticipated the pain of being touched—it hurt, it ached, it burned like a sunburn in the mere expectation of being touched.

She had awakened one morning—or maybe it had happened in midafternoon, or during an evening—anyway, at some moment or other she had looked at herself. Studied her face and body in the bathroom mirror, intensely and without fear. Acknowledged and accepted her gift.

She saw that it had been contemptible to try to resist. Not many people were called upon to fulfill a destiny. She was among the privileged.

And so she had capitulated, with grace.

The enterprise had proven more physically and emotionally exhausting than she had anticipated, however. She had wondered, often, how long she could continue. But she was pretty sure, now, that she was going to make it.

It was seven-thirty when Mrs. O'Hara opened her back door again, wide this time, and peered out at her territory. She had a need of blooming, growing things but kept no plants inside her cabin because of the plentitude in her woods—there were wild-flowers, such as roses, columbine, orchids, and bleeding hearts; cedar and arbutus trees, as well as alder, maple, birch, mountain ash, and wild cherry; and several kinds of berry bushes, too—gooseberry, currant, blueberry and blackberry—that bloomed in the spring and provided her with fruit in the summer and fall.

Mrs. O'Hara looked around, warily, before stepping outside. She didn't mind surprising deer or raccoons or even skunks, but once she had burst outdoors and found herself face to face with a cougar.

She called out a couple of times—"Hey! You there! Scram!"—to make sure no animals were near, and imagined a cougar, or maybe a black bear, fleeing her land, careering through the woods and down the steep bank that led to the lake.

She pushed through the greenery at the side of the house and made her way down the path to the van, which started right away, as always.

An hour later she was entering Earl's Café in Sechelt.

"Miz O'Hara!" Earl called out to her, his eyes crinkling, almost disappearing into his grin.

"Hi, Earl."

"Good to see you," said Earl, looking around for a copy of *The Province*. "Here. Take this."

"Thanks."

"What can I get you?"

"Just coffee, I think."

But Earl clasped his hands in front of him and gave her a look both worried and reproachful. "You're gonna turn into skin and bones."

"I don't think that's likely, Earl."

"You need to eat, Mrs. O'Hara."

"Yeah? Well, nothing appeals to me."

"How about I make you a nice soft-boiled egg and a piece of sourdough toast with real butter? And maybe a glass of orange juice."

She could pick Earl up and hurl him through his plate glass window, if she had a mind. Which of course she didn't. This small, tidy man, with the shiny black shoes and the big white apron, he was no sinner.

Mrs. O'Hara nodded approvingly. "You know, that sounds good."

"Good," said Earl, grinning at her. "Right," he said, nodding vigorously, and he went off to fix her breakfast.

Mrs. O'Hara sat back in her chair, holding the newspaper but not reading it. The table at which she sat had a glass top and round metal legs, painted red. This was a recent change. Mrs. O'Hara knew that Earl's Café & Catering was up for sale, and that Earl had probably replaced the old, sometimes-tottery tables in an attempt to spruce things up. But she also knew that whoever bought the café would be paying for the goodwill that came with the place, not for the tables and chairs.

She glanced over at Naomi, who was waiting on a couple of people sitting at the counter. She was a small, wiry woman in her thirties, with dense black hair that today was scraped away from her face and fastened in the back with something that looked like an enormous clothespin. She was scrubbing the surface of the counter, polishing the napkin container, wiping the salts and peppers, and keeping up a running conversation with her customers that was neither cheerful nor polite. She was wearing tight blue jeans, cowboy boots and a shapeless black sweatshirt with lettering that Mrs. O'Hara was too far away to decipher.

Mrs. O'Hara folded the newspaper and set it aside. She tried to remember what she'd been told about Naomi. She knew that Naomi had two little kids. And that her husband was in jail—for drug trafficking, Mrs. O'Hara believed.

Mrs. O'Hara watched Naomi, a thin, restless little person, tightly wound, and wondered about her character.

"Excuse me," said a voice behind her, and Mrs. O'Hara whirled around, her skin prickling unpleasantly.

"I'm sorry. I didn't mean to startle you." A young woman with a huge leather bag slung over her shoulder thrust out her hand toward Mrs. O'Hara, who took it automatically. "My name is Cindi Webster. May I sit down? Just for a minute?" She was pulling out the chair opposite Mrs. O'Hara's, but kept her eyes on Mrs. O'Hara's face, waiting for permission.

Mrs. O'Hara asked, "Who are you?"

"I'm a reporter. With the local paper."

"What do you want with me?" asked Mrs. O'Hara, alarmed.

"Well, I'm doing a series of stories," said Cindi, shifting her bag higher onto her shoulder, "about people and their work."

Mrs. O'Hara looked at her incredulously. "Their work?"

"Yes," Cindi continued. Mrs. O'Hara observed that her face was growing pink. "And I was wondering if I could talk to you sometime, about your work, if you'd, uh, agree—" She was floundering, now, sounding like a person who might be drowning. "Uh, to talk to me, uh, about, about—"

"About my work," said Mrs. O'Hara, taking pity on her. She wondered if the girl was always so red-faced and tongue-tied.

"Yes," said Cindi. "Right." She expelled her breath in relief—Whoosh!—and looked at Mrs. O'Hara expectantly. "So. What do you think?"

"Here you go, Mrs. O," said Earl, setting down a plate that held an eggcup and two slices of buttered toast, and a large glass of orange juice. "Listen to me. 'Here you go, Mrs. O.' I'm a gol-darn poet and I don't even know it." He burst into laughter as he sailed away.

Cindi hefted her bag again. "Here," she said, sliding a business card toward Mrs. O'Hara. "Maybe you could give me a call? At your convenience?"

"Maybe," said Mrs. O'Hara, smiling slightly. She tucked the card into the breast pocket of her overalls. "I wouldn't hold my breath, however."

ELEVEN

Alberg got to work early that morning, but not as early as Eddie Henderson. By the time he arrived, the search for Janet Maine was well underway.

He made himself tackle the paperwork in his IN tray, and worked steadily away. But he was always aware of time passing.

Halfway through the morning he put down his pen, took off his reading glasses, and rubbed his eyes. He sat back in his chair and stretched, then studied, curiously, the new photo of his daughters that sat on his desk. Janey and Diana had their arms around one another's shoulders and they were laughing. It was a picture taken by the damn musician . . . but Alberg had to stop calling him that. Daniel, he corrected himself. It was a picture taken by Daniel. His son-in-law.

His daughters kept telling him to get e-mail, but Alberg didn't want e-mail. Isabella handled that sort of thing. Alberg had only recently become comfortable with the computer that had its own table in his office. He had absolutely no desire for an electronic mailbox.

His daughters had told him, though, that if he got one they'd write to him a lot.

"Why can't you write real letters?" he had complained.

But Janey had said, "It's so much easier, Dad, to press

one key, than to print the thing out, and fold it up, and put it in an envelope, and address the envelope, and find a stamp to go on it, and then a mailbox to drop it into."

So he wasn't permanently committed to his aversion to e-mail.

He had to get a picture of Cassandra, too, he reminded himself. For some reason this brought to mind his new sergeant.

Alberg went out into the reception area to refill his coffee mug. "Where's Sergeant Henderson?" he asked.

Isabella turned from her computer. "The sergeant and Constable Mondini went out to check the place where the Granger girl was found." She shrugged. "Kind of a long shot."

Alberg was staring into space.

"Don't you think?" she said.

Denise was in Zellers, her arms full of towels. She had chosen four bath sheets, four large towels, four hand towels, and four face-cloths, deep blue in color.

Now she was in women's wear, looking hastily through racks of sweatpants and sweatshirts. Suddenly the pile of towels toppled and fell. She grabbed at some, but the rest landed on the floor.

Denise squatted down to retrieve them, and was surprised to find that she was weeping. But the alarm that this created in her quickly dried her tears.

She picked up the towels and set them down on a chair that someone had placed next to a full-length mirror. Avoiding the mirror, she returned to the rack and selected a pair of dark gray pants and a bright pink sweatshirt, size medium and took them and the towels to the check-out counter.

•   •   •

Cindi returned to Earl's in mid-morning for a take-out coffee. There were no other customers in the café. As she paid Naomi she asked, "So how long have you worked here?"

"A while," said Naomi, wiping the table next to Cindi's.

"We haven't met. My name's Cindi Webster. I'm a reporter with *The Record.*"

Naomi picked up the napkin dispenser and gave it a swipe with her dishcloth.

"You know—just up the street?"

Naomi, vigorously cleaning the salt and pepper shakers, made no response.

"I'm working on a series of stories about work," Cindi went on bravely, "you know, about the various kinds of work that people do. And I was wondering, would you, uh, be interested, because, uh, I'd like to do one about a waitress."

"Sounds dead boring to me," said Naomi, moving on to another table.

"Not to me," said Earl, from behind the counter. He had donned the huge apron bought for him years ago in Paris by one of his regular customers, now deceased. "Talk to her," he said. "A story in the paper about my waitress? Good for business." He disappeared through the swinging door that led to the kitchen.

Naomi, stone-faced, looked at Cindi Webster in silence, then flicked the dishcloth onto the counter and sat down on a stool with a sigh. "So whaddya want to know?"

"Well, first of all," said Cindi, reaching into her voluminous shoulderbag for her notebook and pen, "what do you like about your job, and then, what do you dislike about it."

"I don't like anything about it," said Naomi promptly. She was in her late twenties or early thirties, small, with a lean, wiry body and hair whose extreme blackness Cindi thought was probably not natural. She wore very tight jeans and a big baggy sweatshirt that said LAS VEGAS on it, in something that glittered.

"Why do you do it, then?" Cindi asked.

"I got kids to support," said Naomi, rubbing against the counter, easing an itch in her back.

"Well, but—"

"I kinda slide through it, you know?" said Naomi, waving her hands in the air. "Pretend like I'm two people, and only one of them's doing the waitressing."

Cindi looked down at her notebook, uncertain. She decided she'd come back to this remark, which she didn't entirely understand.

Naomi sprang from the stool and picked up the dishcloth. "Shit," she said, regarding it critically. She went behind the counter, rinsed it in hot water, and wrung it out.

"What hours do you work?" said Cindi, trying another angle.

"Too damn many." Naomi was wiping another table, removing smudges from another napkin dispenser, ridding more salt and pepper shakers of stickiness and grime. She straightened and looked over at Cindi. "I mean, I'm glad for the money and all. But he needs another waiter in here, you know what I'm saying?"

"Yeah," said Cindi, nodding. "You'd like to spend more time with your kids. Who takes care of them when you're at work?"

Earl came through the swinging door and walked over to the blackboard, now blank, on which the day's specials were to be displayed.

"You know that, Earl, don't you?" said Naomi sternly. "You need more staff."

"More staff," said Earl, printing, slowly, with chalk.

"Huh. I'm selling out pretty soon. Any day now. I don't need more staff."

"He did hire somebody once," said Naomi, moving to the next table. "Last fall."

"Yeah," said Earl. He stepped back and peered at the blackboard. "Is that straight?" It read, "SOUP OF THE DAY: FRENCH ONION. LUNCH SPECIAL: CHICKEN CACIATORE."

"I think there're two c's in 'cacciatore,'" said Cindi helpfully.

Earl studied his printing. "I got two c's in it," he said.

"No, I mean—" She got up and went over to the blackboard. "There," she said, pointing.

"Oh," said Earl. "Okay." Carefully, he made the correction.

"So if we needed somebody last fall," said Naomi, angrily scrubbing the last tabletop, "we need somebody now."

"I hired that girl and what happened?" said Earl, turning to glare at her. "She comes one day, two days, three days, and then, whuff!" he said, throwing his hands in the air. "I never see her again."

"That doesn't mean the next one'll do the same," said Naomi. "Look at me. I stayed, didn't I?"

The bell over the door jangled and a quartet of young women entered. Cindi recognized two of them. This was a good feeling. It warmed her. She was getting to know people, getting to know the town. She waited until Naomi had taken their orders, then, "Listen," she said, "maybe we can get together later? And finish the interview?"

"I thought we *were* finished," said Naomi.

"Let me buy you a coffee after work," said Cindi. "Or a beer, if you like. Please?"

Naomi considered this for a moment. "I'll think about it."

•   •   •

Eddie Henderson came into Alberg's office fast, bursting through the doorway, almost as tall as Sid but a whole lot thinner. Her face was flushed. She stood there looking at him, temporarily incapable of speech.

"You found her,' said Alberg quietly.

The sergeant nodded.

"Buried in the clearing."

She nodded again.

Denise put the towels and her new sweats through the wash, and when they were dry, she hung the clothes in her side of the closet and folded the towels.

She opened the door to the linen closet and slid the towels onto the top shelf, which was empty: bath sheets on the left, large towels on the right, hand towels and facecloths in the middle. It was very satisfying to see that shelf filled.

Denise checked the time. Four o'clock. Lots of time for a bath before going to Penny and Harold's for dinner.

She reached for the interior knob of the linen closet door, glancing casually in that direction as she did so . . . and somehow she knew immediately that she should not have done this. She tried to shout, No! in an effort to distract herself, to cause her head to turn quickly in another direction—

But it was too late. She had seen it.

She hissed, and clapped her hand over her mouth.

Denise couldn't scream, couldn't run, could only stand there, paralyzed, unable to look away from the bloody handprint that shrieked at her from the inside of her linen closet door.

TWELVE

It was very late when Eddie parked in front of her house. She got out of the car, locked it, and walked swiftly to the front door. She was physically tense, and shook her hands energetically in front of her as she walked, trying to dispel some of her energy and frustration. If she had had her way she would still be at work; god, she'd probably have stayed the whole damn night, if they'd let her.

Eddie knew about excess, and obsession. She had been cautioned about them, and genuinely wanted to establish more control over herself in these matters. But she felt proprietary about this homicide. She had written her report, made sure the various aspects of the investigation were well underway, and was poring over the report of the earlier homicide when she had been reminded that her shift was up.

"Okay, right," she had said.

And later: "Yup. Just give me a minute."

"Sergeant," Alberg had finally snapped at her. "Get the hell home."

She unlocked the door and went inside, stripping off her jacket and tie, and headed for the kitchen, where she grabbed a bottle of lime-flavored mineral water from the fridge and drank from it greedily. Then she went into the bedroom, where she took off her white shirt and the dark blue pants with the wide yellow stripe: both were crumpled and dusty. She'd take them and the jacket to the cleaners on the way to work in the morning. She put on shorts, a T-shirt, socks, and sneakers, and stepped onto her treadmill, after putting the water bottle and a hand towel on a table within her reach.

She'd been working out for less than fifteen minutes when the phone rang. When she picked it up she saw the flashing light—the answering machine had recorded three messages. "Damn," she said under her breath.

"Where've you been?" said Frank Henderson plaintively.

"Sorry, Dad," said Eddie, wiping her face with the towel. "Had to work a bit late."

"How are you enjoying your house?" he asked.

She had bought the house, instead of renting something, because her father had told her it would be a good investment.

"You can get into the market now," he had said when she told him about the promotion and her new posting. "This is good news, Edwina. The Sunshine Coast's about the only place on the Lower Mainland you can afford," he'd said. "It's a perfect opportunity."

In Burnaby she had lived in a rented apartment, which had been fine with Eddie, for whom domicile wasn't terribly important.

"It's fine," she said. "I like it."

"And the job?" he said.

"I don't think my new staff sergeant likes me much," she confessed.

"What do you mean? What did he say to you?" asked her father indignantly.

"Nothing, Dad. It's just a feeling." She climbed back on the treadmill.

"I'm sure you're mistaken, Eddie. And even if you're

right—you can come on a bit strong, after all—well, he'll get over it."

He didn't ask her about her day and she didn't volunteer anything. They didn't discuss her work. Her father was a bank manager and had never understood Eddie's desire to become a cop. It had developed during her adolescence, which occurred without incident; that is, she maneuvered through it without angering either her parents or her teachers. Her attention was always focused on what was to come afterward. She was impatient to get there, and worked hard so that when she did arrive she would have choices. Although she knew from junior high school that she wanted to be a police officer, she hadn't decided how to go about this. Should she become a lawyer first? Or get some kind of science degree? In the end, she decided to get a basic bachelor's degree and then apply for admission to the RCMP training academy in Regina: she wanted to serve with a federal force, doing police work in more than one part of the country.

Her high school was host to a series of resident cops during her last two years there, when there were starting to be lots of drugs around. She watched them intently but they never noticed this because she hadn't reached her full height yet, nor had she filled out as her mother kept promising she would. Eddie was on the girls' basketball team, and although she got good marks, she was casual about her academic achievements, so most people liked her. But the cops, they didn't even see her. They saw only the guys who were the troublemakers, and the girls with shiny hair and big boobs who sashayed slowly past them, offering oblique glances and crooked smiles: the cops' eyes followed these girls helplessly. Edwina laughed to herself, watching this, and felt enormously free, knowing she could smoke dope or carry a knife around in her backpack and the cops would never know. You had to be aware of someone, in order to suspect them. She also knew that the guys whom the cops had decided were the troublemakers were not the only troublemakers in the school.

"How's the unpacking going?" asked her dad.

Eddie reached for the water bottle and took a swig, then looked wearily at the boxes that crowded the bedroom, some of which had been opened and partially emptied. Their flaps sprawled, gaping, and packing paper littered the floor around them. Eddie had been dipping into them as she needed things. The iron, for instance. She had needed the iron that morning, and since she had never gotten around to listing which things had been packed in which boxes she had had to tear open several before coming across the iron, which had been packed with a carton of laundry soap, a container of bleach, the battered pink telephone with the long cord, a small lamp, and a skipping rope.

"It's going as you'd expect," she said defensively, striding on the treadmill, beginning to get out of breath.

"Mmmm."

"For pete's sake, Dad, you know me. I'm trying to get up to speed on the casework here." She didn't tell him about the homicide. "And this place is no fun to come home to empty."

"Why don't I come over on the weekend," suggested Frank, "and help you draw up a list of priorities."

"Oh Dad. Not another damn list. Please." She wiped her face again and tossed the towel on the bed. She was panting now. Good. Maybe she'd be able to get to sleep tonight after all.

"First you get everything unpacked and put away. Then we look around, decide what's got to be done to the place, and in what order."

"Yeah, sure, fine." Eddie looked around the bedroom, squinting, forcing herself to actually see the bare walls, the dusty floor, the boxes stacked haphazardly. She noticed that a large box at the bottom of one pile had started to cave in. It was probably full of bedding, she thought, and the smaller ones on top were where the books were. I'd better do something about that, she thought, because maybe there was a lamp wrapped in the bedding, or a mirror.

"Inside isn't bad, as I recall," Frank was saying. "Maybe you should do some painting, though."

"What are you talking about, do some painting? Who's got time to paint? Who's got time to empty all these damn boxes?" She stopped, expelling her breath in a whoosh. "I've got to get curtains or blinds or something on all these windows. Oh, for pete's sake."

"Don't worry about it," said her father, sounding worried himself now.

Eddie got off the treadmill and slung the towel around her neck. Her heartbeat was faster than it ought to be: she'd overdone it again. "I don't want to think about this crap. When you get an apartment, you get all that stuff with it. Paint. Curtains."

"So don't think about it, that's what I'm telling you. It'll get done."

"Yeah, sure." She took another swig of mineral water. "Hey, Eddie?"

"What."

"I'll come over on Saturday. We'll do the boxes. Get some curtains."

Eddie sighed. She didn't want to encourage him. But she'd be working all weekend, anyway, if she had anything to say about it. He could do it on his own: unpack her boxes, make up the list of priorities. Her absence would exasperate him, would remind him of all the things he didn't like about his daughter's chosen career, and he'd go home in a huff and maybe not bother her again for a while. "Yeah, okay, Dad," she said. "Thanks." Eddie started unbraiding her hair, the phone clutched between chin and shoulder.

"Eddie?"

"Yeah?"

"Your mother would have been so proud of you."

Eddie looked at her reflection in the mirror propped on top of her dressing table. Her T-shirt was blotched with sweat. Her damp face glowed. She saw herself, plainly—yet she didn't. It was her mother's face that looked back at her.

Eddie shook her head, hard, and looked again. She focused on her hair, long and thick. She watched it ripple through the air and sprawl upon her shoulders.

"Yeah, Dad," she said politely into the phone. "I know."

After she hung up, she checked her messages.

Three calls. Three hang-ups.

June 1985
Abbotsford, B.C.

———

Mrs. O'Hara's physical injuries were healing. She had learned how to wrap a scarf around her head to hide the shorn hair that surrounded her stitched-up gash. Her elbow, although still swollen, was hurting much less—she was off the painkillers. She was back at work, and life was back to normal. Except that it wasn't, of course.

Not a word had she heard from Tom. He had sneaked into the house while she was working and removed his belongings. He'd taken some of her belongings, too. She was still noticing things that were gone—incongruous things like a cheese grater, a potato peeler, a toilet brush. He had come into the house more than once and had never left his key behind, so finally Mrs. O'Hara had had the locks changed.

She knew she ought to see a lawyer and start divorce proceedings, but she didn't have the heart. It had never been one of Mrs. O'Hara's ambitions to become a divorced woman and she was still reluctant to do this even though god knew she had no wish to live with Tom again and in fact wouldn't have taken him back if he'd asked her, which he hadn't. Yet she had an urgent, aching need to put some kind of finishing mark upon her relationship with Tom. Her mind kept returning to divorce as the obvious way to achieve this, but divorce felt unemotional and impersonal, and far removed from the real-life situation. Divorce would certainly cause Tom no pain, or even any inconvenience. Divorce must be what he wanted, since without it he could hardly marry somebody else.

No, thought Mrs. O'Hara, almost reluctantly, divorce was out of the question. It would be immoral to reward Tom for his transgression. It was her responsibility to make sure he was justly punished: in fact, she owed him this.

She lay awake brooding about precisely how to accomplish it, snuggled into the comfortable hollow in the middle of the bed that she and Tom had once shared. She thought about it while wielding a hammer on the rickety outside staircase. She mulled it over as she raked the patch of earth next to the house that served as a half-hearted lawn. She considered it while brandishing the vacuum cleaner, while wiping up slopped-over coffee at the restaurant where she worked, while having a bath, while doing the laundry.

It wasn't revenge that she wanted. She only sought a way to bring things to a satisfactory completion, to make things even again, to balance the scales, to expunge the offense that had occurred and mitigate its deleterious, rippling effects.

One day on her break she found herself walking from the restaurant down to the end of the street, around the corner, up the hill, and across what used to be the highway to the diner, which was located near the police station. As she approached, she felt a number of eyes staring out at her, biting at her skin like gnats: this, she knew, was a product of her imagination, but it was no less painful for that. She eased up to the window and peered between the apostrophe and the "s" at the end of the word "Harvey's" that had been painted on the inside of the glass. There were tables right below the window and two decades of idle-minded patrons had scratched at the lettering with dimes and pennies. There had once been three layers of paint outlining each of the letters in "Harvey's Diner"— one red layer, one blue, one white. The white one, which was the bottom-most layer, was almost completely gone around its lower edges, scraped, scoured, and sniggered away over the years.

Mrs. O'Hara peered between the letters through the glass into the diner, which was practically empty, and after a moment's hesitation she went inside and sat down at a table at the far end. The metal chair made a harsh squealing sound as she dragged its legs across the floor.

Mrs. O'Hara could see no sign of Raylene.

She spread her hands out flat on the table but lifted them quickly because the surface was unpleasantly sticky.

Soon a potbellied man with greasy hair and a sweaty face erupted from the kitchen. With a flourish, he picked up a coffee pot and sashayed through the diner, refilling cups and making loud, hearty comments to his customers: an elderly woman with a large, brown paper shopping bag between her feet, two teenage girls who ought to have been in school, and, at the opposite end of the diner, two policemen. When the proprietor spotted Mrs. O'Hara he hurried over to her, coffee pot in hand.

"What can I get for you, ducks?" he asked, and Mrs. O'Hara told him that a coffee would do.

The clock on the wall said it was almost three-thirty. She had to be back at work by three-forty-five.

The coffee, when it arrived, was surprisingly good—plenty strong enough, which was more than Mrs. O'Hara could say about the stuff she served all day long.

She had been sitting there, quietly, for only five minutes or so when Raylene came in.

She slipped through the door shyly, slyly, like a living ghost, a smile on her pale face, her pale yellow hair rippling, falling in waves upon the shoulders of a man's gray overcoat she had probably bought at the Sally Ann. She looked backward as she entered, her hand stretched out behind her. And then Mrs. O'Hara saw that she was hand in hand with Tom.

As Tom followed Raylene inside the diner, Mrs. O'Hara hardly dared to breathe. She had only a few seconds before they would spot her; only a few seconds in which to glimpse the world that was inhabited by her husband and this whore; only a few seconds to assess the situation truly, to see their authentic, guileless selves, undefended and vulnerable.

. . . In those seconds it was as if Raylene were clasping not

Tom's hand, but his penis, which in Mrs. O'Hara's imagination, under her astonished scrutiny, grew longer and longer, like Pinocchio's nose. Raylene disappeared into the kitchen but Tom, at the end of his lengthening member, remained by the door, staring after her, clothed only in a silly, mindless grin. . . .

They both turned at the same moment, saw Mrs. O'Hara, and became rigid. They looked to her like recalcitrant children. She felt as powerless before them as if they had been children, innocent, exempt from responsibility and blame.

Mrs. O'Hara took hold of her purse and stood up. It was only then that she became fully conscious of her rage. She couldn't have spoken at that moment. She could not have said a single, solitary word. If she had blurted out even a syllable, she would have gone berserk.

Carefully, she edged between the two rows of tables to the door, where Raylene and Tom still stood frozen, their mouths agape. Mrs. O'Hara paused for a moment to look at them, memorizing the sight of them. She saw that there was a sheen of moisture on Tom's face and she thought that he was trembling slightly. Mrs. O'Hara felt extremely large and strong as she stood next to him, very close to him, looking down upon him, as usual. Then she swiveled her head to gaze upon Raylene. And her fast-beating heart achieved a sudden thunderous velocity, filling her ears with noise. She saw Raylene's lips move, saw her mouth open, and realized that Raylene was speaking, but she heard nothing except the sound of her own heart. She did, however, see the sly triumph at the back of Raylene's eyes and oh, that was a shame, such a shame. Before that moment Mrs. O'Hara had expected that Raylene would emerge from the whole thing relatively scot-free. But in that instant things changed.

She turned to look at the police officers, who were oblivious, staring moodily out the window of the diner.

And Mrs. O'Hara there and then made a slight change in her plans.

THIRTEEN

Wednesday, March 27

———

Susan Atkinson emerged from the elevator and traveled down the hallway to her apartment. The halls were outside galleries that ran along the back of the building, roofed but otherwise largely open to the elements, with waist-high concrete walls. Ivy covered the outside of the walls, frequently stretching green tentacles over the top, and clusters of large potted plants stood here and there. Susan ignored these as she passed them, door keys in her hand, carrying a Future Shop bag.

Inside her apartment she stood still for a moment, and heard the beep of her answering machine, but delayed retrieving her messages until she had hung up her jacket and put the bag containing her new portable telephone down on the kitchen counter. The answering machine was hooked up to a cheap, plastic, turquoise telephone. She couldn't remember where or when she had come into possession of this shockingly ugly thing, but when the portable had packed it in she had been glad to be able to rummage around in a trunk in the storeroom and come up with it as a temporary replacement. She could get rid of it now—but thought she'd better put it back in the trunk, just in case.

Three messages. Susan dropped her purse onto the kitchen table and pushed the machine's button.

"Hi, dear, looking forward to seeing you on Sunday,

and I just wondered—would you like to bring a friend? Rick and Barbara are coming, too. I thought I'd do a pot roast. Try to get over early so we can have a good visit. Bye, dear."

"Susan, it's Marge at the bookstore. Your two-volume *Shorter Oxford Dictionary*'s in. Boy, it's gonna set you back a pretty penny. You know that, I guess, huh? Wow."

"Ms. Atkinson, it's the Diabetes Association. We'll be making a pickup in your area next Thursday. Please let us know if you'll have anything to put out for us. Thanks."

Susan sat at the kitchen table and considered the extent of her disappointment.

It was unusually quiet in her apartment. She had turned on neither radio nor television.

She went out onto the balcony. Some kids were throwing a Frisbee on the beach, and there were several strollers on the walkway that followed the shoreline. The sun was shining almost directly upon Susan, who shaded her eyes, averting them from the water and looking across at the town, at the new-leafed trees, explosions of green, at cherry blossoms like great wafts of cotton candy. She listened to the water lapping at the stony shore, and the cry of a seagull, and the shouting children.

Soon she went back inside, closed the balcony door, and sat on the sofa with her chin in her hand.

Up to now, she hadn't seriously considered the possibility that he wouldn't call. She hadn't heard from him the previous day, but she hadn't expected to; he usually didn't phone for a couple of days after they'd been together. She had always considered this a matter of delicacy. Of tact. But now she wondered if he, too, hadn't been completely honest with himself about their relationship. She wondered if he felt guilty despite himself, after they had made love, and maybe for a day or so had been thinking about ending their affair.

"There is no profit in this kind of speculation," said

Susan, out loud. She would go out again, she would buy some groceries.

Before she left, she unplugged the answering machine.

Later, she sat at her tiny desk with the new portable phone and went through her list of things to do, methodically: she called the nursery, the cleaner, the dentist. And her mother. Yes, she too was looking forward to Sunday. No, she wouldn't be bringing a friend. But thanks for asking.

Wednesday. Four more days off, and they were looming large and empty. She felt helpless to fill them.

But fill them she must. She would go swimming, for one thing, every day except Sunday—Sunday would take care of itself: she would turn her mind to work that day, preparing to go back to school; and then there would be dinner at her mother's.

So that left only three days, really. She could spend one of them in Vancouver, shopping for spring clothes. After all, she wouldn't get another chance to shop on a weekday for months. She would do that tomorrow, Thursday.

And today she would go through the trunk and the boxes in the storeroom, selecting things to be given away to the Diabetes Association. She would be hot and dusty and cranky by the time that was done, so she'd have a bath and then take herself out to eat. Maybe she would call somebody, see if Frances or Hedy wanted to join her.

That left only Friday and Saturday.

If she hadn't heard from him by Friday, she would call him. They were, after all, colleagues.

What was going on, though? she wondered, in the elevator, on her way to the storeroom. Could something be wrong?

"No, I'm sorry," Denise told Ivan's mechanic on the phone, "he's out of town, he must have forgotten." She watched through the window an enormous throng of birds sweep in unison from one treetop to another, describing an exaggerated many-winged arc against the blue, spring sky. "I—yes, of course, I'll tell him."

She had decided to take the whole week off. It wasn't only teachers who deserved a break now and again. Two weeks' holiday in a year simply wasn't sufficient. And so the flu she had invented on Monday was going to last the entire week.

She had been letting the machine take her calls. Those who had been told she was ill would probably think she was in bed. And friends, of course, believed her to be at work. Denise was glad she worked in Gibsons instead of here in Sechelt. Now she needn't feel furtive when she left the house to do errands or go for a walk on the beach.

She had answered the phone just now, however, because for an instant she had been certain it was Ivan calling. Now she hung up the receiver feeling disappointed, but surprised to discover that she was also relieved. Why had she been relieved? It must mean that she didn't want to speak to him, at least not at this particular moment. She thought about that—or rather, played with the thought, skittered around the edges of it—and decided that yes, it was true, she didn't want to talk to Ivan.

There was an enormous restlessness within her body, a sensation far too large and powerful to be contained. She needed to dig a huge hole in the garden, or go for a run. But she didn't want to do either of these things: she wanted, suddenly, to cry. She had had this experience several times in the last few days. A terrible need to weep.

"What can I do?" she said out loud.

And knew the answer. She could, and must, clean the house. She had been putting it off, inventing other tasks, other urgencies: stocking the cupboards, doing the laundry, ironing things that didn't need to be ironed—sheets, for example, and the new towels. And she had spent hours at the little desk that was crowded into a corner of the bedroom, paying bills, getting the accounts in order. She had even made a start on a Christmas list.

But now there was nothing left to do, except clean. Denise couldn't think of a single thing—except working in the garden. But, doing what? she wondered, looking out the window. She didn't know one plant from another.

Besides, the outdoors didn't threaten her. And the indoors did.

She turned from the window. The branches she had torn from the underbrush were dropping tiny pink petals onto the bookcase, and the water in the vase had become clouded and brackish. Denise went to the kitchen to get a black garbage bag, bending to take it from a bottom drawer, and standing so swiftly that she made herself dizzy for a moment and had to clutch the edge of the counter. In the living room she wrapped her fingers firmly around the branches and dumped them into the bag. She opened her stinging hand and saw new scratches on its palm.

"I must clean this house," said Denise.

She filled a pail with hot water and added a cleaning fluid. She began in the bedroom, stroking a yellow sponge over the walls, as high as she could reach; removing framed prints and two small oil paintings Ivan had bought from artist friends; wiping; rehanging the paintings; rinsing the sponge in water that was almost too hot for her hands to bear, squeezing away excess water; and wiping again: the top of Ivan's bureau; the surface of her dressing table, pushing cosmetics and silverbacked brush, comb, and mirror first to one side and then to the other. Denise made her systematic way around the bedroom, concentrating, missing nothing. She cleaned the desk, tidied now, unlittered, financial records filed neatly away in drawers. She cleaned Ivan's nightstand, the headboard, then her own nightstand, wiping the lamp, lifting the clock radio and cleaning beneath it, running the sponge around the edges and down the sides. She needed to rinse the sponge again. She pulled back from the nightstand, glanced at the sponge—and a small puff of air was expelled from her lungs, as if she had been rapped, softly, once, on the chest.

Denise sat back on her heels and swallowed several times. She looked again at the sponge, at the red smear on it.

Her skin contracted as she thought about how much cleaning there was still to do.

"We'll get the autopsy results tomorrow probably," said Eddie, "but the preliminary findings indicate there was no sexual assault." She referred to her notebook. "Just like Rebecca Granger."

Alberg was sitting at his desk. Eddie occupied the black leather chair he kept for visitors, and Ralph Mondini had dragged in a folding metal chair from the interview room.

"Assuming there's a connection," said Alberg, "—and you're right, Sergeant, two homicide victims deposited in the same clearing virtually guarantees a connection between them—what do we know?"

"Rebecca Granger was struck on the head, then strangled," said Eddie, leafing through a file folder.

"Right," said Alberg.

"We don't know about Janet Maine for sure yet," said Mondini, "but if she was killed in the same way, well, it might suggest—" He stopped, flushing.

Eddie felt immediate sympathy. She had endured this affliction ever since she was a teenager with sexual urges that were crucial to conceal. She had been betrayed by her own blood—every time she felt lustful, her face got red. Eventually she learned to feign anger or outrage whenever she felt a blush coming on. This had proven amazingly successful. She thought it was at least partially responsible for her reputation as an aggressive officer.

"It might suggest what?" asked Alberg.

Eddie couldn't tell whether he was impatient with Mondini. In fact, she couldn't ever tell what was going on in Alberg's head. He was not a person who needed to worry about blushing—about revealing himself in any way at all. His face was smooth, his eyes were hooded. He hid himself, skillfully, retreating behind the flat, guileless planes of his face.

"Well, it occurred to me," said Mondini, "that—well, a couple of things occurred to me."

"Give me one of them," said Alberg.

"It could be that the perpetrator isn't particularly strong."

"Uh huh," said Alberg.

"Because it looks like he had to knock them unconscious before he smothered them," said the constable. "Like he didn't have the strength to just, you know, strangle them to death."

"Or else he didn't want it to be that intimate an experience," said Eddie.

"What do you mean, Sergeant?" asked Alberg.

"If they're unconscious, it may be like he's killing somebody who's already dead."

"Maybe," said Alberg. "They're conscious, though, when he hits them, of course."

He was pulling apart paperclips and bending them into stick people. Although Eddie knew he was paying attention to the conversation, she nevertheless found this irritating.

Now he arranged his stick people into a circle, feet together. "Anything else?" He glanced up at them over his reading glasses.

"Well, the fact that they weren't buried deep," said Mondini, "that might mean he didn't really care when the bodies would be found."

"Why bury them at all, then?" said Alberg.

"To give himself time to get away from the scene," said Eddie. "To get home. Or onto a ferry."

"You're probably right." Alberg studied Mondini, who reminded him of a constable who had been at the detachment when Alberg took over. Sanducci was Italian, too. But he'd been extremely good-looking, unlike Mondini, who possessed a sallow complexion, thinning hair, and a tall but scrawny physique. Alberg had recently heard that Sanducci, an inveterate womanizer, had actually gotten married, settled down, and become a father. Alberg found this hard to believe.

"Okay," he said. "I want the autopsy report as soon as it gets here. And the scene of the crime report. And officers' reports on interviews."

Mondini's chair scraped against the floor as the two of them stood up to leave.

"You realize," said Alberg softly, "that if we'd found this son of a bitch last summer, Janet Maine would still be alive."

Mondini and Henderson hovered awkwardly in the doorway.

"Neither of you was here then," Alberg went on. "But I was here."

"It was—the body—six months had gone by, Staff," said Eddie hesitantly, clutching the file folder to her chest.

"I know that, Sergeant." Alberg took off his glasses and rubbed his eyes. "Nevertheless." He folded the glasses and put them aside. "But we've got a second chance at him now."

"Right," said Mondini.

They shuffled out into the hall, closing the door behind them.

"So what kinda stuff do you report on?" asked Naomi. She banged her empty beer glass on the bar and signaled that she wanted another. "Besides people and their jobs, I mean."

Cindi figured that Naomi was bringing the interview to an end. "I'm a general reporter," she said, closing her notebook, "so I do whatever comes along." She stashed the notebook in her immense shoulderbag, which rested against the legs of the bar stool she was sitting on.

"Like that murder?" said Naomi. She turned avidly to Cindi, displaying more interest than she had all evening. "How about that, eh? Two bodies, dumped in the same spot." She gave a low whistle, shaking her head.

"No," said Cindi. "There's a guy who covers police and courts. He's handling it."

"Thanks, Paul," said Naomi to the bartender, as he put another beer in front of her.

"What about you, Miss?" asked Paul, but Cindi smiled and shook her head.

"Makes you wonder," said Naomi, "just how safe anybody is." She glanced at her watch. "Jesus. I got to get home pretty soon. Tuck in the kids." She brushed some ferociously black hair away from her forehead.

It was still early, and the bar was far from crowded. Cindi let herself gaze around the room, appraising, assessing.

"Shit," Naomi mumbled. "I'm bushed." She had her back to the bar, hands loose in her lap, and her eyes were closed. "That son of a bitch Earl, he's gotta get another waitress in there. Waiter. Whatever." She began humming to herself, a country and western tune that Cindi recognized but couldn't identify. Naomi's heels drummed against the bar stool railing in time to the music.

"What happened to the last one?" asked Cindi. Naomi's skin was extremely pale, which made her black hair look even blacker. She would be attractive, Cindi decided, if she weren't so combative.

"I don't know," said Naomi with a shrug, her eyes still closed. "One day she's there, next day she's gone. Didn't even pick up what was owed her."

Cindi watched as an out-of-uniform Mountie entered the bar with three male friends. Not bad looking.

"She wasn't a happy person," said Naomi. She opened her eyes and reached behind her for the beer, which she drank straight from the bottle this time.

"What, you mean—she was depressed?" asked Cindi.

"Guilty."

"What about?"

"Put her mom in a home. Or maybe it was her dad." Naomi took another swig. "Or a grandparent. Shit, I can't remember. Anyway, she stashed some old relative or other in some kind of a home, and so she felt guilty." She looked again at her watch. "Shit. I really do gotta go. They're gonna already be in bed if I don't." She swung herself off the bar stool. "Coming? Or are you gonna stay and flirt with that cop over there?"

Cindi reached quickly for her shoulderbag, grateful for the dim light in the bar that might hide her expression. She dug out some money and dropped it on the bar. "Coming. I'm coming."

FOURTEEN

Thursday, March 28

The next day the weather had changed. Gray clouds were piled against the mountains and had spread across the sky. Rain fell in fitful showers, then in downpours. Susan, drinking coffee on the ferry, had forced herself to make the trip to the mainland and was already regretting it, for calmness and certainty had possessed her, unexpectedly, here in the cafeteria, and she had remembered with reassuring clarity his leave-taking late last Monday night.

"I'll call you," he had said. "We'll find a way to spend a couple of days together, out of town."

This rang in her head, now, and she heard unmistakable affection in his voice, obvious attachment, and saw the light tremble in his eyes as he bent to brush his lips across her cheek in what had become a ritual goodbye.

Susan felt a sudden urgent uneasiness. Maybe something *was* wrong. Maybe somebody had died. Or he had gotten sick, had had a heart attack or something, even though he was only forty-two and supposedly healthy.

She hurried from the cafeteria and out on deck, where the wind felt strong enough to knock her off the ship and into the frigid waters of Howe Sound. Anything could happen to anybody at any moment, she thought, wrapping her arms protectively around her body. He might be lying in a hospital bed with an oxygen mask over his face, hooked up to an IV bag.

When the ferry docked, Susan drove off through Horseshoe Bay and back up to the freeway, where she turned left and joined the lineup for the return trip to Langdale.

An hour later she was home.

Mrs. O'Hara had breakfast at Earl's again that Thursday morning, but encountered nothing and nobody of interest there.

As she ate her softboiled egg, she remembered a day years ago when she had decided to poach a chicken. She had placed the bird in a large pot and held the pot under the kitchen tap. And as she watched the water level rise, covering the chicken, she realized that the chicken wasn't a chicken at all. It wasn't a creature that had lived and squawked and feared and fluttered. It was merely food.

And so it was, she had thought, that her sinners weren't people. Not once they had sinned.

The first one, after Tom and Raylene, was a man who owned a hardware store that Mrs. O'Hara frequented. He treated his employees badly, with rudeness and contempt. Mrs. O'Hara had several times sent conspicuous disapproving frowns his way but this had had no effect and so one day she rebuked him, sharply. He turned small, black, porcine eyes upon her and Mrs. O'Hara began to stammer and was gripped by a full-body shudder. The storekeeper slapped her purchases into a paper bag with unnecessary force, turned to one of his feckless employees and ordered the man to do something. Mrs. O'Hara couldn't remember, later, what his directive had been: the tremor of apprehension, or fear, or aversion, or whatever it was, had mutated into rage, and she was too angry to hear. All sound had clotted into a solid, pulsating din. She blundered out of the store and slid open the side door of her van with shaking hands.

That night in the fragrant dark, gasoline slurped from her red plastic gas can: Mrs. O'Hara listened to it splash against the side of the hardware store, then heard the flames bawl as they consumed the building.

He had insurance, of course. And soon there was another hardware store, on the same lot. But Mrs. O'Hara burned that one to the ground, too, and this time he gave up and moved away.

Mrs. O'Hara hoped that he had suspected one of his employees, and that this would result in his treating future staff members with more respect.

Mrs. O'Hara finished her breakfast and pushed the plate aside. Before she left Earl's she used the toilet, because it was very clean. She knew that Earl scrubbed it himself at the close of business hours, and also made regular checks throughout the day. Mrs. O'Hara didn't like using the facilities at the places she cleaned—it felt inappropriate. But it was sometimes necessary, of course.

She climbed into her van, which had no windows in the sides, and as she slid behind the wheel Mrs. O'Hara realized that her energy had returned, and she felt her spirits start to rise. She sat in peace for a moment, looking out through the windshield.

None of the businesses on the street were open yet, only Earl's Café and the sandwich place down the block. Hardly anybody frequented the sandwich place anymore. Mrs. O'Hara reflected on this, marveling. How on earth had Earl's become the café of choice? The sandwich place was a lot spiffier. And although the food wasn't as good as Earl's food, it had been, once; it had in fact been a lot better than Earl's. Yet people went to Earl's. They didn't talk about this. They hadn't made a community decision. They just went there, regularly, day after day.

It was only March. She had—not lots of time, not plenty of time. But time.

Soon there would be hanging baskets of summer flowers up and down the street, and tourist traffic would clog the roads again.

Mrs. O'Hara turned on the engine, put the van into gear, and set off for the first house on her list.

She did the Newmans' place, and then the Mackenzies'.

It was almost noon when she pulled up in front of the Dyakowskis' house, stuffed her keys into the knapsack she used as a handbag, and got out of the van. She hauled back the side door and started to unload her supplies: a metal pail, a plastic pail, a scrub brush, containers of liquid cleanser, gritty cleanser, glass cleanser. She reached for the paste wax, and then reminded herself of where she was—there was nothing in the Dyakowskis' house that needed waxing. The van's door rumbled loudly as Mrs. O'Hara shoved it closed. She picked up the pails full of her supplies and headed through the broken gate across the unmown grass to the back door.

She reached for the key on the window ledge, but before she could insert it in the lock the door opened a crack and Denise looked out, her hair disheveled, her eyes squinted. "Mrs. O'Hara," she said dully.

Mrs. O'Hara was startled: she hadn't expected anyone to be home.

"Mrs. O'Hara," said Denise again.

Mrs. O'Hara found her tongue. "Right. It's me. I've come to clean, like usual."

Denise continued to peer out at her, blinking.

It began to rain. Mrs. O'Hara heard it scattering itself on the roof of the overhang under which she stood, waiting, a pail in each hand, her knapsack hanging around her neck. "You've forgotten," she said. "Okay, then. Do you want me to come back another day?"

"Oh," said Denise, dazed.

"Are you sick?" Mrs. O'Hara asked suddenly. She thought Denise might be looking a little pale. Although it was hard to tell, seeing only a small strip of her face.

"No," said Denise, but she didn't sound completely certain. "Oh well," she said, and pulled the door fully open. "I'm sorry. Come in."

Once Mrs. O'Hara was inside, Denise began chattering, which was uncharacteristic. Mrs. O'Hara watched and listened in amazement.

Tying her robe tight around her waist, Denise said, "Yes, I have been sick, I've had the flu all week. And I didn't stay in bed like I should have, either. Ivan would be so mad." She scuttled into the kitchen and filled the drip coffee maker. "Do you want some coffee, Mrs. O'Hara? And perhaps a cinnamon bun? I think I've got some cinnamon buns," she said, hunting through cupboards. "Oh dear. I'm wrong."

"I don't want anything, thanks," said Mrs. O'Hara, opening the living room curtains.

"It's Thursday, isn't it?" said Denise, rubbing her hands vigorously. "Ivan will be back on Sunday, from Penticton, he's there on some sort of course, I think. I have to be better by the time he gets home," she said seriously.

"Your face is flushed, it's true," said Mrs. O'Hara. "Have you been to the doctor?"

"I mean—can you imagine? A whole week. I've missed almost an entire week of work. But I've kept myself busy," said Denise, running her hands through her hair, which Mrs. O'Hara noticed needed washing. "Cleaning, cleaning, cleaning, you wouldn't believe how I've scrubbed and scrubbed."

Mrs. O'Hara looked slowly around. "What am I doing here, then?"

Denise stopped talking and looked intently into her face.

"I mean, if you've cleaned the place yourself, you don't need me. Right?"

"Oh no," said Denise. "I do need you, Mrs. O'Hara. Really I do." She nodded her head in affirmation. "I haven't done all that wonderful a job, I'm afraid." She scraped her hands through her hair again. "Please."

Looking at Denise, Mrs. O'Hara was somehow reminded of Raylene, although they didn't look at all alike.

What was going on here? she wondered.

Susan picked up the portable phone and dialed his number, standing at the glass doors, watching the rain batter the waters of Trail Bay.

The phone rang several times. She had resigned herself to getting an answering machine, and was trying to decide whether or not to leave a message when the phone was picked up and a soft, breathless voice said, "Hello?"

"Hello," said Susan. "May I speak to Ivan, please?" She sounded calm and controlled, even to herself.

"Oh, I'm afraid he isn't here. Can I take a message?"

"When do you expect him?"

"Oh, not until Sunday, I'm afraid. Shall I get him to call you?"

"I—Sunday?"

"Yes, that's right."

Susan stared out at the weather.

"Hello? Do you want to leave a message?"

"Oh no," said Susan, stammering a little. "No—that's fine. Thank you."

"You're welcome," said Ivan's wife. "Goodbye."

"Goodbye," said Susan, and hung up.

Denise. That was the woman's name.

Susan didn't move for a while. She held on to the phone.

Gone until Sunday.

Okay. He had decided to go ahead on his own, then, and call to tell her where to meet him.

But then why hadn't she heard from him? She sat down to think. Maybe he hadn't been able to get away until today. He might still be on his way to wherever it was he'd decided they should go. Susan was slightly irritated by this high-handedness: she would like to have had a say in where they spent their days together.

But that was nit-picking.

She would wait, then, to hear from him.

When the telephone rang, Mrs. O'Hara had just finished doing the rugs: the sound of the vacuum cleaner still echoed through the small house. Denise answered on the portable phone in the kitchen, and the eagerness in her voice created in Mrs. O'Hara's heart a sympathetic leap.

"Hello?" said Denise, and she might as well have said, "Ivan?"

Mrs. O'Hara, winding the cord around the plump body of the vacuum cleaner, listened, in spite of herself.

"Oh," said Denise listlessly.

Mrs. O'Hara shook her head.

"I'm afraid he isn't here," said Denise. "Can I take a message?"

Mrs. O'Hara put the vacuum cleaner away in the closet.

"Oh, not until Sunday, I'm afraid," said Denise. "Shall I get him to call you?"

Mrs. O'Hara pushed the sleeves of her sweatshirt up past her elbows and picked up one of her pails.

"Yes, that's right."

She poured a thick yellow liquid into the pail.

"Hello?" said Denise. "Do you want to leave a message?"

Mrs. O'Hara put the pail in the kitchen sink and turned on the hot water tap.

"You're welcome. Goodbye."

Mrs. O'Hara glanced at Denise, who was replacing the telephone in its cradle.

Then she looked at her more sharply.

"That was somebody wanting Ivan," said Denise. "A woman." She went to the kitchen window and looked outside. "It's raining again. Or maybe it never stopped. Did it stop, for a while?"

Mrs. O'Hara scratched absently at the flesh of her arms. She thought about Ivan Dyakowski, about how he was always late going to work. She had never considered him a particularly attractive man, physically.

A familiar intoxicating euphoria began bubbling in Mrs. O'Hara's veins. She shivered with gratitude.

"Do you want to have children?" she asked Denise.

"What?"

Mrs. O'Hara didn't repeat the question, just swung the pail out of the sink and set it down on the floor.

"Yes," said Denise finally. "Of course." Her voice acquired more confidence as she said this. "Eventually," she added, more hesitantly, as if her husband had just whispered in her ear. She stepped out of Mrs. O'Hara's way and backed from the kitchen into the living room.

Mrs. O'Hara submerged the sponge mop in the pail and waited while it absorbed water.

"She didn't say who she was," said Denise, behind her.

Mrs. O'Hara listened carefully.

"I told her he'll be home on Sunday. I'm sure she'll call again then," said Denise.

Mrs. O'Hara looked behind her, thoughtfully, at Denise, who was standing in the middle of the living room, looking at the wall, hugging herself. "Oh, I'm sure she will," she said. "Perhaps, if she calls before he gets here, you should ask for her name."

Denise turned and looked at her sharply.

Mrs. O'Hara raised her eyebrows. Then started scrubbing the kitchen floor, humming to herself as she worked.

FIFTEEN

Sunday, March 31

———

On Sunday morning, simultaneously with the fluttering open of Denise's eyes, came the ringing of the telephone. She lay for a moment looking at the ceiling. And with astonishing certitude and grace, the world shifted. Changed.

Denise sat up in bed, slowly, listening to the phone ring, knowing that it was not Ivan calling; knowing who *was* calling; knowing everything.

She sat still, waiting for the ringing to stop, but it rang on and on—Denise had turned off the answering machine. She began counting the rings and had counted nine when it stopped, abruptly. But the noise it had created hung in the air like a miasma. Denise could hear it echoing, shimmering; an auricular illusion that racketed from wall to wall and then, gradually, faded away.

She pulled up her knees, wrapped her arms around them, lowered her head and wept, for Ivan, for her loss. Her body ached for him . . . for his flat stomach, his hairy genitals, his wide shoulders, the blunt, brutal thickness of his neck; she whispered to herself, recreating him, his brown eyes, his thin lips, the space between his front teeth. . . . She grieved the loss of his laughter and his disdain, his restless ambition, the children they would never have.

Mourning was good, she realized. Funerals were good. It was necessary to have a sense of the world stopping in its tracks for a moment, giving the bereaved person time—not to adjust—the world couldn't afford to stop long enough for that—but to prepare, as one prepares for a voyage.

She wiped her face with the sheet and got out of bed, standing cautiously on legs that trembled, hobbled to the window and pulled the blind. Spring sunshine shone once again on the tumult of vegetation that was their backyard—her backyard, now.

Too shaky to stand any longer, she sat down at the desk and ran the palm of her hand over its smooth surface, pale and shiny, lacquered pine. No dust was to be found there. Between them, Denise and Mrs. O'Hara had vanquished dust and grime, fingerprints and skid marks. And blood . . .

She wouldn't have believed she had the strength, let alone the will. Denise bent her head, obedient to anguish, and wept again softly, hopelessly, wondering who might help her: oh! such a pickle she was in.

But totally in the wrong? Was she?

She pushed herself wearily to her feet and shuffled into the kitchen, where she turned on the radio for company. She ate some cereal, sitting on the love seat. She glanced at the rocking chair as she ate and wondered if she would keep it. She spooned up the last of the sugared milk and put the bowl in the sink.

In the shower, Denise washed her body with tenderness and compassion, for it was the body of a young widow and deserved these attentions. The warm, soothing water stroked her skin like the hands of a lover. Denise observed once more, admiringly, how selective the mind could become, capable of closing the door firmly on great chunks of its own churning contemplations, perfectly willing to eschew rationality in the service of its own well-being.

She turned off the shower, stepped out of the tub, and was suddenly acutely aware of sounds: her own breathing, the settling of the shower curtain, reluctant waterdrops easing down the drain. The rubbing of the towel against her legs, her arms, her torso sounded to Denise like the purring of a cat. She enjoyed, briefly, a sense of immense well-being.

She dressed in shorts and a sweatshirt and exited the bathroom, leaving the door open so that the steam could escape. It was because of steam that the paint in there had puckered and flaked. I may move, Denise thought. Maybe to Gibsons.

Or farther, she thought, standing at the living room window, looking out at the front yard, which was every bit as crammed full of untended greenery as the back.

She sat down again, in the rocking chair this time, her hands on its wooden arms, and rocked. She had not meant to hurt him. She had not meant to cause him pain.

Denise rocked, grieving.

Then she rethought. No, that wasn't right. She *had* meant to hurt him. She *had* meant to cause him pain. What she hadn't intended was to kill him.

There she was—Denise, last Monday evening—reclining on the love seat, doing her nails, with the television on for company. She bent her head to her task, paying scant attention to the local—which was to say Vancouver—late news, listening for Ivan's car and concentrating on her manicure, wiping each nail with a tissue soaked in polish remover, working a file under each one, then gently stroking them smooth with an emery board, taking her time about it, on the lookout for every single chip and crack. The news came to an end and she changed channels, looking for a *Law & Order* rerun. She watched the screen until she had identified the episode, turned her head slightly and muted the set for a moment, listening—then re-established the sound.

Ivan's car pulled up outside, present first at a distance

and then proximate, impending, emerging from the night like a swell of music.

On the television screen an agitated Logan was telling Greavey about his abusive, alcoholic mother.

Outside, the car door slammed shut. He hadn't bothered to be quiet about it because he could see from the glow of the lights through the living room curtain that Denise was not only awake, but up.

Law & Order was having a commercial break. Denise muted the sound again and imagined Mike, during this break, imposing calm upon himself, and Greavey deciding not to inquire further into his partner's relationship with his dead mom. At least Denise had assumed that she was dead. But why? she wondered, watching the front door, watching for the knob to turn. Maybe she wasn't dead. Denise liked this idea. Perhaps someday the producers would do an episode in which Mike's mother made an appearance. Denise was very curious about her.

The knob turned, the door opened. "Hi," said Ivan.

"Hi," said Denise.

"It's late," they both said, almost in unison. Ivan laughed, and Denise stretched the corners of her mouth upward.

"The meeting ran late," he said, holding up his briefcase, as if in verification of the irrevocable passing of time. It was the first day of spring break. Denise noticed an alteration in her heartbeat, which had become a quick shallow thrumming that she felt not in her chest but in her wrists. She lowered her feet to the floor and sat on the edge of the love seat. Her mouth was dry—she drank some stale ginger ale from a glass sitting in a puddle of water on the coffee table.

"Your program's back on." said Ivan, gesturing at the television set. He looked at his watch. "Boy. Yeah, it is late. I'm off to bed, hon."

Denise gritted her teeth against a sudden battering of

anger and contempt. She reached for the remote and turned the sound back on. This was her favorite episode of *Law & Order*. She tried to watch it, struggled to find and re-harness her concentration. But it had been splintered: the pieces of her concentration hung in the air like shards of brittle light.

Denise got to her feet, feeling aimless and large-footed. Was her hair disheveled? Was her face mottled? distorted? She tried to make it smooth and stood straight, forcing her shoulders out of a huddle.

"I wanted to be calm about this," she said. "Yes, I had really and truly wanted to be calm."

Ivan must have heard something new in her voice. Perhaps she sounded unnaturally dispassionate, Denise thought, and she tried to lengthen her body, to draw her shoulders back, elevate her chin, stretch her spine. Detached and elegant, that's what she would be.

But it wasn't working. Her shoulders wouldn't budge from their protective hunch, her neck had shrunk, and her chin was tucked into the hollow between neck and chest. She heard herself screech at him: "Where have you been?!"

How ghastly, that she should shout such a thing. How mortifying, that she should feel so ugly.

Ivan pivoted in the doorway, one hand lightly on the doorjamb. She watched him thinking. Denise, looking at the long weary stripe of male thing that was Ivan in the damn doorway, thought he was too close to her, much too close to her, even though he was across the room. There ought to be a great chasm between them, some sort of gorge, with rocks, and wickedly rushing water in its bottom. Instead, there was only an expanse of familiar floor, so familiar as to be nauseating.

"I don't know what you're talking about," said Ivan. But he did. Of course he did.

He didn't turn to leave the room, to head for the bathroom or the bedroom. He continued to stand quietly in the doorway, waiting. Patiently expectant, that's what he was. Maybe a tiny bit tense, but not much.

Denise flapped her hands, but couldn't think of anything to say, and for an instant he looked amused. And then this was gone, and he was hiding again behind his blank face.

Denise, snared among furniture, stumbled toward the window and lacking a purpose there created one, hauling the venetian blind ceilingward and tethering it. Her image in the glass stared back at her, fists on hips, head thrust forward, shoulders still hunkered. Behind her, in the glass, Ivan leaned against the doorjamb and folded his arms, right shoulder leaning, left leg straight, right leg slightly bent, hip thrust slightly forward, and—was this deliberate? The son of a bitch, thought Denise. She turned quickly around, appalled by the sensations in her groin, the silent moaning, the growing dampness: the cotton crotch of her underpants would soon be sticky with sex.

"You're having an affair," she said. "You're sleeping with somebody else." Ivan lowered his jaw and widened his eyes but he didn't fool Denise. "And I won't have it," she said.

She stalked into the kitchen, but once again found herself without an objective. She was fluttering, pointlessly. Confronting him, but not really confronting him. Hurling accusations over a hunched shoulder, then skittering face first into a corner while he considered his possibilities. You are a spineless chick, she said to herself, contemptuously. Well, somebody said it. This was not a phrase Denise had ever used and she titled her head inquisitively, listening for more. But there wasn't any more, only the same phrase again: You are a spineless chick, Denise.

Ivan had come into the kitchen by now. Denise felt him behind her. She wiped the countertops, vigorously. And noticed that she hadn't cleaned up after her dinner of scrambled eggs and toast. She had cooked the eggs in butter with a little cream, slowly, with some chopped chives added at the end. The cast-iron frying pan that had been her mother's sat on the stove with shreds of dried egg clinging to its sides and bottom. Toastcrumbs littered the breadboard, and her dirty dishes sat in the sink. Denise swept the dishcloth across the countertop, rearranging the crumbs.

"Don't try to deny it," she said to the sink. Then she leaned heavily against the counter, gripping the edge with her fingers, her palms facing upward. The dishcloth fell to the floor, and a moment of silence was created—poignant, unencumbered. Then Ivan reached down, picked up the dishcloth, tossed it onto the counter.

"Yes," he said quietly.

Denise couldn't begin to assimilate the variety of consequences, repercussions, that she knew would flow from this unequivocal monosyllable. She blinked her eyes, rapidly, her lashes brushing them free of sudden tears whose warmth astonished her. She remained where she was, her back to Ivan, wrists crooked, bare, thrust upward like a pair of pale vein-threaded offerings.

"Good," she said. "Thank you for that, anyway." But bitterness had seeped into her voice.

"Denise," he said. "Do you want to talk about it?"

She pushed herself away from the counter and rubbed her wrists, which were aching now. "Talk about what, exactly?" And this was better—she sounded almost conversational. She even felt able now to turn and face him, and did so, folding her arms, giving her head a little toss. She directed her gaze straight into his eyes and felt a small prick of satisfaction when his lashes fluttered and he looked away from her. "You're prepared to give me details, perhaps?" she said.

"I mean, talk about what happens now," said Ivan, patiently.

Denise rubbed her big toe through a splotch of what

was probably butter and glanced across the floor at Ivan's shoes, black and polished, with jaunty leather tassels. She imagined him slipping off his loafers in somebody else's bedroom. They were probably all over each other, the two of them, while this was happening. She glanced up, higher: was his shirt misbuttoned? Was a button gone? But no. If passion were to send their buttons flying, one of them—not Ivan, definitely not useless, bloody Ivan—would sew them back on again. Before or after the shower? she wondered. Which they would have together. . . . Denise stamped her bare foot on the floor, splintering these apparitions.

"Perhaps I should leave," said Ivan, very seriously. "Tonight, I mean."

Denise felt her lungs deflate, and looked sideways for deliverance.

"We can talk later," he said solicitously. "Tomorrow, maybe. I could come by in the evening."

Denise couldn't speak. She picked up the dishcloth and started wiping again, but her hands were trembling.

"Denise?"

She shook her head.

"Ah, Denise. Listen. Who knows, right? Who knows what's going to happen?"

Her hands were shaking so badly now that the dishcloth slipped through her fingers and again landed on the floor. It has to go into the laundry now, Denise thought. It should have gone into the laundry the first time it fell. She couldn't look away from it, a crumpled square of fabric with a blue and white pattern huddling on the kitchen floor.

"We'll talk about it," said Ivan. "And we'll do what's right for both of us."

Denise continued to stare at the dishcloth, her hands entwined in front of her. She watched Ivan reach down and pick it up. She looked at the frying pan and wondered what size of a lump it might effect upon the back of Ivan's head, which he was even now offering to her, stooping before her as if in placation, his hair as shiny black as his polished loafers.

She had thought it would be a cuff, something merely tentative, she was still trembling so. But when her fingers wrapped around the familiar handle she stopped shaking. Even then she expected to land only an insignificant blow, a trivial clout which Ivan would accept with a groan and a manly flinch, as something justly deserved.

But when she struck him, a crevasse opened in his head and Ivan fell like a tree, his blood pouring over the kitchen floor.

SIXTEEN

Have you heard from Alan since you got here?" asked Eddie's father that morning, casually, over breakfast.

"That's over, Dad," she said abruptly. "I told you."

"Yes, but I just wondered; you're bound to feel lonely, at first, a new place, a new job—and—"

"I'm not at all lonely, Dad, but thanks for asking."

"I thought he cared for you, Edwina. I thought you cared for him."

"Dad. Can we talk about something else, please?"

He had made pancakes and bacon for their breakfast. He had brought the pancake mix with him—and the bacon, too, and even a pound of butter and some syrup, realizing that Eddie's cupboards would probably be bare.

"Okay," he said, with a sigh. "Sure."

Eddie was pushing a piece of buttermilk pancake around in a pool of syrup. This was her father's favorite breakfast. It wasn't hers. She thought that if he had really wanted to do something for her, as opposed to doing it for himself, he would have brought eggs and hash-brown potatoes.

"I think you're going to feel somewhat strange," he said thoughtfully. "Living as a policewoman in this community."

"What on earth do you mean by that?" she said, looking up at him in surprise.

"Everyone will know who you are. Your neighbors.

The people in all these houses"—he waved expansively—"up and down the street."

"Everyone knew who I was in Burnaby, too. Everybody up and down the hall. Everybody on every floor. So what?"

"It'll be different here," said her father, nodding sagely. "What's the matter? Don't you like your pancakes?"

"I like them fine, Dad. I'm just not very hungry. Too much on my mind."

He looked around the kitchen. "We've made a dent, though," he said. "And at least you've got your windows covered now."

"You're right, Dad," she said. "And I'm glad of it, too."

He had insisted that she provide him with precise measurements of every window, and had brought with him, as well as food, venetian blinds for the whole house.

"And I thank you again," said Eddie.

He touched his napkin to the corners of his mouth. "You're welcome." He sat back with a sigh, resting clasped hands on his paunch, and tilted his head at her. "And what is life like, exactly, in the Sechelt detachment of the RCMP?"

Eddie laughed. "You don't want to know, Dad. Why pretend that you do?"

"No, really," he protested, smiling. His thinning hair was tousled and his short-sleeved shirt was open at the throat, revealing loose skin. He wore slippers over bare feet and trousers that were baggy at the knees. These were the same clothes he'd worn yesterday, but today Eddie sensed in the casualness of his appearance a studied intimacy that she resented.

She studied him across the table. "Okay, Dad. A woman disappeared last Monday."

"Probably missed the last ferry from the mainland," said her father with a smile.

"We found her body the next day, in a shallow grave, an

indentation, really, no more than that, earth and leaves scattered on top. She'd been murdered."

Her father was frowning now.

"Yeah, and it's the second body buried in that same spot. Can you believe it? The first one was found sometime last year." Eddie leaned forward, resting her forearms on the tabletop. "Dad. How many homicides do you think I worked on in Burnaby?"

"I don't want to know," he said quickly, reaching for his coffee cup. "This is not a fit subject for mealtime discussion, Edwina."

She sat back. "You did ask, Dad."

After a while Eddie started to clear the table, and when her father offered to help with the dishes she poured him more coffee and made him sit down and tell her about his garden.

An hour later she drove him to the ferry.

When she got home her phone was ringing. But it stopped before the answering machine kicked in.

"Shit," said Eddie. She knew the detachment would have waited and left a message, but she called in anyway and was disappointed to learn that nobody at work had been trying to reach her.

She sank into a chair and looked around the living room, which she had to admit was a lot more welcoming now. Her house was actually starting to look like a home, thanks to her father, who had unpacked every single box in half a day. It had taken a lot longer than that to find a place for everything, of course, but he had insisted on doing this, over Eddie's protests. She would have to rearrange her bookshelves, and she had refused to let him put away her clothes, which were stacked in piles on her bed, and she knew she wouldn't be able to find things at first because her father's idea of where stuff belonged was frequently poles apart from Eddie's. But there was hardly any clutter left, and Eddie hadn't realized until it was gone just how much the disorder had been jangling her nerves. She needed to feel some permanence, and this was now starting to happen. And she was grateful to her father.

She only hoped that he wouldn't find it necessary to visit her often. She could say no, of course—but she knew how much he still missed her mother, and doubted that she'd have the heart to refuse him, at least for a while. But maybe his garden would keep him busy, she thought, now that spring had come.

Eddie pushed herself up from the chair, surprised by the extent of her weariness. She would have a long, hot bath and put away her clothes, do some laundry, have a light dinner— and then go to bed early. And first thing in the morning she would once more turn her mind to the homicides. She felt a shiver of impatience, wishing it were already tomorrow.

She stripped off her clothes—socks, jeans, denim shirt, underwear—remembering to close the blinds first, turned on the taps of the bathtub, then walked around her house, enjoying the fact that she actually owned it. Maybe her father was right, a little painting might be a good idea. A blue accent wall? Or should she stick to off-white?

The phone rang and Eddie picked up the portable in the living room. "Hello."

There was a pause, and then, "Hi."

She became rigid. "How did you get this number?"

"Come on, babe. Give me some credit."

Eddie looked around for something with which to cover herself. She went quickly into the bathroom and grabbed her robe from the hook on the back of the door. "I said, how did you get this number?" She returned to the living room and sat down, huddling into an easy chair, and began rubbing its arm with the palm of her hand; the touch of the nubbly fabric against her skin was comforting.

"How're you doing over there, anyway? How much do you miss me?"

The chair was quite worn. Eddie had bought second-hand furniture and now she wished that everything in the place was brand new.

Abruptly, she hung up. She turned down the volume on the portable phone and switched off the answering machine.

When she walked into the bathroom and lowered herself into the steaming water, she was shaking with rage.

"Thanks for coming, Bernie," said Mrs. O'Hara. "I appreciate it."

"No problem," said Bernie Peters, placing her handbag on the table as she sat down. "I gotta eat lunch. Might as well eat it here as anywhere." She settled into the chair, patting her bright auburn curls, encased in a hairnet, with both hands, then folded her hands in her lap.

"So, what'll you have, ladies?" said Earl.

"Tomato soup, brown toast, and two percent milk, please," said Bernie.

"I'll have a shrimp sandwich with fries," said Mrs. O'Hara, "and a glass of water."

"Okeydoke," said Earl.

Mrs. O'Hara glanced around the restaurant, which was filling up with the after-church crowd. "You used to do some cleaning over at the school, didn't you?"

Bernie nodded vigorously, whisking crumbs from the table with the edge of her hand. "For a while I did. Gave it up though. Too much work. And it was no fun anyway, not with all those damn kids running around." She cocked her head and regarded Mrs. O'Hara shrewdly with small, bright eyes. "Are they looking for somebody? Oh well. They're always looking for somebody."

"I thought I'd look into it," said Mrs. O'Hara vaguely.

"So what do you want from me?" said Bernie, as Earl delivered a glass of milk and another of water.

"I know you as a tolerant person, Bernie," said Mrs. O'Hara, "and I know you're observant, too. You mentioned the kids. Kids I can deal with. But what about the staff? Are they bossy? Do they get in your way?" She smiled across at Bernie. "I like to know all I can about my clients. So what can you tell me about the teachers?"

How long has he been lying there? thought Denise. All scrunched up in the trunk of his car, his bloodied head on a pillow—a quixotic touch, that, cradling his poor dead cranium on a pillow—with his limbs awkwardly folded: how long?

Not that Ivan cared how long it had been.

How much—deterioration—would have occurred by now, given the unseasonably warm weather? What effect would that have had on his carcass? Denise was surprised by her mind's choice of word, and wanted to find another one, but it was too late. And besides, it was the right word: it wasn't Ivan lying there. It wasn't even Ivan's body. It was only a carcass.

I must have been mad, she reflected, rubbing her palms together, splayed fingers clinging to their opposites. Mad. And for these last several days some kindly god or other had set Denise's life in abeyance and waited, patiently, for her madness to retreat. But now that she was sane again, something was required of her. She knew this: she just couldn't think what it might be.

Denise rose from the rocking chair and wandered through the house, looking at things that were Ivan's: his shaving kit in the bathroom, on the back of the toilet; the clothes that overflowed a closet and several drawers; a golf bag leaning against the wall by the back door; in the drawer of his bedside table, a package of mints, a paperback book about investing for early retirement, a ballpoint pen and a notepad, and some condoms. They had only recently begun to use condoms. Denise, closing the drawer, acknowledged that she was a very stupid woman.

She would have to get boxes from somewhere and fill them with his belongings. Would his mother like to have them, Denise wondered? Or should she give everything to the Salvation Army?

She gripped her head with both hands. How was she going to deal with this? She wanted things to go on as they were, quietly and serenely, in the continuing absence of Ivan, away at a conference. But she knew that was impossible. It was Sunday, now, and that woman would be calling again. And even if Denise put her off, it would be temporarily. As soon as she was back in school tomorrow morning, and Ivan didn't show up . . .

She thought suddenly about the car; Ivan's car. Since nobody had come to her door to tell her it had been found, perhaps it hadn't been found. Although that seemed unlikely. Had she locked it? She must have. But stuck off in the middle of the woods as it was, surely nobody coming across it while walking their dog or looking for whatever people look for in the woods—mushrooms (was it mushroom season?) or blooming things—anyway, anybody coming across Ivan's car would surely think it abandoned. And if they didn't report it, they'd smash it up for fun.

Or else they'd try to find a way to steal it. It could be broken into it without much difficulty, and she knew there was a way to start a car without its key. So perhaps somebody had driven away in it.

With Ivan in the trunk . . .

How long before he would begin to smell? And what

would the thief do then? Denise grew dizzy considering the possibilities, both likely and improbable.

If she were to go back there and find the car gone, what would that mean? How would it change things?

Rain was falling again, from a sky dank and heavy with gray clouds that hovered so close to the surface of the earth they left scarcely enough air for people to breathe. Or so it felt to Denise, standing at the window, clutching her cardigan closed at the throat.

She put on a navy slicker with a hood, plucked the car keys from the empty sugar bowl in the cupboard and put them in her pocket, and stepped out into the rain.

Denise trudged along with her hands in the pockets of her slicker, her eyes mostly on the ground to keep the rain out of her face. As she walked, she observed the toes of her sneakers, which were pink and gray, dirty and torn. She slowed and stopped and stared down at her feet in their tired old sneakers, while the rain flung itself against her slicker like handfuls of marbles. She wanted to retreat, to withdraw to her bed with the blinds drawn and the covers over her head. She wanted to stay there until she fell asleep and, once asleep, never waken.

But there was something massive and unpredictable teetering directly above her head. It was preparing to fall on her, to kill her in her sleep, if she allowed herself to sleep before dismantling it, whatever it was—a house of cards, perhaps; a chimera, anyway. But it was a fantasy with substance; a nightmare with authenticity. Denise shivered and plunged on, through puddles, splashing rainwater onto the legs of her jeans.

When she reached the end of her street she turned right and walked through the village, past cafés and the hardware store, past a tearoom and a crafts shop, past an occasional pedestrian huddled beneath an umbrella, splashed sometimes by slow-moving vehicles. Now there were houses on her right and the shopping mall on her left, rain bouncing from the roofs and hoods of the automobiles and four-by-fours crowding the parking lot. Denise proceeded past the houses, along the edge of the highway, then around a bend and up the hill. She was very cold, now, beneath the slicker, and wished she had worn gloves. Her face was wet with rain despite the hood. She had no idea where she was going. But something in her head apparently had a map, so she kept on walking.

Her legs had started to ache, and she tried to slow down—she was traveling uphill, after all—but she was unable to slow down, her body simply wouldn't do it. This created in Denise's blood a shudder of panic, but she beat it down, beat it out like a brushfire and quick-marched up the hill as if this pace were her own personal choice, swinging her arms with counterfeit enthusiasm. The hood fell back, allowing rain to smear her cheeks and forehead. It leaked into her eyes, and crept under the slicker at the back of her neck. Denise strode along, panting, her thighs throbbing. She was hurled around a corner and past a group of houses that were so new they looked raw: the new, tender grass in their front lawns was so vividly green that Denise thought for a moment there was concrete there, slathered with DayGlo paint.

Then, abruptly, there were no more houses and no more pavement, and Denise was being propelled rapidly along a wide gravel road. The rain fell in bursts, slapping fretfully at her face and her ungloved, swinging hands, directed by impish gusts of wind. Denise pulled the hood back over her head, but it had gotten wet inside and stuck to her hair and the sides of her face, clammy and mean, so she brushed it off again. She was panting heavily. She had a stitch in her side and she badly needed to rest, or at least to slow down but, helpless, she continued her swift passage along the road, which was turning into a lane now, narrow and rutted. Denise stumbled frequently but her legs, although almost spasming from this unaccustomed effort, possessed extraordinary strength and refused to let her fall. They churned savagely, her arms flailed, and she remained upright, driving onward.

Soon she was brushing aside wet leaves and branches, greenery having encroached upon the narrowing lane. She barreled ahead, ducking when necessary, raising her arms to protect her face. Eventually the forest enveloped the lane completely, and whatever had been propelling her onward evaporated.

Denise's body trembled in its wake. She leaned forward, her hands gripping her screaming thighs, her eyes shut tight, and rested, panting, waiting for her heartbeat to decelerate. When it did, she opened her eyes and stood upright.

The sound of the rain flew among the trees of the forest like slightly discordant notes of music. The scent of the earth was strong, musky and fecund. From far away the barking of a dog drifted toward Denise on the cool, moist breeze.

Directly ahead of her, perhaps fifty feet away, Ivan's metallic blue Cavalier was barely visible.

She looked at it for a long time before moving toward it, slowly, pressing through the brush, elbowing aside salal and blackberries, treading on ferns and weeds and infant trees. The Cavalier squatted in the embrace of foliage, practically invisible. In six months, if left alone, it would be engulfed by the rainforest.

Denise pulled the keys from her pocket. She lifted a branch of salal away from the trunk and unlocked it. The trunk door lifted several inches and hung there, suspended. Denise closed her eyes, wrenched it all the way open, and stepped back, hurriedly, blindly. Her back found a straight solid treetrunk to lean against. Oh please god, please god, she was saying under her breath.

When she opened her eyes and looked into the trunk, she didn't know whether god had answered her prayers or not. The trunk was empty. There was no Ivan. No bloodied pillow. No flattened black plastic garbage bag. Denise turned slowly around in a full circle, peering through the trees, her eyes scouring the ground. But Ivan was gone.

Denise stood rigid in the forest, listening to the rain.

"Look at this," said Cassandra, scrutinizing a wedding photograph displayed on top of one of her mother's bookcases. "It's an awful picture. We aren't even smiling, for heaven's sake."

"Marriage is a serious business," said her mother. "It's nothing to get all giddy about."

Helen Mitchell's room was reasonably large and comfortable. She would like to have had a separate bedroom, but such accommodations weren't available at Shady Acres. The bed took up a large portion of the room. She had tried—with modest success—to make it look less intrusive and institutional by draping it with a handmade quilt from Nova Scotia and several throw cushions. She had perked up the bathroom, too, in an attempt to camouflage the fact that it was equipped for a wheelchair: a bright fabric calendar covered one wall, there was a rubber-backed, rainbow-striped carpet on the floor, and an arrangement of dried flowers sat on the counter.

She was glad of the small refrigerator in her bed-sitting room, and of the television, the telephone, the slim bookcases, the two armchairs, and the small coffee table. Framed photographs were displayed on top of one of the bookcases: one of her son Graham, his wife Millie, and their children; one of her dead husband; and the wedding picture of Cassandra and Karl.

Helen took most of her meals in the dining room with the other residents, having marshaled a small group of women to share her table. Sometimes, though, she ate in her room: today, Cassandra had brought a box of pastries from the bakery and coffee-to-go from Earl's.

Helen brushed crumbs from her lap and observed fretfully through the bay window that it was still raining. "Sit down," she said impatiently. "Stop prowling."

But Cassandra ignored this, moving to the photograph of her father, whom she remembered only vaguely. He had been thirty-six when he died, which seemed to Cassandra at this moment inexpressibly sad. She touched his black and white likeness, gently, watching his eyes to see if his lashes might flutter. "He's been gone for a long time," she said—a murmur; she hadn't really been addressing her mother.

"Don't euphemize, Cassandra, he isn't "gone," he's dead."

"Forty-five years," mused Cassandra.

There was a slight pause. "I suppose you're right," said Helen. "Goodness. That *is* a long time." She shook herself gently, like a bird lifting and shifting its resting wings.

Cassandra bent to sniff the daffodils that filled a large green glass vase sitting between her mother's handbag and the photo of her brother and his family. "So, Mom—are you going to tell me why Uncle Barry left me this money or not?"

Helen slapped the arms of her chair, exasperated. "Just spend the damn money, Cassandra, and stop fussing about it. Make up your mind what you're going to do with it—then do it."

"I'm trying, Mom. It's difficult. It's hard to imagine myself doing anything else but what I'm doing." She sat on the edge of Helen's bed. "I mean, is it really credible, Mother? Me running a bookstore? Or operating a café?"

"Those aren't your only options. If they don't appeal to you, fine—do something else. For god's sake, spend the damn stuff. Blow it on a trip around the world. Don't— don't just keep tripping over it." She looked at her watch.

"I'm going for a walk." She pushed herself up and stood still for a moment, leaning heavily on the back of the armchair.

"Are you okay, Mom?"

"I'm seventy-nine years old. How okay can I be?"

Her tone was bleak, and Cassandra looked at her sharply. Helen gazed back . . . and Cassandra held her breath. Within her chest grew a conviction that something momentous and terrible was about to happen—some kind of dreadful accident, perhaps—and that there was nothing she would be able to do about it. She wondered if her mother was about to die, right there in front of her, and suddenly—quickly—she reached for her . . . just as Helen gave her head a little shake and moved away from the chair.

"Just around the block a couple of times," she said, picking up her handbag.

Cassandra watched her make her way to the door, back straight, head erect, silver hair a sweet stunning contrast to her deep gold sweater, which as she passed the daffodils in their green glass container reflected their sunniness.

Her mother paused in the open doorway. "Well, come along then."

"It's raining, Mom."

"I know it's raining," said Helen. She stepped out into the hall, looked left and right, then returned to her room to take an umbrella from a hook hanging on the wall near the door. "We'll need this, I guess." She threw Cassandra a glance over her shoulder and then turned to face her, umbrella in one hand, handbag in the other. Light from the hall bounced on the lenses of her eyeglasses. "You're far too old, Cassandra, to be cultivating such an active imagination."

Cassandra began to protest.

But her mother interrupted. "Who else was he going to leave it to? He was unmarried. He had no children of his own. Who else but to his brother's child?"

"Graham," said Cassandra. "Why didn't he leave some of it to Graham, then?"

Helen's gaze brushed the daffodils, and the side of Cassandra's face, and settled on the view through the window. "He always preferred you to Graham," she said.

"But why, Mom? That's what I mean. He hardly knew either of us. Why would he prefer me?"

Helen looked directly at Cassandra now, and sighed. "I guess we'll never know. Close the door behind you, please," she said, and moved along the hall, out of sight.

Denise backed Ivan's Cavalier along the lane and even though it was daylight this time, it was hard to see properly—brush obscured the rear window, making it almost impossible to tell whether she was on the existing track or forging a new one. Sometimes she felt the tires sink into the soft, sodden, muddy shoulder and expected them to get stuck, but they never did. She didn't really care if she got stuck or not, didn't care if she couldn't get the car back to the house. She was only trying to get it there because it seemed the reasonable thing to do.

It was putting a dreadful strain on her neck and shoulder, though, as she craned her body backward. She needed both hands on the wheel because of the roughness of the terrain, and this increased the physical stress on her body. If she got stuck, she would just leave the damn car.

But she didn't get stuck.

The car lurched spasmodically backward along the track, sometimes uphill, sometimes downhill, slurping mud, stumbling on rocks, until finally it shot out onto a proper road and Denise got it turned around. She drove it home and parked it in front of the house.

She sat in the car for several minutes before getting out—not thinking, exactly. Absorbing, maybe. Or trying to.

At the front door, a chill that was unfamiliar and frightening enveloped her.

She opened the door slowly, cautiously, and peeked around it before entering the house.

"Ivan?" she called.

He could be here, she thought. He might be here.

But the silence was profound, and Denise knew the house was empty.

It was emptier, in fact, than when she had left it.

The golf bag was the first thing she noticed. Not the bag itself, but its absence. She looked swiftly around the living room. His camera was gone from the top of the bookcase. In the bathroom, there was no shaving kit. His closet and drawers still held a few of his clothes, but most had been removed. She opened his bedside table drawer and laughed, then removed the drawer and emptied it over the wastepaper basket: paperback, notebook and pen, mints, condoms. Then she jammed the drawer back into the table.

Denise sat down on the edge of the bed. Now what? she thought.

Now what?

———

Mrs. O'Hara sat at her kitchen table, waiting, holding one of her grandmother's handkerchiefs, a small linen square surrounded by a wide lace border. It was pretty but impractical. Mrs. O'Hara had a dozen of them, and kept them in a zippered fabric bag that had also belonged to her grandmother.

Through the open window sunlight entered the kitchen and stroked her arm warmly. She listened, while she waited for the sound of an approaching car, to the chittering of birds, and she noticed that autumn was materializing, merging with the last days of summer: she saw this in the goldenness of early turning leaves, in the bright reds and yellows of the dahlias, in the row of sunflowers out by the fence, their shaggy heads dipping in a breeze from the west.

It had been full summer, still, two weeks ago, when Mrs. O'Hara had gone to visit Raylene, who lived in a small cramped house off the Mission Highway. She had gone there in the late afternoon, and Raylene had been cooking, making some kind of a stew for herself and Tom, who, Mrs. O'Hara knew, could soon be expected home from work. Mrs. O'Hara had been wearing sweatpants, a T-shirt, and an old flannel shirt that Tom had left behind. She didn't have a plan, but there was a concept in her head, and she was prepared to improvise.

Raylene looked horrified when she opened the door and saw Mrs. O'Hara standing there.

"Hello, Raylene," Mrs. O'Hara had said politely. "I guess we have some arrangements to discuss."

Raylene's relief was obvious. Mrs. O'Hara was going to do the civilized, gracious thing. She was going to give up her husband without a struggle. Well, Raylene had been right, in a way. By this time Mrs. O'Hara wouldn't have taken Tom back on a platter.

"Okay, sure," said Raylene, her pale face aglow. "Come in, come in."

The house was filthy, but Raylene herself glinted and sparkled, frail and white though she was, dancing around her kitchen with a big spoon in her hand as if she were in some kind of a commercial.

At least that was how Mrs. O'Hara remembered things now, as she waited.

She had been to Raylene's house several times—Tom had frequently persuaded her to make up a foursome with Raylene and her husband Dean, who had now taken off for parts unknown—but never before had she seen it so dirty. She hadn't realized what a salutary influence Dean had had on Raylene's housekeeping.

Mrs. O'Hara had sat quietly on Raylene's rickety kitchen chair with her hands folded in her lap. Raylene, meanwhile, stirred the stew and set the table, grateful, now, that Mrs. O'Hara had shown up on her doorstep.

"I'm really glad you're here," she said fervently. "I'm really glad you're gonna let bygones be bygones. Because we really do want to have kids, Tom and me." She frowned at the table, set for two. "Are you sure you won't have supper with us? Because there's plenty." And then she giggled and pressed her pallid fingertips over her mouth, realizing the ludicrousness of the suggestion.

"Tom'll be home pretty soon, won't he?" said Mrs. O'Hara, and Raylene nodded, blushing. "I've got an idea," said Mrs. O'Hara. "If I know Tom, he'll be real happy that I've come to make peace."

"Oh, yes," said Raylene eagerly, hands clasped over the wooden handle of the big spoon she was still holding. "He will be, he surely will."

"Let's surprise him," said Mrs. O'Hara, standing up. "Where can I hide? What about the basement?"

And so Raylene had rushed to open the basement door, with Mrs. O'Hara right on her heels.

Mrs. O'Hara, sitting now at her kitchen window, couldn't see around the corner into her front yard, but when the car arrived she heard its tires crunch slowly up the gravel driveway, the sound becoming louder before the vehicle came to a stop.

The car's engine was turned off and Mrs. O'Hara heard the door open—only one door. She had thought there might be two of them. It was probably a good sign that there was only one—but then, what did she know about such things? She was about to tiptoe through a minefield here.

Suddenly an exhilaration that Mrs. O'Hara realized could be dangerous sprang through her nervousness. She tamped it down as she rose from the wooden chair and walked slowly to the door, the lace-edged handkerchief trailing through the fingers of her left hand.

She opened the door and watched the policeman approach, glance up at her, and start climbing the stairs. Neither of them spoke until he had reached the top. He was a tall, strong young man, slightly taller than Mrs. O'Hara. He nodded to her, touched his hat, and removed it.

"Morning, Ma'am."

Mrs. O'Hara invited him inside and offered him coffee.

She and the policeman sat down in what she felt to be companionable silence—although a small, stern voice in her head warned against jumping to conclusions. And for a few minutes the officer made small talk. Mrs. O'Hara found this very interesting. She had assumed that policemen didn't bother with idle conversation.

Eventually, he pushed his coffee cup slightly away from him and produced a long, narrow notebook from an inside pocket of his jacket and a ballpoint pen from another pocket. His hat sat on the table near his left elbow, rather like a small, cherished, well-trained pet. The police officer straightened, flexing his arms, and something creaked, as if he were wearing leather.

"This is just routine, Ma'am," he said, in a tone of voice that was almost soothing.

Mrs. O'Hara imagined him on the road in his patrol car, wearing sunglasses in which other people could see their reflections, hiding behind his impenetrable lenses so that nobody would see his youth. She leaned back in her chair and crossed her legs, deliberately relaxing her body, regarding him solemnly, attentively.

"Now," he said. "You and your husband separated, when?"

"About three months ago," she told him.

He wrote something in his notebook. "And that was because of his—relationship—with the deceased?"

Mrs. O'Hara nodded. "Yes. Of course."

The officer wrote more words in his notebook. He examined her, a stare that brought coldness to the surface of Mrs. O'Hara's skin. She looked back, calmly. He said, "What kind of a relationship did they have, the two of them?"

Mrs. O'Hara permitted her eyebrows to rise. "I assume it was a sexual one."

The police officer shifted his feet under the table. "No, I mean—did they get along, do you know? Apart from the—apart from that? What I want to know is, did they ever fight?"

She shook her head wearily. "I don't have any way of knowing, for sure. But my guess would be yes, they did fight."

"And why would you guess that?"

"Because he used to fight with me." Mrs. O'Hara rested her elbow in the palm of the opposite hand and winced, as if reflexively.

"I understand you had some kind of an accident recently?" The policeman flipped backward through his notebook. "In May?"

She looked at him steadily, but didn't reply.

"Mrs. O'Hara? Is that right?"

"I—sustained some injuries. Yes."

"Falling down the stairs, is what they told us at the hospital. Right?"

She hesitated, glancing out through the window at the sunflowers. "Down the stairs. Yes."

"*You were lucky,*" *the police officer told her grimly.* "*That's what happened to Raylene. Right down the basement stairs, smashed her head on the concrete floor.*"

"*I know,*" *said Mrs. O'Hara softly. She cultivated sorrow, enough to fill her eyes with moisture but not to overflow.*

"*He said he found her there,*" *said the policeman.* "*Tom. But in the laundry room, in a pile of dirty clothes, was one of his shirts. With her blood all over it.*"

"*Yes, well—*" *Mrs. O'Hara manufactured a shiver, tilted her head into the sunshine and touched her grandmother's handkerchief to her glinting tears.* "*He—he does have a—a temper.*"

"*Your fall. It wasn't an accident, was it,*" *said the policeman sympathetically. He leaned slightly toward her.* "*Maybe you didn't even fall at all.*"

Mrs. O'Hara turned her head away and gave it an almost imperceptible shake.

"*The charge is second degree murder,*" *he said.* "*It could get reduced to manslaughter. That depends on how good his lawyer is. Whatever it ends up being, though, we'll want you to testify.*"

Mrs. O'Hara took a shuddery breath. "*Oh dear. About—about my fall, you mean?*"

"*Yes.*"

Mrs. O'Hara sighed. "*Of course,*" *she said reluctantly.* "*Of course I'll testify. It's my duty, isn't it?*"

And she had testified.

And Tom—bewildered, desperate, but utterly helpless—had gone to jail.

SEVENTEEN

Monday, April 1

———

Sunlight was squeaking into her bedroom between the slats in the new blinds when Eddie woke. She was lying on her back. She must have been dreaming about Alan, because her mind was full of him. She swept him out of there, though, and got up and dressed.

She had decided when she bought the house to have more meals at home, but she hadn't started doing this yet and couldn't do it today, either—not breakfast, anyhow. She was afraid that Alan might call her again and wanted to be on her way quickly, before this could happen. But Eddie, as she brushed her hair and braided it, acknowledged that eventually she'd have to talk to him. She hadn't decided what to do about this situation, but she had a couple of ideas. Meanwhile, she thought, leaving the house, she'd grab another breakfast at Earl's.

She found a parking spot halfway down the block from the café, and as she locked up her car she noticed Andrew Maine across the street, opening up the menswear store.

Eddie knew that Janet Maine's body hadn't yet been released for burial. Should the grieving husband really be back at work so soon, even before the funeral? Yet what was he supposed to do, she asked herself, her hands clasped, leaning on the roof of her Mazda—sit around the house feeling sorry for himself? Andrew disappeared inside the store, closing the door behind him, and Eddie turned, tugged at her jacket to straighten it, and decided somebody had better have another talk with Andrew.

The café was crowded with people and was noisy, fragrant with breakfast. As Eddie entered, setting the bell ajangling, two people vacated a table by the window and she headed in that direction, picking up a few curious stares as she went. But Eddie was used to that. Her face might occasionally redden but at least her body never seized up on her: she moved easily across the room, aware of her height but comfortable with it, and took possession of the empty table, slipping into one of the chairs just as Naomi arrived to clear away the dishes.

"You could've waited till I'd wiped up here," said the waitress irritably, loading up her tray with cups and saucers, plates smeared with egg yolk and maple syrup.

"Yeah, I guess I could have," said Eddie, amused.

Naomi held the tray on the palm of one hand while she swiped the tabletop with a cloth held in the other. "So what're you gonna have?"

"Two eggs over easy, hash browns, brown toast, and coffee, please. And a small tomato juice," said Eddie, while Naomi looked out the window, feigning boredom.

When she'd gone, Eddie pulled a notebook and a pen from her breast pocket and flipped it open to a blank page. "Re-interview Andrew Maine," she wrote. And let her eyes wander around the café as she thought, What else? What else?

A certain amount of forensic evidence had been collected—upholstery fibers had been found clinging to the victim's coat, the mud on her sneakers didn't correspond with the mud in the clearing, there were sweater fibers in her hair, but they hadn't come from the sweater she was wearing—and these leads would be followed up.

And they had received more information from the autopsy, as well, of course. It had confirmed that Janet Maine had been struck on the head, then strangled. The blow to the head hadn't killed her, but had probably knocked her out. There were no indications that she had struggled with her assailant, or tried to get away. Her clothing wasn't torn or disarranged. Nothing had been found under her finger-nails. And there were no wounds anywhere on her body—however minor—except the bump on her head.

Eddie rested her chin in her hand. How had the woman been persuaded to get into the vehicle? She must have known the guy, and trusted him. But then what? How had he managed to distract her long enough to smack her on the head? Did he do it in the car? Yeah, thought Eddie, he must have done it in the car. For surely she wouldn't have driven off to the damn clearing with him—she was on her way home, for god's sake.

Unless, of course, it was Andrew who had picked her up. Andrew who had struck her, strangled her, then scooped out a shallow grave and dropped her into it.

"What the hell are you staring at?" said Naomi, stand-ing before her with a mug of coffee and a glass of tomato juice.

"What?" asked Eddie, startled.

"You've been staring at me," said Naomi accusingly, setting down the dishes harder than was necessary. She planted her hands on her hips and stared coldly at Eddie.

"Sorry," said Eddie. "I didn't realize."

Naomi's hair fell to her shoulders today. It was so black, Eddie marveled, that it didn't reflect any light. Her ears were rather large, and protruded through the frizzy mass of her hair like things separate and alive; like tiny animals—gerbils, perhaps, or hamsters, Eddie thought, fascinated. Naomi's ears were neither flat against her head nor still, like ears ought to be. They made compulsive twitching movements that disturbed the hair that was trying to conceal them. She wore no makeup. Her skin was fair, her eyes were brown, there was a dimple in her chin. She was also a very short person, which Eddie figured she probably found irritating.

"Sorry," Eddie said again, offering a smile.

"Humph," said Naomi, turning away.

Eddie, taking a sip of black coffee, noticed a young woman getting up from a stool at the counter. But instead of heading for the washroom, or the front door, she made her way through the tables straight over to Eddie.

"Excuse me," she said. "I'm sorry to intrude, but do you mind if I introduce myself?"

"Go ahead," said Eddie.

"My name's Cindi Webster. I'm a reporter. With the local paper."

"Hi," said Eddie, extending her hand. "Edwina Henderson."

They shook hands, and Cindi asked, "Do you mind if I sit down?"

Eddie, who did, smiled at the reporter and closed her notebook. "No. Sit. Sure."

"I'm doing this series," said Cindi, pulling out the other chair. She settled herself in it while she talked, parking an oversize shoulderbag on the floor. "Feature stories about people and their jobs. And I was wondering if I could talk to you. About being a police officer." She tucked her hair behind her ears and looked earnestly at Eddie. "You're new here—it'd be a good way to introduce yourself to the community, maybe. What do you think?"

"It's an interesting idea," said Eddie cautiously. The relationships she'd had with the press so far had been tolerable—her attitude toward reporters was wary, but neither positive nor negative. And Eddie had resolved to construct for herself here in Sechelt a social life that would for once include people who were not police officers. She was bloody determined to do this. And the reporter looked friendly enough, leaning forward, awaiting Eddie's decision. Eager. Guileless.

On the other hand, Cindi Webster was probably every bit as ambitious in her field as Eddie was in hers.

But then, was this a bad thing? A reason to mistrust her?

Maybe she ought to do it, Eddie thought.

She did, after all, have a few good stories to tell. . . .

But how could she talk about her career without talking about Alan?

"I'm sorry," she said finally, with at least a small amount of real regret.

"Oh dear," said Cindi with a sigh. "How come?"

Eddie laughed. "Maybe I'll tell you, someday."

"I think I understand, though," said the reporter, gathering up her bag. "It's hard to know what's professional and what's personal. When you're female, anyway."

"Uh huh," said Eddie.

Cindi plopped the bag into her lap and sat back. "At least, that's been my experience." She was smiling a little, eyes narrowed politely, to diminish the curiosity that gleamed there.

Eddie laughed out loud.

"You want to go for a beer sometime?" said Cindi.

"Sure," said Eddie. "Why not? And meanwhile, for your feature—have you asked Staff Sergeant Alberg?"

The forensic evidence wasn't going to get them anywhere, thought Alberg, paging through Janet Maine's file, unless and until they had a suspect.

Interviews with friends and family had produced absolutely nothing. The woman's husband was the obvious suspect, of course. But his grief seemed genuine and nothing had been unearthed—so far, at least—to indicate any marital difficulties. Besides which . . .

. . .

Alberg tossed the file aside and sank back in his chair. Besides which, whoever killed Janet Maine had killed Rebecca Granger as well, and Andrew had been vacationing in Hawaii with his wife when the teenager disappeared.

His phone rang.

"Yeah? What is it?"

"There's somebody out here wants to see you," said Isabella.

Alberg took off his reading glasses and dropped them on the desk. He sat up straight and stretched his shoulders, wincing. "Who? What's it about?"

"It's an attractive young woman," said Isabella. "I don't know what it's about. She wants to tell you herself."

Alberg aimed a cautious glance at his IN basket and was gratified to see that it had shrunk considerably. If he kept pounding away at it all day long he could shrivel the damn thing into nothing. "I need a break anyway," he said. "Send her in."

He gazed expectantly at the door and soon heard a soft knocking. "Come in," he said.

The door opened and Cindi Webster poked her head around it. "Hi," she said. "We've met. Do you remember me?"

"Sure," said Alberg, getting to his feet. "Cindi, isn't it? Come in. Sit down."

"I'm doing this series," Cindi began, advancing across the room. She looked at the leather chair.

"Go ahead. Sit down," said Alberg again, and she did.

"It's a series of feature stories," said the reporter, "about people and their work."

"Uh huh," said Alberg.

"I was wondering if I could talk to you," said Cindi, "that is, if you'd be one of the people in the series. It isn't a personal kind of a thing," she said hastily. "I mean, it's about your work, you know? Not your personal life."

"You'd better tell me more," said Alberg, the office chair squeaking as he sat down. He had lost some of his mistrust of reporters since his younger daughter Diana had joined their ranks. But he remained healthily leery of those whose work he didn't know. And he couldn't remember reading anything written by the young woman sitting across from him.

"So far," she told him, "I've interviewed a vet, a lawyer, a waitress, a logger, a fisherman, a teacher, a painter—the artist kind. And I just talk to them about their work, or I mean they talk to me about their work. Why they decided to do this kind of work, and what they like about it, and what they don't like about it." She looked at him expectantly. "So what do you think?"

"And I'd be your police officer," said Alberg dryly.

"Yeah."

He leaned back in his chair and folded his arms. "You'd have to let me read some of your stuff first," he said.

She nodded vigorously. "I've got some clippings with me."

She waited, trying to look patient, but he thought she was nervous. Her hair was light brown and her eyes were green. She wore jeans, a collarless blouse, and a dark pink cardigan. She was slightly overweight, which Alberg found attractive. "How old are you?" he asked suddenly.

"Twenty-eight."

Christ. She was two years younger than Diana. Alberg gave an involuntary sigh. "Yeah. Okay."

"Oh, good," she said, smiling broadly. "When?"

"Hand over your clippings," said Alberg. "Go get a coffee. Come back in twenty minutes."

•   •   •

"I don't know where the hell he is, Susan," said the principal, a short, rotund man with almost no hair. "I've been calling his house all day. There's no answer. I haven't got a bloody clue where the man is."

"Well, aren't you worried?" Susan resisted an urge to grab him by his narrow shoulders. "Shouldn't you be calling—I don't know—the hospitals or something?"

He screwed up his forehead and placed his fists on his hips. She thought for a moment that he was going to break into some kind of obscure folk dance, despite the obvious strain on his jacket buttons—this was mostly because the heels of his small shiny shoes were fitted tightly, neatly together, and the toes were splayed apart, reminding her of Dorothy in The Wizard of Oz, except that the principal's shoes were black, instead of ruby red.

"For god's sake Susan, have you no sense of propriety?" She leaned forward slightly, as if to hear him better.

He lowered his voice. "I know what you're up to, the two of you," he said, wagging a finger in her face. "It's none of my business, but my god, don't you think if anybody starts calling the hospitals it ought to be the man's wife?" The last word—wife—shot from his mouth in a sudden volley of spittle from which Susan quickly withdrew.

She watched him hurry away, plump arms pumping, head tucked into his shoulders, and realized for the first time how intensely she disliked him.

She had gotten to school early that morning, long before most of the staff. The gravel parking lot contained large puddles and only two other cars when she arrived—neither of the cars was Ivan's.

But she hadn't expected to see his car there. Ivan was never early. In fact, he was seldom even on time. He attempted to make up for this by staying later than almost everyone else.

Susan wasn't sure how good a teacher Ivan was, or how

much he liked his job—it was possible that he didn't like teaching at all: there was an ambiguous, noncommittal element to their conversation when they talked about work that Susan found disturbing.

She had rushed across the parking lot, hunched over inside her coat, holding her briefcase awkwardly above her head to keep as much rain as possible out of her hair. Inside, the halls echoed and the ceilings seemed higher than she remembered—it felt as if she had been away a lot longer than a week.

In her classroom, Susan opened both doors, turned on the lights, and sat at her desk. And as she looked out over the several clusters of small desks awaiting her five-year-olds, and smiled at the colored chalk drawings of spring flowers that filled the corners of the blackboards, she gradually became calm. She took from her briefcase a thick folder containing eight-by-ten paintings done by her students just before the break—they loved it when she took their work home in a briefcase—and tacked them up on the walls. She became absorbed in this task and soon found herself humming under her breath.

He wasn't there at recess.

He hadn't arrived by noon.

Ivan never did come to school that day.

Now, as Susan watched the principal disappear down the hall, the air seemed to shudder and shimmer as if the hallway were a mirage and the principal a figment of her imagination.

She drove slowly home through the rain, certain now that something was wrong. Even if he had decided to unceremoniously dump her, which she was reluctant to believe but had to confess was possible, if only because anything was theoretically possible, his unexplained absence from school was a clear, unequivocal indication that something was very, very wrong.

The principal was right, of course. It wasn't Susan's place to go looking for him.

But she had to.

She would have to call his wife again.

This shouldn't be difficult, she told herself, swinging into the parking lot underneath her apartment building. She would say she was a colleague, which of course she was. She would say that they were supposed to work on a report together, she and Ivan, and were to have had their first meeting at noon today, and she was wondering, she would tell Ivan's wife, had he fallen ill? And was she, his wife, so worried about him that she had forgotten to notify the school?

Susan got out of the car and locked it, remembering that the principal had been phoning Ivan's house all day and getting no reply. Well fine. Susan would go there in person, if necessary, pretending to be angry with Ivan, exasperated with his irresponsibility.

And if his wife refused to come to the door, thought Susan, getting into the elevator, she would wait for—well, for what felt like an appropriate amount of time.

The elevator door opened and she started down the outside hallway. What would be an appropriate amount of time? she wondered. She might have to wait all night, she thought, inserting the key in her apartment door. Fine. She would sit out there in her car all night long, if necessary. As soon as a light went on in Ivan's house she'd be back at the door, pounding.

She stood motionless in her apartment. Listening. But heard no beeping from her answering machine.

Susan dropped her briefcase and rested her forehead against the wall. Her whole body ached. She hadn't realized how much she had been hoping to hear that dreadful beeping.

Slowly, she took off her jacket and hung it in the closet. Yes, she would do that, she would sit in front of his house all night, and if no light ever came on inside, in the morning she would damn well go to the cops.

"Susan."

She froze, then turned so quickly she banged her head against the edge of the closet door.

"Susan."

Ivan stood in the entrance to the living room, silhouetted against the late afternoon light, a gray figure outlined in darker gray, wearing a large white bandage on his head.

Susan cried out, and flung herself down the hall and into his arms.

Cassandra would be astonished when he told her. Alberg was pretty astonished himself. Two whole hours that reporter had been there. He'd talked about himself to a total stranger for two entire hours.

He squirmed on the cushion, getting comfortable, rubbing his spine against the large rock that was serving as his backrest. There was a swell of excitement in him that threatened to disturb his digestive system. And he had come here to this quiet place to try to figure out what it was. To confront it, really, this inexplicable eagerness. He was reminded of children at Christmas. He felt somewhat like that, as if he were anticipating something splendid but didn't know—or couldn't remember—what it was going to be.

He sat quietly now, his knees raised, poking at the earth between his feet with a stick he had picked up as he made his way through the woods from the road. The sea was a congregation of shades of silver, moving restlessly, talking to itself in a low, seductive murmur.

Alberg had gone through almost his entire working life for Cindi Webster. He had told her about his personal experience with "scarlet fever," the infatuation of some young women for RCMP officers. He'd told her about his first arrest, his first car chase, the first time he'd had to draw his weapon. He had described for her riots, break-ins, domestic disturbances, homicides. . . . Alberg shook his head, marveling.

"Have you ever shot anybody?" It was a question he'd been waiting for, because it was a question every civilian wanted to ask. And Alberg had opened his mouth to evade the issue, smoothly, as it had become easy for him to do, over the years: there were plenty of dodges available to him, plenty of platitudes, equivocations, dissemblings at his fingertips, on the tip of his tongue.

"Once," he had said, instead.

And when she began to make the obvious follow-up query, he had interrupted her. "He died," he had told her flatly.

She had looked at him intently for several seconds and apparently had realized that he wasn't going to talk about it, for she had moved then to another subject.

He'd left out a lot, of course, but still, he had told Cindi Webster more about his life as a cop in those two hours than he'd ever told either Cassandra or his ex-wife.

And there it was again—a sudden churning in his stomach that he knew was a precursor to something important.

Alberg leaned back against the rock, resting his head, looking up. The sky was silver, too, but the trees crowding the fringes of his vision were brilliantly green. It's spring, he thought. The mysterious commotion inside him moved into his throat—and to his astonishment, he was suddenly blinking tears from his eyes.

Alberg looked around quickly, to make sure that he was alone there, in the damp grassy place near the sea that was his own private hideaway . . . and suddenly he knew what had happened to him.

EIGHTEEN

Tuesday, April 2

———

Denise had sat in the rocking chair for most of the night, shivering, occasionally rubbing her arms, but refusing to wrap herself in a blanket or turn the heat up. Maybe the cold would sharpen her thinking. And there was also a need to punish herself for what she'd done.

She had gone over it again and again. Her memory was clear, now. She had—somehow—wrestled his body into the trunk of his car. She didn't know why she hadn't considered at the time that he might be merely unconscious—she just hadn't. She had folded him into the trunk—she was sure she had done this with tenderness and regret. Hadn't she? And now, it seemed that he hadn't been a corpse after all.

It was a good thing the Cavalier had a big trunk: he had had lots of room in there.

But how had he gotten out?

And when? His belongings had disappeared only yesterday—had he been in the trunk all that time? Or had he escaped almost right away and spent the intervening days lurking around the yard waiting for Denise to leave?

And now that he had his things, where had he gone?

Denise's head sank forward. She was so tired. But she knew she wouldn't sleep. It was too late for sleep now. Oh dear god—what was she going to do?

Suddenly, someone knocked on the door. It's Ivan,

Denise thought immediately, not surprised that he should knock: this seemed completely appropriate, under the circumstances.

She didn't move from the chair at first. She hadn't the faintest idea what to say to him. But after all, she told herself, the banging of her heart loud enough to deafen her, there was no law that said she had to say anything at all. Perhaps she'd just listen, let him do the talking.

It occurred to her as she stood up—which set the chair to rocking slightly—and crossed to the front door, that Ivan, horrified and angry though he must certainly be, would be every bit as frightened of her as she apparently was, at this moment, of him.

And it wouldn't matter what happened between them from now until the end of their lives, her fear would fade, was already fading, but Ivan would continue to be afraid of her. Was this a good thing, she wondered, or a bad thing?

Mrs. O'Hara stood on the Dyakowskis' porch, without pails or cleaning supplies, although she was dressed for work in a T-shirt, overalls, and a denim jacket, with her hair pinned up in a bun.

"I see his car out there," she said, with no preliminaries, when the door opened. "I guess I was wrong."

"Wrong about what?" said Denise, whose eyes were narrowed against the morning light. She raised a hand to shade them.

"He's back, then, is he?" said Mrs. O'Hara.

Denise looked toward Ivan's car. "No. Actually, he isn't." Her head dropped, slowly, until she was looking at the ground. She stepped out onto the porch. "It's a lovely day, isn't it?" she said, still looking down.

Mrs. O'Hara put a large hand on Denise's shoulder.

"I don't know where he is," said Denise, calm but detached. "He's alive, though," she went on. "Which is a relief. I guess they'd have put me in jail."

Mrs. O'Hara squinted upward, toward the rusty gutter that ran unevenly along the eaves. "Did you try to kill him, then?"

Denise quickly lifted her head. "No!" she said, shocked. "I mean to say, that wasn't my intention."

Mrs. O'Hara looked at her sturdy wristwatch. "I've got time for a cup of coffee. How about it?"

Denise stepped back and Mrs. O'Hara went inside, straight to the kitchen, and put on a pot of coffee. While it dripped through, she leaned against the counter and said to Denise, "What happened?"

Denise sank into a chair at the kitchen table. "We had an argument. I hit him with a frying pan. He bled so much—" Her bottom lip was trembling uncontrollably.

"Sometimes they do," said Mrs. O'Hara. "Sometimes not."

The fragrance of coffee was filling the room and through its burbling Mrs. O'Hara heard the clock on the wall ticking loudly.

"He bled so much I was sure he must have been dead," said Denise, hurrying now. "I put him in the trunk of his car and drove the car into the woods and left it there. And I forgot what I'd done—" She looked imploringly at Mrs. O'Hara. "I really did, I really truly did."

Mrs. O'Hara nodded.

"As soon as I remembered, I went back there. But he was gone. He's gone!" she said, clasping her hands, clutching them to her chest.

"Have you called the hospital?"

"No," said Denise.

"Do you want me to call them?"

Denise nodded, and Mrs. O'Hara went to the phone.

"He was there," she said to Denise a few minutes later. "He told them there was nobody he wanted them to notify.

They kept him for a while because he had a mild concussion. He was released yesterday."

Denise leaned forward and rested her forehead on her hands, which were folded in her lap. "Oh god, oh god."

Mrs. O'Hara waited.

Finally, Denise sat up and wiped at her face with her fingers. Mrs. O'Hara got a box of tissues from the bathroom and gave her a handful. "Thank you," Denise mumbled.

Mrs. O'Hara poured two cups of coffee and sat down, checking her watch again. "What was the argument about?" she asked.

"Oh . . ." Denise looked vaguely around the room. "It was about . . ." She looked directly at Mrs. O'Hara. "He was having an affair."

"Huh," said Mrs. O'Hara.

It was still on, then. Mrs. O'Hara acknowledged the presence of destiny, that familiar figure, black, with winged arms.

Denise, dabbing at her eyes with a tissue, said, "It's somebody at school, I think. I think it must be." Her voice was thin and fragile, pushed out with effort on a shelf of pain.

Mrs. O'Hara remembered that Raylene's back had been warm, yielding, and slightly damp when Mrs. O'Hara had flattened her hands against it and pushed. Raylene had made an exclamation of surprise, then had grunted three or four times, as she tumbled down the stairs. There was a cracking sound when her head hit the concrete floor. Mrs. O'Hara had known immediately that she was dead because of the angle of her neck. As Raylene fell, Mrs. O'Hara had yelled, "Raylene! Raylene!" as if she hadn't actually expected her to die. And perhaps she hadn't. While Raylene lay still at the bottom of the steps Mrs. O'Hara, standing at the top, had pressed her hand against her chest, to quiet the thumping there.

Mrs. O'Hara studied Denise for a while, watching her sip coffee, stare at the floor, run her hand through her hair. Then she looked again at her watch. "I have to go," she said.

Denise walked to the door with her.

"You get yourself to work today, young lady," said Mrs. O'Hara.

"Oh no," said Denise faintly. "I couldn't possibly."

"Oh yes you can." Mrs. O'Hara took her by the shoulders and gave her a gentle shake. "You must. Whatever's going to happen next, you need to have something to hang on to. Your job's about all you've got, as far as I can tell." She shook her again, less gently. "Go back to work."

Eddie went down the hall to Alberg's office and tapped lightly on the door. He waved her in, but he was on the phone, so she stayed out there until he called out to her to enter.

"Just wanted you to know, Staff, I'm going to talk to Andrew Maine again."

He nodded. "Now?"

"Yeah," said Eddie.

"Good," said Alberg. "Because I'll be away this afternoon and you'll have to hold the fort."

"What time are you leaving?"

"Twelve-thirty or so."

"Okay. I'll make sure I'm here." She ducked out into the hall, but Alberg called her back.

"How are you settling in?" he asked her.

She shrugged. "Fine, I think. What do *you* think?"

He remained expressionless. "Yeah, fine. So far."

"Good." She hesitated. "Well, I'm off, then." He didn't respond, so she backed out again.

Shit, she thought, furious, hurrying down the hall. She hated it that she still craved, if not kindness, then a considerateness of which that goddamn Alberg was clearly incapable. She rushed through the back door, letting it bang closed behind her, heading for one of the patrol cars parked in a neat row in the fenced compound behind the detachment, reminding herself that it was this hunger for appreciation and approval that had made her vulnerable to goddamn Alan, that psychopathic son of a bitch.

She got into the car, opened the driver's window and sat still for a few minutes, her hands on the wheel, recovering her calm.

Then she set off for Andrew Maine's townhouse.

The menswear store was open late on Tuesdays and Fridays: Andrew's hours on those days were noon to closing.

It was shortly after ten o'clock when Eddie knocked on Andrew's front door. It took him a while to respond and when he did, he opened the door just a crack, revealing a strip of white face, one bloodshot eye, and a small chunk of hair. He said nothing, only looked at her.

"Can I come in, Andrew?"

"Did you catch him?"

"Not yet, I'm afraid. Can I come in?"

"Why?"

"I'd like to talk to you."

"You already did."

"I know. But I'd like to talk to you again. Maybe you'll remember something new, something that'll help us find out who did this. Okay?"

He hesitated. Eddie thought he was frowning now. "I haven't had breakfast yet."

"This won't take long."

"What time is it?"

"It's about ten, Andrew," said Eddie, controlling her exasperation. "How about it?"

"Could I have coffee while you talk to me?"

"Sure." He pulled the door open wider. "Okay."

Andrew was wearing rumpled blue pajamas, the lapels edged with cord that was a darker blue, slip-on leather slippers, and a white terry cloth robe, the belt dangling from its loops. He tied the belt as he shuffled into the kitchen. Eddie followed him.

Andrew filled an electric kettle with water, plugged it in, and heaped instant coffee from a lidless container into a mug sitting next to it. There were only a few dirty dishes lying around: Andrew hadn't eaten much, Eddie figured, in the week since his wife's death.

He stood by the window, looking outside, while the kettle came to a boil. "The funeral's in two days, I think," he said.

"Andrew," said Eddie; "are you alone here?"

A few seconds passed before he turned to look at her, clearly baffled. "Alone?"

"Yeah. Haven't you got anybody staying with you?"

"I don't know what you mean. Of course I'm alone. She's dead." His eyes filled, and overflowed.

"I'm sorry, Andrew." Eddie crossed the room and touched his arm. "I didn't intend to upset you. I meant, don't you have a relative, or a friend, who could stay with you? Because you're so unhappy."

"Yeah, I know I am." He pulled away from her and filled the coffee mug. He stirred the coffee with a spoon and sat down at the table. Eddie sat opposite him. He drank some coffee. Eddie took her notebook and pen from her pocket. "I'm sorry," said Andrew, "do you want some coffee, too?"

"No thanks." Eddie smiled at him and flipped her notebook open to a blank page. "Okay. Now, the day Janet disappeared, last Monday, tell me again why you were working late that day, Andrew. Because you don't usually work late on Mondays, do you?"

He was looking at the window, maybe looking through

it, at the cloudless April sky. "Yeah," he said, "I did have somebody staying with me. My mom and dad were here. They had to go home, though. They went home on Sunday, I think," he said, eyes on his coffee now.

"Andrew? Why were you working late that day?"

"It was the last day of the month," he said. "So we were taking inventory."

Eddie nodded, and made a note. "Okay. Now—I saw you going into the store yesterday morning. Why are you back at work so soon?"

He poked at his coffee with the spoon.

"Andrew?"

Carefully, he scooped something out of his coffee—a teabag. He looked at Eddie in astonishment. "Look at that," he said.

"I see it," said Eddie.

"I don't like tea." Andrew frowned, his head craned to stare closely at the teabag. "It must've been my mom's. Jeez."

Eddie sat back with a sigh that was almost a giggle.

Andrew peered into his coffee and took a cautious sip. "Can't taste it, though. Good thing."

"Andrew."

"Yeah?"

"I said, you were back at work yesterday—"

"Oh yeah. Yeah." He shuffled his feet under the table. "Yeah, I'm going to work again." He put his elbow on the table for support and pressed his head into his hand, clutching his temples tightly.

"This is a bad time for you, I know," said Eddie.

After a few seconds Andrew lifted his head. "My mom's gonna help me pack up Janet's things."

Eddie nodded.

"When she comes back for the funeral. She's gonna stay

a couple more days and help me do that." He sat back. "My mom, when Janet and I got married, she said she had only one piece of advice to give us." He pushed the mug of coffee away from. him. "She said, never let the sun go down on a quarrel."

"That's good advice," said Eddie.

"But I did. I did." His face was contorted with misery. "I—she—I couldn't make it up with her. I just couldn't."

It flashed into Eddie's mind that she ought to have been doing this at the detachment, in an interview room, with another officer present and a tape recorder going. Shit, she thought. Had she screwed up here? But she decided that if Andrew would confess here, he'd confess again; he'd confess as many times as anybody wanted him to.

"What did you quarrel about, Andrew?" she asked softly.

He planted his hands on the table, tears streaming. "She told me this thing, Janet did, this awful thing, and I—I just couldn't—she killed it, see?" He was sobbing now, hanging on to the edge of the table, as if this were the only thing preventing him from floating away. "She didn't call it that, of course—I needed to talk about it. I tried to talk to somebody at work, but it was no use, the vacuum was on, and I talked to my manager, and Norman that I bowl with, but they wouldn't call it killing either, but—" Andrew made a fist of his right hand and banged the table "—but that's what it *was,* that's what an abortion *is,* right?" He leaned across the table, toward Eddie. "Right? *Right?*" Eddie didn't reply. He sank back into his chair. "It hurt me," he said dully. "That's all I could think about, was how much I was hurting. And so. And so. We didn't make up. And the sun went down." He raised trembling hands to rub at his face.

Slowly, Eddie closed her notebook and put it away.

•   •   •

"You might be interested to know, Miss Atkinson," said the principal, catching her in the hall at lunchtime, "that we have heard from the errant Mr. Dyakowski."

Susan, her jacket half on and half off, arrested in midflight, looked at him with wide eyes and an open mouth, and elected not to speak.

"He'll be here tomorrow," said the principal, his eyeglasses glinting in the overhead light.

"Oh good," said Susan. "Good." She nodded, and continued to nod, feeling like a mechanical bird—perhaps a woodpecker—as he darted skillfully through the throngs of children who clogged the hallway, heading in helter-skelter fashion for the lunchroom. Susan shrugged her jacket on and hurried in the opposite direction, toward the parking lot.

Less than fifteen minutes later, she was letting herself into her apartment.

Ivan, no less whitefaced than yesterday, no less grim, had made a plate of sandwiches and brewed a pot of coffee, and they sat in the living room to eat lunch together.

"I'm not going to press charges," said Ivan. He got up and moved toward the balcony. Halfway there, he turned. "Do you mind?" he asked, gesturing toward the sliding doors. Susan shook her head and he pulled the doors open, admitting a cool rush of air and the sounds and scents of the sea. He stood still for a moment, looking out. Susan felt that she ought to get up and embrace him, but decided that it would be better to keep her distance from him now, and in the immediate future—until he gave her a sign.

"I think she must be crazy," he said. "That's what I've decided." He turned around. "Not because she hit me. I can understand that. But because—because of the rest of it." His car keys had been in his pocket, with the remote opener attached. Susan knew that if this hadn't been the case, he probably would have died. "She wouldn't have done that," he said with conviction. "She couldn't have done it. Not Denise. Not unless she's gone crazy."

"I don't know her," said Susan. "So I can't say."

Ivan crossed the room and sat down again. "I don't know if I should phone her, or write her a letter. Or what."

"What do you want to say to her?"

Ivan sighed. "I don't know, exactly."

Susan said, slowly, choosing her words with care, "Do you think that you want to explore the possibility of—of resuming, or renewing, your marriage?" The sandwiches were still untouched. Perhaps they could have them for dinner, she thought. She glanced at Ivan.

He looked astounded—then he burst into laughter. He stood up, and sat down again. "I can't believe this." He looked at her curiously. "No, Susan. I don't want—I think, Susan, that when your wife clobbers you on the head, stuffs you into the trunk of your car, and abandons the car in the middle of a forest, I think that's a pretty clear indication that the marriage is over."

Susan agreed, of course. And why wasn't this realization creating euphoria? Why did she feel so damn uneasy about Ivan's sudden freedom?

"So what's your advice to me?" asked Ivan.

"My advice?" Susan responded. "Okay. I think you should write her a letter. 'Dear Denise: This is to inform you that we're getting a divorce. My lawyer will be in touch with you in due course. Sincerely, Ivan.' " She tilted her head and smiled at him.

It was probably the melodramatic way in which the marriage had ended, she thought, that was causing her to feel solemn about the whole business. Instead of overjoyed. Like she ought to.

NINETEEN

Alberg swung through downtown Vancouver, hands in his pockets, savoring the mild breeze that made its way up from the ocean that could be glimpsed at the northern end of the streets, even noticing the spring flowers overflowing the curbside planters. He was enjoying his anonymity.

Alberg was aware that his enduring wish to remain unnoticeable was often antithetical to his effectiveness as a police officer. But there you are, he told himself: life was full of contradictions. He was known by sight to the whole damn town of Sechelt, even though he continued to eschew the uniform in an attempt to remain inconspicuous. This had been at first wholly successful, but after more than ten years . . .

What freedom, he thought exultantly, wheeling along the street. Nobody even glanced at him—he might as well be invisible. Except of course for those who wanted his money. There was a battalion of them—men and women, boys and girls—spread throughout the downtown core like sentries, or infiltrators. Many were pathetic indigents: most of these were addicts, many of them were sick, and some were half as old as Alberg's daughters. He tried to look away from them, from the figures draped against the corners of buildings or huddled on threadbare coats spread on the pavement. He found it interesting that today, anyway, their requests for cash were all so polite. "Spare change, ma'am?" they would say to a woman hurrying past, her smooth nyloned legs scissoring, head high, briefcase swinging; and when she ignored them, they nonetheless offered a quiet, "Thank you." Alberg sensed the background rage, though, and felt reluctant admiration for their self-control. In the three blocks between Pacific Centre and his destination he gave a loonie to every panhandler he passed, and ended up at the office of Reg Washburn, private investigator, eight dollars poorer.

As he entered the building he resolved not to describe to Reg the decrepit digs in which he had expected to find him. He had certainly not expected a soaring glass tower with potted trees and a fountain in its lobby.

He took the elevator to the seventeenth floor, less than halfway up, and walked silently along the carpeted hallway to a wide wooden door flanked by narrow windows of clouded glass. A small brass plaque identified the business within. Alberg pushed down on the bulky brass door handle and went inside.

Behind a long low desk sat a middle-aged receptionist who was talking on the telephone, the receiver clutched between her shoulder and her chin, while typing furiously away on a computer keyboard. She looked up at Alberg and smiled.

"Okay, sure, I understand," she said soothingly into the phone, "you're upset. Who wouldn't be? I'll give him your message and I'm sure you'll be hearing from him later today." She listened for a moment. "Okay. Sure. No problem." She hung up and spun her chair around. "I'm Louise," she announced. "And you must be Mr. Alberg. He's expecting you."

A few minutes later he was sitting in Reg's office with a mug of coffee steaming on an end table next to his chair. Reg was at his desk, hands behind his head, grinning at him.

Reg Washburn had spent twenty years in the RCMP, the last six with E Division in British Columbia, before taking early retirement. "So you want to know what it's like being a PI," he said.

"Yeah," said Alberg.

"Which means you're thinking of getting out."

"I guess I am," answered Alberg.

Reg lowered his arms and rested them on the desk. "Must admit, I'm surprised."

"So am I," said Alberg.

Reg looked at him appraisingly. "What do you see yourself doing, as a PI?"

Alberg shrugged uncomfortably. "I don't know, for god's sake. That's why I'm here—I don't have a real clear idea about what to expect."

"Yeah," Reg persisted, "but if you had your druthers, what kind of stuff do you think you'd want to take on?"

"Pretty much what I'm doing now, I guess," said Alberg. "Except I want to make all my own decisions, I don't want anybody breathing down my neck, and I want somebody else taking care of the goddamn paperwork."

"You won't be able to pick and choose, you know, Karl," Reg said seriously. "Not at first. You gotta establish your specialties—find yourself a niche. This takes time. And meanwhile, you gotta take what's offered."

"What's your niche?" said Alberg. "Fraud?"

"Fraud, yeah," Reg agreed, nodding. "As you might expect. But I've got two partners, so fraud's not all we do. And some stuff we contract out to other agencies."

The large window behind Reg's desk looked out on a collection of mostly new downtown buildings that had been built to look old, most of them constructed of red brick and crowned with incongruous triangular embellishments of glass framed in blue-painted wood. The shorter, humbler structure immediately next door, however, was an older vintage. A wide puddle had collected in a depression in its flat roof, and a large seagull was standing in the middle of the puddle, cleaning itself.

"Sometimes we're hired to investigate open cases," Reg was saying. "If the family of a dead guy isn't happy with the pace of the police investigation, for instance. We had one of those last year."

"Oh yeah?" said Alberg. "You got any at the moment?" Reg shook his head.

"Okay, so tell me what you *are* working on," said Alberg, picking up the coffee mug.

Outside Reg's office was a larger space containing two desks, each with a telephone, a computer terminal, and a printer; a write-on bulletin board that took up almost an entire wall; a water dispenser; a table that held a coffeemaker, several clean mugs, bowls of sugar and sugar substitutes, and some spoons; and a small refrigerator.

Reg reached for some folders and thumbed through them. "A missing person. Another missing person—both adults. A stalker." He looked up. "That one's a doozy. Plus we've got one, two, three—six insurance frauds, altogether. And here's an employee theft. And a domestic. This one's a cheating spouse. The wife. Our client's the husband." He put the files back.

"Do you get a lot of domestics?"

"Yeah, well, we could take on a lot more than we do. Mostly they're process serving, surveillance—not very interesting stuff. But sometimes—missing kids, for instance—they can be good cases." He narrowed his eyes, assessing Alberg. "You'd do well at this, Karl."

Two large trees stood at either side of the window behind Reg's desk: Alberg thought they were the same kind that were in Cassandra's library. The office also contained two more plants—cacti, he thought they must be—that were almost as tall as he was.

"Oh yeah?" he asked. "Why?"

"I mean once you get established, maybe find yourself a partner. And assuming that you're not gonna need to take cases strictly for the money." Reg lifted his eyebrows in tactful inquiry.

"I haven't done the number-crunching yet," Alberg admitted. "I'm jumping the gun a bit here."

"You've put in the years, though, right?" said Reg.

"Yeah."

"The reason I think you'll do well, and have a good time, too, is—" He took a quick slurp of coffee and set his mug down: it was a dark purple mug with his name on it in white script. "First off, I tell my people that their best source of information is always the client. The client always knows even more about the target than he thinks he does. So I tell them that interviewing is of primary importance. And that they should—especially during the first consultation—shut up and listen. You know where I learned all this? I learned it in Kamloops. From you. Watching you work." He sat back, folded his arms, and grinned at Alberg, rocking slightly, back and forth in his chair.

Alberg, mildly flustered, lifted his hand to smooth his hair. "Hmmm," he said.

"And secondly," said Reg, leaning forward again, "there's a lot of flakes out there, Karl. And some of them—well, you take—well you know that in the elite squads, for instance—police squads—homicide, drugs, like that—there're occasions when it gets hard for some of them to walk the fence. Hard for them not to see a deal. So, you get a guy like that, he's persuaded to resign—he's a rogue cop. And where does he go? He hangs out his shingle." Reg shrugged, opening his arms wide. "So it's important to have guys like you and me out there, too."

"Huh," said Alberg. He looked around the office at the prints, tastefully framed, that hung on the walls. And inspected Reg, white-shirted, wearing a tie, his suit jacket hung over the back of his chair. Reg looked relaxed and prosperous.

Reg said, "Now you're gonna want to know the ins and outs of income versus expenses and all that, right?"

"Whatever you can tell me, I'd be grateful," said Alberg.

An hour later Alberg left the building, feeling somewhat dazed but mostly exhilarated. He checked his watch and decided to treat himself to fish and chips at Troll's in Horseshoe Bay before catching the six o'clock ferry.

He might want a partner. And he'd have to get registered. And decide where to set up shop, and what kind of work he'd try to get. Did he want to take on a bunch of cases for lawyers, usually defense attorneys? Reg had talked about locating witnesses, reconstructing crime scenes, conducting murder investigations—that stuff sounded interesting, Alberg thought, striding toward the parking lot beneath the Pacific Centre shopping mall, where he'd left his car. And some of the domestics Reg had told him about had sounded interesting, too.

He remembered Cassandra asking him soon after they had met what he liked about his job. "Figuring things out," he had replied. "Talking to people, thinking, finding out what happened, who did it, why they did it—that kind of thing."

And Cassandra had said, "What about justice?"

Justice wasn't in his purview, he'd told her. He had said this almost lightly, as if justice were a thing probably unobtainable, maybe insignificant, and certainly beside the point.

Alberg realized that he felt differently now, about justice as a philosophical reality and a worthwhile goal. But he still saw little relationship between genuine justice and the legal system he served.

He found himself whistling as he walked along, meditating on his future.

When he got to the end of the block and had to wait for a light to change, he glanced to his left and saw a man approaching, driving a motorized scooter that had three large wheels. The man's withered legs were partially wrapped in a blanket, and he was wearing a peaked cap. He was about Alberg's age, with gray hair and a thick, neatly trimmed gray beard. An antenna had been attached to the back of the scooter. The man swiveled and came to a stop beside Alberg. He glanced up at him and gave him a wink, his face otherwise expressionless. Alberg nodded back. A small, tattered pennant flew from the scooter's antenna and as the light changed and the man steered deftly into the crosswalk, Alberg saw that there was printing on it: Vancouver City Police, it read.

Alberg followed him, slowly, across the intersection.

Eddie unlocked the door to her house, went inside, pulled off her jacket and hung it up, loosened her tie, and threw herself down on the living room sofa. She couldn't get Andrew Maine out of her head. Hunched over like a turtle, he had been, hurting so much that he hadn't been physically able to straighten his body. Alone in his house, she knew that he would lie on his bed in the fetal position, reliving again and again those painful conversations with his wife that had not ended in reconciliation. Eddie knew she shouldn't do this. It was like prodding a partially healed wound, or an aching tooth. Inquisitiveness in itself was neither good nor bad; in fact, it was obviously a useful tool. But it sometimes became self-indulgent, and led to extravagant leaps out of the realm of logic and into exaggeration, occasionally even fantasy. Imagination was a vital ingredient in good police work—but only when firmly disciplined and controlled.

Eddie knew a lot about discipline, about control.

All she had seen or sensed in Andrew Maine was pain, plus a certain amount of righteous anger. She was disappointed not to have found a suspect, but she was also disappointed in Andrew himself. Although she envied his naïveté, the simplicity of his thinking—even the austerity of his attitudes—she now judged his sweetness to be compromised by prejudice.

Eddie covered her eyes with the back of one hand and let her other arm hang down toward the floor, her fingertips brushing the carpet. When the phone rang she reached for it automatically, pre-occupied with Andrew, and with his wife's so far inexplicable homicide.

"Ah, good," said Alan. "I refuse to talk to your machine."

Eddie sat up. "Why are you doing this?" she said evenly.

"Why am I keeping in touch?" he asked, pretending to sound astonished.

Eddie put the receiver down, gently, and pulled the jack from the wall.

Quickly, she showered and changed. Plugged the jack back in. And left the house, furious with herself.

Half an hour later she was in a bar, nursing a beer and waiting for a roast beef sandwich, when Cindi Webster materialized next to her.

"Is it okay if I sit down?" asked Cindi. "Or are you waiting for somebody?"

"Go ahead," said Eddie, glancing at her watch.

"I almost didn't recognize you," said Cindi. She waved at the bartender and ordered a beer. "Out of uniform."

The place was almost empty, but then it was only seven-thirty. Eddie wondered what kind of social life was available to her, while living on the Sunshine Coast, outside the detachment. Would she get desperate and end up fleeing to Vancouver whenever she got the chance?

"Are you eating?" asked Cindi.

"Yeah, I've ordered a sandwich."

"Who's that guy, that officer, he's—I don't know his name, but I saw him in here one day last week." Cindi pushed her hair back. "I'm letting it grow," she said, "so I can put it in a ponytail or something. It drives me nuts hanging around my face like it does." She glanced at Eddie, who had pinned her braid onto the top of her head and covered it with a Roughriders cap. "How long did it take for yours to get that long?"

"I haven't had it cut for five or six years, I guess," said Eddie. She drained her glass and signaled for another beer.

"Anyway. He's tall and he's got dark hair and a mustache."

Eddie looked at her blankly. "Who?"

"The officer I told you about. Do you know who he is? I mean, his name? And is he married?" She drank some beer and looked expectantly at Eddie. She'd dumped her shoulderbag on the floor by her feet. She wore sneakers, jeans, and a pink T-shirt, and a navy cardigan tied around her waist.

"I think I know who you mean," said Eddie. "He's a constable. His name is Cornie Friesen. Don't know if he's married or not. Do you want me to find out?"

Cindi was frowning into her beer glass. "The thing is, I've sworn off sex, so I don't know if there'd be any point."

Eddie shifted on the stool to look at her more closely. "Hmmm," she offered. "And how come you've done that?"

The bartender set a large plate in front of her and drummed on the counter. "Ta-da!" He leaned toward her. "Hope you enjoy it, Sergeant."

Eddie watched him retreat. Jesus. She'd been here how

many days? And everybody in town knew who she was already.

"Because of STDs," said Cindi. "So far so good," she said, knocking on her head, "but I want to have babies someday. And you can't be too careful."

Eddie's stomach took a sudden nosedive, like a broken elevator. She was so lucky. She still couldn't believe her luck, to have gotten out of the thing with Alan not pregnant; not infected with anything in fact, neither germ nor sperm. The only damage she had suffered was some softening of the brain, and she thought she had escaped before that had become irreversible.

She poked at the contents of her plate, a pile of chips on one side and a roast beef sandwich on the other. "Look at that," she said wonderingly to Cindi. "They've cut the crusts off the bread." She lifted the top slice: thinly carved beef, mustard, mayo, plenty of cracked black pepper.

"On the other hand," Cindi was saying, "I've got to try them out, right? I mean I can't wait until the wedding night, right?"

Eddie took a bite and made a sound between a moan and a laugh. "This is so good," she said. "I can't believe it."

"I know sex isn't everything," said Cindi, "but you've got to do it for such a long time, it better be at least good, am I right?"

"You're talking about marriage?"

"Yeah, of course." Cindi leaned back and gathered her hair in her hands. "How much longer's it going to take, do you think? Before it'll all tie back?"

"You're nearly there," said Eddie, checking it out. "Another—I don't know—a couple of months, maybe."

The door opened and two off-duty police officers entered—Joey Lattimer and Frank Turner—stopping off for a drink on their way home, Eddie figured. She watched them scan the bar as they headed toward an empty table, and waited for them to spot her. When she had met them she had entered Turner in the "civilized" column in her own private ledger, and had reserved judgment on Lattimer, who had leered at her, but maybe out of nervousness.

"That's him," said Cindi in an excited whisper. "That's the guy I meant before. The one in the leather jacket—the one with the mustache. Oh jeez."

"Lattimer. Forget it, Cindi. He's married. They're both married," said Eddie.

And now they noticed her, just as they reached the table and started to sit down. For a moment they froze, half standing, half sitting, looking awkward and guilty, as if she'd caught them doing something they shouldn't. Eddie grinned and tossed them a mock salute. They relaxed, grinned back, and sat down.

"Everybody's married," said Cindi irritably.

"Not everybody," said Eddie, and she took another bite of her sandwich.

"I don't believe in going out with married guys," said Cindi.

"Yeah, well, you don't believe in going out with anyone, though—isn't that what you've been saying? Sorry," said Eddie, swallowing, "I shouldn't talk with my mouth full."

"I was asking for your opinion, is what I was doing," said Cindi with dignity. She waved at the bartender and ordered another beer.

"You want another one too, Sergeant?" he asked.

Eddie shook her head. "Just a glass of water, please." She wiped her fingers on a paper napkin and finished her beer. "My opinion about what? About whether you should audition prospective husbands in bed?"

Cindi started to protest. Then she turned around, resting her back against the bar. "Yeah," she said. "Yeah," she said again. "It doesn't sound good, the way you put it. But that's it all right."

"I think you should, yes," said Eddie. She sighed and pushed her plate away.

"You aren't going to eat the chips?" asked Cindi.

"Help yourself," said Eddie. "Check out other stuff first, though," she said.

"Yeah," said Cindi, nodding, munching on a chip. "That's where I've gone wrong in the past. I mean, it's the easiest thing to make sure of, right? So I jump right in there. And then if it's halfway pleasurable—well, my eyes are dimmed to the rest of him, if you know what I mean."

"I do indeed," said Eddie, looking at her watch.

"Don't go yet," said Cindi quickly.

The bartender delivered Cindi's beer and a glass of ice water for Eddie. "Here you go, Sarge."

Eddie said, "Have you got a name, sir?"

"It's Paul." He wiped his hand on his apron and extended it toward her.

"Eddie," she said, shaking hands.

"Cindi," said Cindi, with a peal of laughter, and the bartender shook her hand, too.

"Pleased to meet you," he said. "Are you done with this?"

Eddie looked inquiringly at Cindi.

"Yeah," said the reporter with a sigh. She gestured dramatically. "Take it away."

"I've really got to go, Cindi," said Eddie, watching the door close behind Lattimer and Turner. She'd been sitting here when they'd arrived, she was still here when they left, and she didn't like the image this suggested.

"Wait a minute," said Cindi, placing a hand on Eddie's arm. "You know this series I'm doing?"

"About people's jobs," said Eddie. "Yeah, I remember."

"Yeah. Well I—"

"How did it go with my boss, by the way?"

"Fine. Good. Terrific, in fact. He had lots of great stories."

"He did?" said Eddie, astonished.

"Yeah. But listen, I also talked to that waitress at Earl's, the one with the black hair and the attitude. Did you know he hired another one, Earl did, another waitress, sometime last fall? And she just up and disappeared?"

She had leaned close to Eddie as she spoke, lowering her voice, and Eddie caught a flowery scent that reminded her of her mother. It was something made by Yardley, she thought. Bath powder, maybe. Or body lotion.

"I'm not suggesting anything here," Cindi said earnestly, keeping her voice down. She anchored her flyaway hair behind her ears again. "But what with that legal secretary you guys just found, and that poor teenager last year—"

"Rebecca Granger," Eddie responded mechanically. "She disappeared on Valentine's Day. They found her body in August, on her birthday."

"I know," said Cindi. She clasped her hands and rested them on the edge of the bar. "I've been trying to decide all evening whether to say anything about it. It could be coincidence, after all. It probably is." She sat perfectly still, perfectly relaxed, her face tilted slightly, her eyes on Eddie, waiting.

"Uh huh," said Eddie. "And you're speaking to me here—as what?"

"Not as a friend," said Cindi. "We don't know each other well enough to be friends. Not as a reporter, either. It isn't my story, although I wish it were, and I'm certainly not about to give anything to that rat-turd who *is* covering it." She shrugged. "I guess I'm speaking as a citizen."

"Uh huh," said Eddie.

Cindi shifted on the bar stool. "It's probably nothing. It's probably coincidence."

"Probably," said Eddie.

But there was a fluttering in her stomach that threatened to prevent the easy digestion of her roast beef sandwich.

TWENTY

Wednesday, April 3

———

Mrs. O'Hara had found it hard to sleep. The night had brought a medium-sized wind, so the trees were restless and noisy and the cabin creaked more loudly than usual. Mrs. O'Hara tried to wait for daybreak but couldn't: it was still dark when she climbed out of bed.

She swallowed several aspirin and made herself some tea, then went to the door and opened it. By this time the sky had begun to lighten, although many stars were still visible. It was soothing to stand there in the doorway gazing at the wakening world. Mrs. O'Hara hadn't looked at the clock yet or put on her wristwatch, and for the moment she cared nothing for the passage of time. Time seemed irrelevant. She thought it must be immensely liberating to live life without benefit of clock or wristwatch. When the day of her retirement arrived perhaps she would divest herself of such things and live the months that remained to her only according to the light in the sky.

She couldn't see the lake from here but imagined it, silvery in the burgeoning daylight, the surrounding grasses strong black paintbrush strokes, the trees bending toward the water, leaning toward it as if to see themselves reflected there. Mrs. O'Hara shivered suddenly in the coolness of the pearly blue morning, and closed the door, softly.

She had no wish to dress, no wish to travel, no wish to

clean houses or organize her last sweep. There were aches in her body and aches in her brain, and she was afraid that tiredness would never again leave her.

Soon, however, these things wouldn't matter. Soon the days—and nights—would belong only to her. She wondered what she would do with them.

She had become a church-goer, for a while, shortly after her arrival in Sechelt. She used to drive up and down the peninsula a lot then, getting to know her territory, and a pretty white-painted chapel had caught her eye. It gleamed at her through the thicket of trees that surrounded it, white glints through the bright green of spring, the lush foliage of summer, the gold of autumn, the delicately skeletal bare branches in winter: it was the protective enclosure of the trees that had captured her fancy.

One Sunday she searched her closet for a skirt, climbed into her van, and went to church.

She attended sporadically for several months, gradually becoming acquainted with some of the parishioners—and with the pastor, a thin, stooped man with a durable smile.

Eventually she had accepted the pastor as a client.

One day, while she was cleaning his house, his four-teen-year-old daughter burst in: she had been with her father in the chapel, arranging flowers for services the following morning. Mrs. O'Hara speculated, later, that if she had been standing when the girl came in, things might not have unfolded as they did, for Mrs. O'Hara was a large, imposing woman, possibly even of frightening size. But at that moment she was on her hands and knees, scrubbing the kitchen floor, her face damp with perspiration, her hair coming loose from its bun, and she knew that her expression was one of unthreatening surprise—quickly followed by concern, because the girl was so obviously distraught. "What is it?" asked Mrs. O'Hara. And the girl began to sob, her shoulders hunching, her hands covering her face. And pretty soon Mrs. O'Hara had heard the whole evil tale.

Although she was not a mechanic, she knew a thing or two about cars. She also knew the pastor's schedule, when he made his regular visits of condolence and support, and to whom.

She drove to his house one winter morning before dawn, parked her van on the highway, crept into his yard, and made adjustments under the hood of his vehicle.

The chance of her endangering the pastor's daughter was remote, since the girl walked to and from school and avoided being alone with her father whenever possible.

The pastor's car went out of control on a rambling, graceful hill, spun off the road, and slammed into a Douglas fir, killing him almost instantly. Mrs. O'Hara hadn't necessarily intended for him to die, but was prepared for this eventuality, and accepted it as his due.

The girl, his daughter, went to live with an aunt and uncle in Nanaimo.

As Mrs. O'Hara gazed around her comfortable cabin, a strange, hostile thought unfolded in her brain: when she died—how much time would pass before somebody thought to look for her? And found her body?

"I can't believe there'd be another one," said Alberg to Eddie. "Three homicides? Jesus." His frustration was growing, and so was his anger. "Check it out," he said. "She probably didn't disappear. She probably changed her mind about wanting to work for Earl. But check it out." He turned to Frank Turner. "What did we get from the interviews in the area around the clearing?"

"Nothing, Staff," said Turner, a tall, lean redhead with a scarred forehead and right cheek. "It's pretty isolated there. Nearest house is a couple of miles away. And you can't see the clearing from the road. So the guys didn't come up with much."

"Did they come up with anything at all?"

"Sorry, Staff. No."

Alberg opened the center drawer of his desk and immediately slammed it closed. "Eddie?"

She paged through her notebook. "The victims didn't know each other. Rebecca was a high school student, Janet worked in a lawyer's office—they don't seem to have had anything in common. They didn't go to the same hairdresser, or doctor, or dentist. Neither of them had any formal religious affiliation. Rebecca's mother says she and her husband didn't know Janet, or Andrew." Eddie shrugged, almost apologetically.

"And although Janet Maine had had an abortion," said Alberg, "that doesn't shed any light because Rebecca Granger was uh . . . a virgin, right?"

Eddie nodded.

"That's refreshing," Alberg grumbled. He sat back again, folding his arms. "And even though Janet's husband was upset about the abortion, you don't think he was upset enough to kill her."

"Right," said Eddie. "And besides, his boss says he was working when she was killed."

"So." Alberg looked from one of them to the other. "Does anybody think we've got a couple of random killings here?"

"I don't think so," said Frank Turner, and Eddie nodded in agreement.

"Okay. Why?" asked Alberg.

"There's no sexual assault," said Turner.

"And is sex the only possible explanation for a spontaneous homicide?" asked Alberg.

Frank shrugged. "It could happen in the course of a robbery."

"But neither of these victims was robbed," said Alberg.

"Sex, or rage," said Eddie. "And there's no sign of rage here, either. Both killings were calculated."

"Okay. If you're right, and we're looking at deliberate homicides, there *must* be some damn connection between the victims." Alberg stood up, walked to his office door, and opened it. "Find it," he said, waving Eddie and Frank Turner into the hall.

How did I get him into the trunk? Denise asked herself, sitting in the rocking chair.

She hadn't gone back to work. She had called to say that she still had the flu.

How did I get him into the trunk?

She received a foggy memory of a recalcitrant leg, dangling.

She had folded it carefully at hip and knee, but it sprang awkwardly forward and draped itself over the lip of the trunk. Patiently, she pushed it back.

Tears were very close to the insides of each of her eyelids. Tension wanted to squeeze them free, but they remained where they were.

Ivan's leg had trembled, slightly, as Denise closed the trunk.

This, too, she remembered.

It had been a small tremor—nothing more. She had thought it part of the dying process; a final shudder of protest, significant only of extinction.

She had swaddled his head in a bathsheet and lain it gently on a pillow on a sheet of black plastic.

And once she had removed Ivan from the scene, she had turned to the mess in the kitchen.

She remembered pulling a stack of towels from the linen closet and dropping them into the blood. They soaked it up like the sponges they were. She was interested and relieved to see that the color of the blood changed slightly, became slightly paler, as it was absorbed by the towels.

Denise fetched a broom from the landing on the basement staircase. When she opened the door, that cellar smell wafted upward, bringing to mind cardboard boxes of apples and potatoes, splintery shelves filled with glass jars containing pickles and peaches, chutneys and salmon. Denise's basement held none of these treasures, but it smelled like it did, it smelled like the cellar in her grandparents' house, years and years ago. They were both dead now, both of those grandparents.

But they had died quietly, with dignity, spilling no blood upon their kitchen floor.

Denise snatched the broom from the landing and pulled the chain that turned off the light.

She pushed the towels around in the blood, using the handle of the broom, which frequently slipped off and skidded on the floor, collecting blood drops on the worn handle, drops that soaked into the wood where paint had flaked away, drops that crept into small slices in the handle that had been created by who knows what. Later she would try to scrub the handle clean, but couldn't, could not get it clean. Could not.

When the fluffy towels were soaked—which happened very rapidly—Denise picked them up by a corner and dropped them into plastic garbage bags. She didn't fill the bags all the way because that would have made them too heavy to lift.

Another stack of towels was pitched upon the floor, swirled through the blood, picked up, stowed away in garbage bags.

She used every towel in the linen closet, and the ones hanging limp and soiled in the bathroom, too.

She had to get down on her hands and knees, finally,

and scrub the floor. Some of the remaining blood had dried by then.

She remembered scrubbing vigorously at a curved line on the floor, dark red: a graceful line, wide and thick but with a pretty curve, its inner edge soft and yielding. She had wiped it into oblivion with a single confident swipe, even though the hand towel she was using was worn almost through in the middle, no longer thick and fluffy but thin, almost transparent. . . .

Denise sat in the rocking chair and reclaimed every single terrible memory of the night of Ivan's "murder."

She was still sitting there, inert and silent, at lunchtime, when a car pulled up outside the house. She heard footsteps approaching and knew they were Ivan's. They were firm, measured footsteps and Denise was filled with gratitude, because they were evidence of his continued existence.

She waited for a knock on the door but there was none, only a faint scraping sound as an envelope was pushed through the space between the floor and the bottom of the door. Denise listened to more footsteps, retreating footsteps, and the sound of first one car, and then another, driving away. After a while she scooped up the envelope and unfolded the note that was inside.

He wanted a divorce.

Well, who could blame him?

She looked outside and saw that his Cavalier was gone.

"Who said she disappeared?" Naomi asked impatiently. "And are you gonna sit down and order, or just waste my time here?"

"Yeah, sure," said Eddie, sliding onto a stool at the counter. "I'll have a hamburger and fries. That reporter— Cindi Webster. She says *you* did, Naomi. She told me you said she disappeared."

"I said she didn't show up for work, is what I said. Coffee?"

"Thanks. But didn't you think that was odd?"

"I don't know. Maybe. I'm busy, here, in case you hadn't noticed," Naomi called over her shoulder, bustling out from behind the counter with the coffee pot.

Eddie sighed.

She scribbled for a while in her notebook, exchanged pleasantries with the people sitting on either side of her, ate the hamburger that Naomi eventually banged down in front of her, had a second cup of coffee, used the washroom. . . .

"Can you give me a minute now?" she asked finally.

"Sure," said Naomi, wiping the countertop. "What do you want?"

"I need to know where she was staying. Where she'd come from. I want to know whatever you can tell me about her—starting with her name."

Naomi looked at her curiously. "You think somebody did her in, maybe? Like those other two?"

"I don't think anything yet," Eddie responded patiently. "Okay? Can you help me?"

"I can tell you a few things. You'll need Earl for the rest." She turned to face the swinging door that led into the kitchen. "Earl!" she shouted. "I'll get him," she said to Eddie. "Earl!"

TWENTY-ONE

Thursday, April 4

———

Alberg woke early, according to plan. But he almost didn't get up right away. Cassandra, sleeping, her legs pulled up, her back curved, facing away from him, smelled too damn good. He wanted to press his early morning erection against her butt, and spread his hand inside her panties, over her warm damp bush, inserting his fingers there. . . . Jesus.

He rolled out of bed, almost falling upon the floor, and stood still, holding his breath, as Cassandra stirred and moaned—a sound that animated his erection still further. She settled back into sleep, then, and Alberg tiptoed out of the bedroom, watched by the cats curled up at the end of the bed, and closed the door quietly behind him.

In the kitchen he made cheese omelettes, sliced mushrooms and fried them in butter, toasted whole wheat bread, made coffee, poured orange juice.

Then he ventured into the backyard, still in his robe and slippers, looking for flowers. He eventually found a big red tulip, which he cut and placed in a small vase.

When he had set the table, he went back into the bedroom to waken Cassandra.

"Hey. Wife," he said, kneeling next to the bed, wincing at the pain in his knees. He buried his face in her neck. "Time to get up."

But she wrapped her arms around him.

Good thing I put the food in the oven, he thought, as she dragged him back into bed.

"So what's the occasion?" Cassandra said later, digging into her omelette. She ate the way she did most things, with relish, with expectation of enjoyment.

"Something happened to me the other day," said Alberg. "On Monday, it was."

She gave him a quick look. "Something bad?"

"No. Something good. I think. But I didn't tell you about it right away because—"

"You hardly ever tell me things right away," said Cassandra calmly.

He was momentarily unnerved. "Really?"

"Eat," said Cassandra, waving her fork in the air. "This is very good. Extremely good. Mmmm. Karl. What a treat."

"Good. Thank you. Well, this time, then—this time, the reason I didn't tell you right away was because at first I didn't know what it was. But then I figured it out." He leaned across the table toward her, knife in hand, the blade pointing at the ceiling. "I had an epiphany, Cassandra," he said solemnly. "That's what it was."

She lowered her coffee cup without drinking from it. "Really? What kind of an epiphany?"

Alberg sat back. He took a bite of his omelette but found that despite its mouthwatering fragrance he wasn't at all hungry. There was no room in him for hunger. He was too filled up with tidings, and the need to spread them.

"This reporter came to see me," he began. . . .

When he finished, Cassandra was motionless, her fork in her hand: she hadn't taken a bite for at least ten minutes.

Alberg's omelette had congealed on his plate. "Huh," he said in surprise, gazing at it.

"So what you're saying," said Cassandra finally, picking through the words at her disposal as if through a patch of poison ivy, "—let me get this right, now—you want to quit the Force and become a private investigator. In Vancouver."

"Well, I don't think there'd be enough work to keep both me and the detachment busy over here, Cassandra," he said dryly.

Alberg had initiated the conversation with trepidation. Now there was no hesitation in him at all. He felt enormously optimistic: strong, healthy, and confident that good things lay ahead for both of them. He reached across the table for Cassandra's hand. She withdrew it, though—politely, but deliberately. Her mouth, he noticed, had lost its plump, kissable curve and set itself into a straight line. "Let me try to explain," he said. She began to shake her head. "No," he said sharply. "You've got to listen, Cassandra."

She lifted her eyes to his face. "Okay," she said. "Go ahead."

Alberg sat back in his chair. "When I was talking to this reporter, this young woman—I've given a hundred interviews, for Christ's sake—do you think I was expecting anything like this? So listen. It was like—it was like I was painting a picture for her. Sitting there with a canvas on an easel and paint in one of those things artists hold in their hands—what the hell are they called?"

"Palettes," said Cassandra.

"Right. A palette. And I was painting what I saw, dabbing paint on the canvas, feeling very cheerful about it: that's the way I felt, talking to the reporter.

"But I talked on and on," he said, sounding astonished. "And the more I talked, the more—lightheaded—I got. I went through my whole bloody career, Cassandra. Well, not everything. But most things. I sure as hell hit all the highlights. I talked, and talked, and talked. And when I'd finished . . .

"I stood up and showed her out of the office, shut the door, and then I stood there alone in the middle of the room and I felt like—I don't know, Cassandra—like a teenager. Happy. And I couldn't figure out why. Didn't figure out why until later."

He looked at her in wonder, his eyes so bright that Cassandra thought for one utterly confusing moment that he might be going to weep.

Instead, he laughed. "Later, I realized what had happened." He leaned toward her. "It was as if by talking to her I'd painted my whole damn career on that imaginary canvas, and put it in a big box, Cassandra, and then, still talking, I'd picked the box up in my two hands," he said, miming this, "and just—just put it to one side. And suddenly—there was this huge gorgeously empty horizon. Where there didn't used to be one." He sat back again, apparently finished, and watched her intently.

"But—" Cassandra pushed her plate away and crossed her legs. "It's too—abrupt for me, Karl," she said.

Alberg nodded.

"It's happened too suddenly."

Alberg nodded again. "I understand that."

The mushrooms on her plate, limp and cold by now, looked like large dead insects. Moths, she thought. She moved her chair farther away from the table. "So. What now?"

Alberg shrugged. "I don't know."

"You don't know, but you've already been to see your friend the PI."

"Yeah."

Cassandra rubbed her palms together. "I have to tell you, Karl, I feel extremely resentful. I mean, we're married, for god's sake. And you go off and have your damn epiphany, and then you slink away and visit your damn PI friend—"

"I didn't slink, Cassandra," he protested.

"—without a damn word to me, and now you—you

make love to me, and ply me with omelettes and tulips, and present me with a damn fait accompli."

"It isn't a fait accompli," said Alberg. "I'm discussing it with you, aren't I? We'll decide what to do together, like we always do."

"Bullshit," she blurted.

They stared at each other.

"The epiphany," she said. "That's the fait accompli."

Mrs. O'Hara watched staff members arrive at the school, and then the students. She squirmed from time to time, sitting in the van, because the upholstery on the driver's seat had a rent in it, and the fabric along the edges of the tear tended to curl up and poke her in the behind.

She had drunk all the tea in her thermos.

It wasn't a large school. Bernie Peters, who was indeed an observant woman, had been able to provide a thumbnail sketch of every member of the staff. Mrs. O'Hara figured she knew which of them was Ivan Dyakowski's whore. But she had to make sure.

It was fitting, she thought, to conclude her ten-year project the way it had begun, with an unfaithful spouse. There were—god knew—all sorts of sins; all kinds of worthy transgressors. But there would be a pleasing symmetry in ending the thing the way it had begun.

Mrs. O'Hara stirred behind the wheel, shifting position, seeking strength, seeking vitality: these weren't immediately present.

All the children were inside, now, and the schoolyard was empty.

Suddenly, a blue car hurtled into the parking lot. Two people emerged and hurried toward the school. A loud buzzer sounded inside the building and they broke into a run: one of them was Ivan Dyakowski; the other, a dark-haired, athletic-looking woman who matched the description Bernie Peters had given her of a teacher named Susan Atkinson. Mrs. O'Hara watched them go inside.

She put down the mug and lowered her head, pressing first one temple and then the other against the steering wheel, holding on to the wheel tightly with both hands. A chicken in a pot, she thought. That's all he was. Only one more chicken in a pot.

Mrs. O'Hara lifted her head, started the van, and drove slowly down the hill and along the main street. She had to be at her first house by ten. She wasn't looking forward to working today.

She didn't want to admit it, but she was afraid that she might not be strong enough this time. Ivan would be rattled and wary, because of what Denise had tried to do to him. Mrs. O'Hara didn't know whether she had the strength to physically overpower him.

She thumbed through her memories and recalled Sinner Number Five, a woman she had met soon after moving to the Sunshine Coast, a woman Mrs. O'Hara had thought, cautiously, might even become a friend. But childbirth had transformed her into a maniac.

Mrs. O'Hara had been present when the woman shrieked at her infant son, threw him into his crib so hard that he bounced, and rushed out of the house in a frenzy, leaving the child behind her in hysterics: Mrs. O'Hara had picked him up and tried to soothe him, with little success. The father, fortunately, had soon arrived. He was alarmed by his wife's continuing inability to adjust to motherhood, but clearly was not prepared to do anything about it. But Mrs. O'Hara was.

One day when she knew the woman's husband would be in Vancouver, she took a seafood casserole to her house. When the woman died of food poisoning, the authorities assumed she had been the cause of her own demise.

The husband was remarried within months, to a young woman much better equipped for bringing up children.

Mrs. O'Hara propelled the van through town, past the hospital and down the hill to Trail Bay, where she pulled off the road, facing the sea. Yes. Poison would indeed be so much simpler. . . .

Rebecca Granger had been a strong girl, but so completely self-absorbed that distracting her had been easy. The woman who had aborted her child was a slightly built thing and not a problem. And of course neither of them had had the slightest inkling that Mrs. O'Hara the cleaning lady was a source of danger. The waitress, too: unprepared; entirely unprepared. The astonishment on their faces . . . astonishment . . . and then a fear so gigantic that even to witness it had, the first time, caused Mrs. O'Hara's bowels to move. . . .

She hadn't seen the fear of the others. Those who had died—she hadn't seen their faces as they died. And Tom, and the hardware store man, she hadn't been present when they had realized what had happened to them, what she had done to them.

A terrible thought crept into Mrs. O'Hara's head—although it felt as if it had entered her body through her heart. She thought of the orange and white snake in her dream. Perhaps it hadn't been tender and compassionate after all, for this ghastly thought eased its way through her with the suppleness and the cunning of a serpent. And the thought was this: what if she had changed her modus operandi because she had wanted to see their faces as they died?

What if this had been the reason?

Out on the water, a tugboat traversed the bay, and Mrs. O'Hara for the first time after all these years wanted to be gone from this place, wanted to see the village of Sechelt receding forever behind her.

• • •

She found him sitting on the steps in front of the detachment, hands resting on his knees, wearing sunglasses. "Staff?" she said uncertainly.

"What is it, Sergeant?" he responded, without turning to look at her.

"I think we're going to have to go back to the clearing again. Dig it up again."

She was standing with her feet slightly apart and her hands behind her, holding on to her notebook. The silence lengthened and Eddie waited, counseling herself to be patient. But as it continued to lengthen she felt an unexpected rush of mirth. She looked away from him, across the street into the woods, because she thought it was the sight of Alberg in street clothes, looking not only like a civilian but like a tourist, in those sunglasses, that was making her want to laugh. That and nervousness.

Alberg took off the sunglasses and swiveled his head around to look at her. Her heart sank—his eyes were so cold and unreadable. "Sit down, Sergeant."

Eddie sat next to him.

"Well?"

"The waitress's name was, or is, Rochelle Williamson. And it looks as if she disappeared, all right."

"Go on."

"She'd rented a room—a bachelor suite—in an apartment building behind the hospital. Nobody even noticed that she wasn't living there until she was two months behind in her rent."

"Did she leave any personal belongings behind?"

Eddie nodded, referring to her notes. "Yeah. The guy let me take a look at them. Clothes, a few books, some—mementos, I guess you'd call them—in an empty chocolate box."

Alberg stretched his legs out in front of him. "What kind of mementos?"

"Some family photographs—snapshots. A couple of Christmas cards."

"Wallet? Money? Identification?"

"No. But if she was abducted, she would have had that with her, right?"

"Abducted. Huh," he said contemptuously.

Eddie gritted her teeth and kept her mouth shut.

"When was the last time anybody saw her?"

"Earl and Naomi, when they closed the café on Friday night," said Eddie. "That was September 15th. She had the weekend off, but she didn't show up on Monday morning."

It had turned into a very warm day, Eddie realized. She was becoming uncomfortable, sitting in the sun in her uniform.

"They must have called her, didn't they?" said Alberg irritably. "To find out where the hell she was?" He was scratching on the concrete step with a rock he'd picked up from the lawn next to them.

"She hadn't gotten around to arranging for a phone yet," said Eddie. "But they knew where she lived, of course. Naomi went over there sometime during the day, and again after work, and banged on the door. But nobody answered. And she did this for a couple more days. Then they decided she'd just skipped out."

"Didn't it occur to them to ask questions in the apartment building?" Alberg's voice was full of frustration.

"Yeah, Naomi did that, Staff. But Rochelle had only been there a few days. Nobody knew anything about her. And two months later, when she hadn't paid the rent—the building manager didn't know where she'd been working, and he had no idea where she might have come from. So he just packed up her stuff in case she came back for it someday."

"And it didn't occur to any of these people to report her missing," said Alberg flatly.

Eddie didn't reply.

"Did any mail come for her?"

"Yeah. A couple of letters from a nursing home in Surrey. So I called them. Her father lives there."

"Has he heard from her?"

"He's got Alzheimer's. But the director of the place says Rochelle hasn't been in touch with him, and she hasn't replied to their letters."

She waited, glad she'd worn a cotton vest under her shirt, imagining it blotting up all the sweat her body was enthusiastically producing.

"Aren't you jumping to conclusions," he asked finally, "wanting to go digging in the goddamn clearing again?"

"Yeah. Maybe."

"I mean—Jesus." Alberg threw the stone. It bounced in the middle of the road and skittered off into the ditch on the other side. "How could we have missed another body, for Christ's sake?"

"Well, see, she disappeared between the other two, Staff. Rebecca's body was there for six months—it was a lot more carefully buried than Janet's. So I figure maybe this poor broad got a deeper grave than Janet. Maybe each one of them got buried a little less deeply than the one before."

Alberg looked at her disapprovingly. "You've got a hell of an imagination, Sergeant." He started pulling grass up by the roots, brooding. "Okay. Go do it. But for Christ's sake be discreet. And I want to know immediately, when you either find a goddamn body, or you know for sure that there isn't one."

Eddie was already on her feet, brushing at her pants. She grinned at him, and he responded with a baleful stare before clapping the sunglasses back onto his face.

•   •   •   •

"We could go somewhere, Mom, if you like."

"I don't really feel like going anywhere, Cassandra."

Helen was wearing white slacks with narrow legs and a long pink blouse that fell to her thighs. Her hair was completely white now, and she had recently had it cut short and permed. Cassandra thought she looked like an elderly angel.

"In a little while they'll be serving tea in the dining room," said Helen. "Can you stay?"

"Yes, of course."

They were sitting on a weathered bench in one of the gardens that surrounded Shady Acres, a bench situated almost directly beneath a flowering cherry tree. A dark-haired, middle-aged man in overalls was digging fertilizer into the ground under some nearby rosebushes, whistling as he toiled.

"That should have been done a month ago," said Helen Mitchell, indicating the gardener disapprovingly. "Still, now's better than not at all." She folded her hands in her lap. "And how's Karl?" she asked politely.

"It's Karl I want to talk to you about." Cassandra stood up suddenly, then just as suddenly sat down again. She felt possessed. A quick, ruthless energy rippled through her, blanking out her day's agenda, generating both bewilderment and euphoria. She bent close to her mother. "He wants to quit."

"Wants to quit what?"

"The Force. He wants to take early retirement."

Helen Mitchell considered this for a moment. "I can' say I'm surprised, really."

"I am," said Cassandra vehemently. "I'm surprised Definitely."

"Have you bought the bookstore yet?"

"No. I decided against it."

"What about that filthy café?"

"No, Mother. I decided against Earl's, too."

"Well, then."

Cassandra looked at her in exasperation. "And what does that mean, Mother? Well, what?"

"I'm sure he's got something in mind," said Helen. "I can't imagine Karl giving up his job without having something to take its place." She looked quizzically at Cassandra from behind her spectacles, which Cassandra noticed were new: they had large round lenses and tortoiseshell frames.

"He wants to be a private investigator," she said, almost too quietly to be heard. She had looked around furtively before making this announcement. Even though she'd thought of this for Karl herself on more than one occasion, now that it was apparently going to happen she couldn't dismiss the fact that most people thought of the private investigation business as more than a little sleazy.

Helen was laughing out loud.

"Yeah, fine," said Cassandra, flushing with embarrassment. "It's fine for you to laugh."

He had said, though, that his friend's offices were in a fashionable high-rise near the courthouse. With trees, and a fountain. And marble floors.

"I think it's exciting," said Helen dreamily, looking up at the blossoms of the cherry tree. "A whole new life . . ."

"Yes, Mother. That's all well and good. For him. I hate to put it this way, but—what about me?" she asked, embarrassed by the plaintiveness in her voice.

"That's why I asked if you'd bought a business yet," said her mother. "And you haven't. So you're as free as the wind, Cassandra."

Cassandra mouthed the words: free as the wind. A small breeze touched her lips, and brought to her nostrils the fragrance of the cherry blossoms.

"You'd already decided to go into business for yourself," said Helen. "Which means you'd already decided to leave the library."

Leave the library. Her chest ached whenever she thought about it. But, "Yes," she said. "I guess I have."

"So you're both beginning new lives. I think that's wonderful."

Helen took Cassandra's hand and stroked it, holding it between hers, and Cassandra felt her hand tremble, as if it were a small creature with a tiny beating heart.

"And since you haven't decided yet what business to buy," said her mother, "may I suggest that you consider investing in your husband's?"

Denise had decided that if Ivan were going to report her to the police, to charge her with assault or attempted murder or something, he would already have done it. And he wouldn't have bothered to send her a note telling her he wanted a divorce. And so she was for the moment grateful not only to whatever gods there were, for causing Ivan to survive his ordeal, but to Ivan himself.

She had called the bank that morning and told them she'd be at work tomorrow.

Perhaps she would save her money and go back to school. The world was full of possibilities, thought Denise tossing Ivan's socks and underwear into a cardboard carton standing on a stool to check the contents of half-forgotten cupboards—determined to eliminate all traces of Ivan from the house as soon as possible. This was not done with anger in her heart. She simply had an enormous need to turn her back on her marriage and get on with whatever was to constitute the rest of her life.

It hadn't occurred to her yet to announce her new status to family and friends. She had to regain some equilibrium first. She wanted to come to terms with her new, soon-to-be-unmarried self before introducing it to anybody else.

When she had finished packing up Ivan's things, she sa

down at the desk in the bedroom to reply to his note. This proved to be much more difficult than she would have anticipated. She tried first to apologize, but couldn't find the words: how on earth do you tell somebody that you're sorry you almost killed him? Perhaps it was something that ought not to be put in writing anyway, she finally decided.

Next she launched into an analysis of their marriage, a summation of memorable events, an affectionate acknowledgment of shared love. . . . But this she found to be equally inappropriate. The wastebasket was by now full of crumpled paper. Her right hand was threatening to cramp. The sun was low in the sky and Denise was hungry for dinner.

"Dear Ivan," she wrote. "Of course you may have a divorce."

Then she dithered a while about whether to write "affectionately," before her signature, or "best wishes." In the end, she just signed it.

She looked at this brief note gloomily. Surely there was more to say. But it seemed not. She folded it and put it into an envelope, and wrote Ivan's name on the outside. She would deliver it to the school tomorrow.

She had propped the envelope up against her purse, which sat on the kitchen counter, when she heard someone knocking at the door.

"I don't want to come in," said Mrs. O'Hara, "but I need to speak to you. I find that I want to tell you what's going on, although this is something I have never done before."

She saw Denise's bewilderment; felt it, as an ache in her chest. She tried to picture winged fate turning away from her and embracing Denise Dyakowski in its dark folds. But the image refused to acquire substance.

Mrs. O'Hara raised her arm, heavily, and rested her

hand on the doorjamb. "I don't quite know how to go about this."

"Are you sure you won't come in?" asked Denise.

"I'm sure," said Mrs. O'Hara.

She thought there must be lots of people who could carry on in her name. That Naomi person in the café, for example, the one whose drug-dealing husband was in jail: Mrs. O'Hara had recently heard that Naomi had had a hand in putting him there, which, if true, made her a kindred spirit.

But Denise, standing here before her, Denise, brushing uneasily at her short, curly hair with ineffectual fingers, Denise had for all intents and purposes done in her first sinner already, all on her own.

"If he had died," said Mrs. O'Hara, "you would not have done wrong."

She imagined many successors, who might form a society and visit her regularly, in the short time she had left. They would sit around her stove on cool evenings, or outside among the sunflowers in the daytime; they would relate their experiences to her, and to one another, and they would seek her advice. . . .

"You realize that, don't you?" she said intently to Denise.

"Oh no, Mrs. O'Hara," said Denise quickly. "I think it would have been wrong, oh yes."

One didn't choose this avocation, of course, Mrs. O'Hara acknowledged, reluctantly. One was, in fact, chosen by it, or for it. And to make this designation wasn't within her power.

"Well. Anyway," said Mrs. O'Hara. "I have just one left, so I've had to choose between the two of them. And I've chosen him. Your husband."

Denise, frowning, shook her head in bewilderment. "Chosen him for what?"

"Her name is Susan, by the way." Mrs. O'Hara glanced at her van, parked on the street. "I haven't decided how I'm going to do it. Or when. But it will be soon." She looked into Denise's face, searching, although she knew she would find no comprehension there. "It's the last one. And I want to have some time to myself. So I have to do it soon." She turned, and headed slowly across the muddy yard.

Denise called after her. "Mrs. O'Hara? Mrs. O'Hara!"

Mrs. O'Hara turned around and waved. "Don't worry. It'll all be over soon."

Denise felt the chimera again, massive and unpredictable, hovering above her head.

TWENTY-TWO

Friday, April 5

———

Alberg got to work very early, full of energy and optimism. He had awakened suddenly, at dawn, absolutely certain that a break in the homicide investigation was imminent. He knew it would happen. He just knew it. He had that feeling—a prickling sensation; almost an itch—that happened when things were about to come together.

He had forgone breakfast, having decided to reward himself, when the intimidating pile of paperwork in his office had been vanquished, with bacon and eggs at Earl's. Of course it was true that he'd had an omelette just yesterday. That was a fair number of eggs in one week. But he'd eaten practically none of the damn omelette—what a fiasco *that* breakfast had turned out to be.

He thought about Cassandra, then, imagining her sitting in her windowless office, bathed in the soft gray glow from the skylight, her chin in her hand. In his imagination her face was blank, expressionless: he couldn't tell what was in her mind. But he knew that she was thinking, furiously, because the more still she became, the harder her mind was working; and she was very still. Alberg felt a bit sick. He wished she'd have an epiphany of her own. He wished he could give her one.

He shook himself free of his musings, and concentrated on his IN basket.

An hour or so later he draped his jacket over his arm and took a stack of completed paperwork out to Isabella. "Do not provide me with any more of this crap," he said to her. "Not today."

Isabella scrunched up her forehead in protest.

"Not until after lunch, anyway," said Alberg irritably, shrugging into his jacket. "I'll be at Earl's."

Outside, he ran into Eddie Henderson, who was just arriving.

"Morning, Staff," she said.

Alberg glanced at her casually, then more sharply. "Is something wrong, Sergeant?"

She stopped and looked at him, and for a moment he thought she was going to blurt out whatever was bothering her. He was immediately dismayed, and wished he'd kept his mouth shut.

"No, nothing," she said slowly. "Why, Staff?"

His new sergeant lacked serenity today, that's what it was. Odd, to find serenity in a police officer. But she had it, all right. Usually.

"You just look—I don't know," said Alberg, uncomfortable now. "A little worried."

"I'm okay. But thanks for asking." She hesitated. "I'm glad we didn't find her there. The waitress. In the clearing."

Alberg nodded. "So am I."

"But I still think something's happened to her."

"I hope very much that you're wrong," said Alberg: "But I'm afraid you're not." He wanted to talk more about this, and was about to suggest that Eddie join him at Earl's, when an aged Toyota pulled up at the curb and a woman climbed out, hurriedly, and rushed up to them.

"You probably don't remember me," she said to Alberg. "I was at your wedding. With my husband. I do hope you have a few minutes free." She glanced at Eddie and lowered her voice. "I really do have to talk to you."

"And you are—?" Alberg inquired courteously.

"My name is Denise. Denise Dyakowski."

"And what do you want to talk to me about?" said Alberg.

"About my cleaning woman," said Denise. "About Mrs. O'Hara."

Mrs. O'Hara, driving home, thought that maybe, when this last one was done, she would be able to stop looking for evidence of man's weakness and transgression everywhere: maybe her last few months could be tranquil ones.

But just because she wouldn't be looking for it, maybe wouldn't even see it, this didn't mean that it wouldn't be there, she told herself, driving rapidly, propelling the van around the turns in the road with uncharacteristic recklessness.

She slowed and turned off the highway, close to home now.

Mrs. O'Hara realized that her life on the Sunshine Coast had been a lonely one. Perhaps that was why she had remained for so long largely untouched by the profundities of what she had done. She had developed a peculiar habit: she would lift her hands into the light and study them, short nails, rough skin, no blood on them, no blood at all. . . . She accepted responsibility, oh yes, but had remained untouched and undisturbed by the deeds she had executed.

Until Number Six.

One of Mrs. O'Hara's early clients was a harassed middle-aged woman who worked in a realtor's office. She lived in an out-of-the-way cottage with her mother-in-law, an excessively talkative person, small and bent, with rheumy eyes behind thick spectacles and large hands so gnarled and leathery that they looked more like tools than living appendages. The old woman liked to totter around the house in

Mrs. O'Hara's wake, brandishing her cane and telling mystifying tales about her past. When her daughter-in-law came home the old woman would turn on her, berating her for the meals she cooked, the way she did the laundry, the untended garden. Mrs. O'Hara paid these harangues little attention, perhaps because the old woman's voice was frail and quavery. But one day she happened to be looking at her when she had one of her outbursts. Although the old lady often brayed proudly that all of her teeth were her own, she didn't have all of them anymore. And Mrs. O'Hara saw with horror that the unkind words hurtling from her mouth toward her weary daughter-in-law were accompanied by spittle. Mrs. O'Hara looked quickly at the daughter-in-law, who had literally turned the other cheek.

Enough is enough, she thought grimly.

The next time she came to clean she waited until the mother-in-law had lain down for her afternoon nap—curtains drawn, spectacles on her night table, cane resting against the wall, shoes side by side on the mat next to the bed. Mrs. O'Hara hovered outside the door, which was not quite closed, until she heard the old woman begin to snore. Then she went into the room, picked up the second pillow, placed it swiftly, firmly, upon the old woman's face, and pressed.

The woman struggled—she had more strength than Mrs. O'Hara had anticipated. Would she remain resolute? Mrs. O'Hara wondered. Because she realized that this was the first time she had actually been present when depriving a person of life. She pushed on the pillow, reluctant to use too much force for fear of breaking any of the old woman's fragile bones. She heard the alarm clock ticking, oblivious, felt the woman's big hands scrabbling at her arms, and hoped the old lady thought it was her daughter-in-law who was doing this to her.

Finally, finally, she was still.

Eventually, Mrs. O'Hara removed the pillow, and looked curiously down at the dead face. The eyes were open. Mrs. O'Hara closed them, gently, with the edge of her hand. She thought the old woman looked very peaceful. Maybe she had even wanted to die.

Mrs. O'Hara finished cleaning the house, then called her client at work. "I can't waken your mother-in-law from her afternoon nap," she said. "I'm afraid she has passed away."

She waited for the daughter-in-law to arrive, and was a strong, comforting presence while they waited for the ambulance.

Later, though, later, in her cabin, sitting in her rocking chair, thinking about the events of the day, Mrs. O'Hara's teeth suddenly began to clatter, very gently at first, then more urgently, and her hands on the wooden arms of the rocking chair shook, and she felt violently nauseated and had not quite made it to the toilet when she threw up.

Mrs. O'Hara had not actually seen the old lady expire. But almost.

And she did see the poor dog die. Maybe that was what had created in her the need to witness the moment of Rebecca's death, as well. Mrs. O'Hara hadn't expected to have any particular emotional response to the event—just felt it as a need. And then . . .

Mrs. O'Hara pulled off the rough, narrow road and under the shelter. She rubbed at her face, hard, wishing she could rub from her body all pain, all weariness, all despair.

She opened the door, stepped out of the van, and slammed the door closed. And headed, through the rain, up the slope toward the cabin.

•   •   •

"All Denise knows," Alberg said to Eddie, "is that her name is Mrs. O'Hara, and she lives somewhere up around Pender Harbour, and she's a cleaning lady."

"And she's threatened to kill this Denise person's husband? The cleaning lady has?"

"Yeah," said Alberg. "Sit down, for god's sake."

Eddie sat in the black leather chair that always reminded Alberg of Sid Sokolowski. "Why?"

"Denise wasn't very forthcoming about that. Her eyes were skittering all over the ceiling: they reminded me of waterbugs. But what she did say was that she and her husband have separated, and Mrs. O'Hara doesn't approve."

Eddie put her hands on her thighs, elbows out, and squinted across the desk at him. "Come on, Staff."

"Yeah, I know. It's probably nothing. But she's taking it seriously—Denise, I mean."

"Has she told her husband that the cleaning lady's out to get him?"

"I don't think she and her husband are speaking to each other. She thinks he's probably gone to live with his sweetie."

"Maybe Mrs. O'Hara's a hitman," said Eddie, brightening. "Maybe Denise hired her."

"Then why tell *me* about it?" Alberg snapped. He sighed. "Sorry. I seem to have lost my sense of humor." He leaned back in his chair. "I know what you're thinking. And you're right—one of them's crazy, and maybe it's Denise. But I promised I'd go talk to this Mrs. O'Hara." He hesitated. "I know the guy," he said reluctantly. "Denise's husband. They came to our wedding."

"So why not go talk to him, instead of this O'Hara woman?"

"Because I'd feel like a bloody idiot, warning him about his cleaning lady, unless I'd checked her out first." He glanced at Eddie. "I want you to run her down. Find out where she lives. Then come with me when I go talk to her."

Mrs. O'Hara studied the contents of the freezer compartment of her fridge, and was reaching reluctantly for a TV dinner when she heard someone coming up the path from the road.

She closed the freezer and tiptoed to the back door. Heard him making his way through the greenery at the side of the house.

Mrs. O'Hara stood in her living room with her fists on her hips, staring at the door. At the first knock, she swung it open.

"Who are you?" she said to the man standing there. She knew who he was, though. He was a policeman. "And what do you want?" He was tall and broad, somewhat overweight, and a scrim of politeness concealed whatever his intentions were. He had on khaki pants, a white shirt that was open at the throat, and a lightweight jacket.

Then a woman stepped around the corner of the house to stand beside him. She was also tall, and wore a police uniform. She had a strong, solid-looking body and an open, amicable face that Mrs. O'Hara decided was a lie—it was the clear blue eyes, the wide mouth and the firm chin that created the suggestion of congeniality. But Mrs. O'Hara knew from her stance, from the way she held her head, from the disturbing directness of her gaze, that it was an illusion.

Eddie thought Mrs. O'Hara looked like a lumberjack. She wore a red and white plaid shirt under bibbed overalls, and hiking boots, and although her face was deeply lined her body was still thick and powerful. She wore her mostly gray hair pinned upon her head in a bun. Wisps had come loose, though, and she occasionally swiped at them, as if they were flies buzzing around her face.

"I'm Staff Sergeant Alberg, Ma'am, with the RCMP in Sechelt. This is Sergeant Henderson. I wonder if we could have a word with you, please."

"What kind of a word?" Mrs. O'Hara had clasped the edge of the door and appeared to be leaning heavily against it.

"It's a routine inquiry, Ma'am. May we come in for a moment?" Alberg's voice was smooth and mellow and held an implication of compassion.

"I was just about to eat," said Mrs. O'Hara.

"I'm sorry to bother you," said Alberg, "but we'll just take a moment of your time." He smiled at her, burying his hands in his pockets. "Really we will."

Reluctantly, she stepped back and pulled the door open, and Eddie followed Alberg inside.

Mrs. O'Hara crossed the room to a large leather recliner and lowered herself into it. With her feet flat on the floor, she spread her hands on her thighs. She looked from one of them to the other. "You might as well sit down."

Alberg sat on a small sofa angled next to the Franklin stove. Eddie spotted a wooden chair in the kitchen area. "May I?" she asked Mrs. O'Hara, who shrugged. So Eddie picked it up, moved it closer to the stove, and sat down.

"What do you want?" said Mrs. O'Hara to Alberg, with a glance at a large round watch she wore on her left wrist. "What do the police want with an old woman like me?"

"We're here at the request of Denise Dyakowski," said Alberg. "She's expressed concern about you."

Eddie watched Mrs. O'Hara with interest so intense that it felt positively prurient. The creases in the woman's forehead deepened: she started to speak, then thought better of it, and snapped her mouth closed. A frown gathered on her face—Eddie could almost hear it rumbling beneath her skin, like thunder. Her eyes became smaller, withdrawing into protective pouches of flesh.

Finally, "It is I," she said, coldly, "who have expressed concern about Mrs. Dyakowski. Whose husband recently left her." She made an obvious attempt to relax, draping loose hands over the arms of her chair and crossing her legs.

"She says you threatened her husband," said Alberg.

"With what?" Mrs. O'Hara smiled and lifted her shoulders, almost apologetically.

"I'm not sure," said Alberg easily. He grinned. "She was a little vague."

Mrs. O'Hara shook her head as if in sympathy. She began to speak again; but changed her mind.

Alberg waited, smiling.

"Well," said Mrs. O'Hara after a minute, "if that's all?"

Alberg looked over at Eddie. "Is that all, Sergeant?"

Eddie felt like a stagehand, suddenly pushed out into the lights without benefit of script or makeup. She blinked furiously. "What do you think of Mr. Dyakowski?" she blurted.

Mrs. O'Hara gave her a swift, harsh look and Eddie almost flinched—she had *felt* that look: the woman might as well have slapped her face.

"I'm afraid," said Mrs. O'Hara, slowly, with infinite regret, "that that man may not suffer the fate that he deserves."

They were plunged into silence. Nobody moved. Eddie didn't dare even turn her head to look at Alberg. Her gaze remained fixed on Mrs. O'Hara, who was squinting intently into the distance in search of Ivan Dyakowski's destiny.

TWENTY-THREE

Denise arrived at the school just before the last bell was to ring, and smiled hello at the receptionist in the office, whom she knew slightly—a young woman named Beth who, because of her red hair, green eyes, and freckles, had always reminded Denise of Anne of Green Gables.

Beth looked at Denise with eyes larger than usual, and a face that was positively white. Oh god, Denise thought suddenly, and her chest emptied and became an echoey cavern. The whole school knows, she realized.

But knows what? she asked herself frantically, as she approached the counter—because what else could she do, turn and run? She certainly wasn't going to turn and run.

"I've got something for Ivan," she said to Beth. She glanced behind her. "I'll wait here," she said, smiling, hoping to project an aura of confidence and composure.

Beth didn't even try to speak. She gave Denise a tremulous smile, ducked her head, and aimed her full and complete concentration at the computer screen in front of her.

They couldn't know about her hitting Ivan on the head and—and—and about everything that then transpired, Denise told herself. Ivan wouldn't humiliate himself by letting that story get around. So what they knew, what Beth must know, what caused her to get all pale and flustered, is that he was having an affair.

Denise suddenly felt as if she weighed five hundred pounds. She seriously wondered if it was possible to lift herself from this bench, and move away from the office, down the hall, out of the building and into her car: she didn't know if she had the strength to do this.

She sat there with her purse in her lap, the note to Ivan inside the purse, her face burning. Of course it would be somebody he taught with—this was not a surprise, not really, she scolded herself. She just hadn't thought about it when she decided to come here. She just hadn't considered all the ramifications of showing up in person, to warn him about Mrs. O'Hara. It had been her original intention, after all, to deliver the note while school was in session. She knew this would have been the civilized way to proceed. But Mrs. O'Hara's pronouncement had changed everything.

But *why* hadn't she acknowledged the presence in the school of his lover? Why hadn't she considered the possibility of running into her?

Probably because if she had, she wouldn't have come.

Denise rearranged herself on the bench, waiting. And then the bell rang to signal the end of classes.

She was a wreck, sitting there, sweaty and jumpy; at risk of bursting into tears at any second. She changed her mind several times, then changed it back, and she was wallowing in one of these troughs of indecision when Ivan strode into the office, mercifully alone.

Denise immediately stood up. Ivan saw her and stopped dead, causing a child to run into him from behind.

"Ivan," said Denise, faintly. "Let's go outside." She brushed past him. He didn't move to follow. *"Please,* Ivan— don't embarrass me. Believe me, this is nothing for you to feel reluctant about. Just for Christ's sake come *outside* with me." Her face must be bright red, she thought: she could feel the blood beating there. Her voice was shaking, with humiliation, maybe, or frustration. "Come on, come *on,"* she urged, and moved quickly through the doorway. If he came, fine. If he didn't—screw him, she thought, furious.

Outside, she stood in the middle of the lawn, waiting, looking up at the gray sky, grateful that the rain had stopped. At last, Ivan emerged slowly from the school, his hands in his pants pockets. Denise experienced a slight shock, looking at him: he had changed, somehow. Or she had. He approached her, but stopped when he was still several feet away. Denise opened her bag. Ivan took a step backward.

"Oh for heaven's sake," said Denise impatiently. She thrust the envelope toward him. "Here. Take it." She flapped it in the air. "Take the damn thing." He took it from her. Denise watched as he opened it and read the brief note inside. He nodded.

Denise regarded him with an interest that was almost theoretical. Maybe the son of a bitch *does* deserve to die, she thought. Maybe she shouldn't have gone to the cops. Maybe she should let Ivan take his chances with Mrs. O'Hara. Yes. After all, she had confided in Mr. Alberg. If Mrs. O'Hara really was a threat, the police would surely take care of it.

They regarded one another warily, she and Ivan, until finally Denise said, "We have things to work out. The house. The furniture."

"I'll call you," said Ivan. "Or my lawyer will."

It seemed a long time since she had last heard his voice. She couldn't remember if he'd cried out when she had hit him; she didn't think so: she thought he'd toppled to the floor in utter silence.

She would have to get a lawyer, too, Denise realized.

She laughed and turned away, heading for her car. Lawyers. Divorce. Who'd have thought it?

"I remembered something in there, Staff," said Eddie, on the way back to Sechelt, "that made my skin prickle."

"Oh yeah?" Alberg's skin had been prickling the whole time they were there. He had felt suffocated by the tiny, opaque windows, the low ceiling, and the massive presence of the potbellied stove.

"It's probably just some kind of fluke," said Eddie.

"Probably," said Alberg. He thought the sky was becoming brighter. If this continued, and the evening were even partly clear, he wanted to do something romantic and—and auspicious—with Cassandra. Somehow he had to make clear to her the power of his dream, and then persuade her to share it. "Tell me anyway," he said.

Eddie turned in the passenger seat and addressed his profile. "I remember Andrew Maine telling me that he'd tried to talk to people about his wife's abortion."

"Uh huh."

"His manager at work. Some friend on the bowling team." She faced front again for a minute. "He was looking for somebody who'd help him accept it. Christ. The poor clod."

"Uh huh. But he didn't really want to accept it, did he?"

"Yeah, I think he did, Staff. Anyway." She turned back to him. "I'm sure he mentioned trying to talk to someone about it while there was a vacuum cleaner going. And I was wondering, who cleans the menswear store?"

"Could have been his Mom," said Alberg, "cleaning her house." But he knew it hadn't been.

"Yeah," said Eddie, watching him.

He lived for these moments, Alberg realized. For the instant in which things toppled willy-nilly into place. The moment when a jumble of meaningless bits and pieces hurled themselves into the air, then with exquisite grace assembled themselves in front of him—not as a complete, intact whole, but as a skeleton, a neat, defining framework within which only one answer could be possible.

He pulled the Oldsmobile to the side of the road. These moments could be equally satisfying when effected by someone other than himself; he knew this. He just hadn't known that his new sergeant could do it.

"I'll be damned," he said to Eddie.

She hardly dared to breathe. Her hands clutched each other in her lap. She wanted to laugh out loud, Alberg could see it in her face. But she just stared at him, intently, waiting.

"It could be that Mrs. O'Hara has a pretty interesting client list."

"But, Staff—if we're right—why?"

Alberg checked the rearview mirror, the side mirror, and pulled out onto the highway. "Let's ask Ivan Dyakowski why. He's a teacher, right? What time is it—is school out yet?"

"Yeah, it is."

"Okay. Let's go talk to him."

Mrs. O'Hara remained calm after the police left, even though she knew that a life-changing event had occurred: she felt the weight of it in her body. It was like when she had realized for the first time that she would die at sixty-five.

The police officers hadn't said anything remotely threatening, of course. But for Mrs. O'Hara, simply their arrival at her door had been enough. She knew that their curiosity wouldn't dissipate. She had always known that if ever they looked at her, and wondered, they would quickly find the connections. She had never seriously worried about this, because she had been confident that no actual evidence of what she had done existed. But this had been true only of the first ones, which had been meticulously and intelligently planned.

What had she been thinking of, forsaking prudence as

she had, with the last three? Perhaps she been more weary than she knew, for longer than she knew.

As she sat in her big chair, looking at her big strong hands sprawled on her thighs, Mrs. O'Hara felt a loneliness that made her dizzy. She had counted on retirement to put an end to her loneliness but now realized that retired or not, she would never escape the judgmental, condemnatory aspects of her own nature: the better she got to know someone—anyone—the more of his or her corruption Mrs. O'Hara saw. And this was unlikely to change just because she would no longer be in a position to wield punishment.

Mrs. O'Hara sat there for a long time, letting the ramifications of her new situation soak into her bones. After a while she realized that despite the gravity of this situation she was actually calmer, more tranquil, more determined and confident than she had been in a long time.

For the first time, she could act without giving the slightest consideration to detection or her own escape. These things were irrelevant now.

The door was opened by a woman with dark hair: this was all Eddie could determine at first, because the woman opened it only slightly. She might have been a one-eyed woman, for all Eddie knew, and this thought led to speculations about whether Susan Atkinson might have been born with only one eye, or had lost one to illness or an accident, and about how she explained her one-eyedness to her students, who were young enough to be terrified by the mildest of abnormalities. Eddie didn't know why her mind flew off on tangents like this but she had learned to accept them, hoping only to keep under control the unseemly hilarity they sometimes wanted to produce.

"Miss Atkinson?" said Alberg, holding up his badge.

Eddie, wearing the uniform, decided that a display of her badge would be redundant.

"Yes? What do you want?"

"I understand that we can find Ivan Dyakowski here. We need to talk to him."

Susan Atkinson peered through the crack at them, apparently considering this. "Who told you he might be here?"

"The school principal," said Alberg patiently.

A murmur was heard from within the apartment. Susan Atkinson stepped back and the door was pulled all the way open.

"Hi, Ivan," said Alberg genially.

"Why do you want to talk to me, Karl?" Ivan Dyakowski looked at them grimly, holding on to the door handle, barring entrance to the apartment. "Does this have something to do with Denise?"

"In a manner of speaking," said Alberg. He lowered his voice. "I really think you ought to let us in."

Ivan hesitated, then stepped back, and they entered Susan Atkinson's apartment.

Which Eddie scrutinized enviously. It was tidy, but not oppressively so. Things matched—the sofa and chair in the living room, for example—or else they definitely didn't: the dining room table and chairs were painted in bright colors, harmoniously jumbled—the blue chair had a bright red seat, the yellow one had purple rungs. Beneath them all lay a straw mat, and framed posters of art shows hung on the walls.

"You might as well sit down," said Ivan, as Susan hovered near the entrance to the kitchen. Eddie figured she was probably trying to decide whether she ought to offer them coffee. Ivan glanced at her, probably wondering the same thing. "Oh—sorry. This is my friend, Susan

Atkinson." He moved closer to her. "I'm staying with her for the moment. I—I've left Denise. We've split up."

"I'm sorry to hear that," said Alberg cheerfully, sitting on the sofa.

Eddie took the matching chair.

"So, uh—what brings you here?" asked Ivan cautiously.

"Your wife's worried about you," said Alberg. He sat back and rested his arm along the back of the sofa. "She thinks you might be in danger."

Ivan gave an explosive snort of laughter and put his arm around Susan. "Yeah, well, she ought to know."

Alberg gave him a smile. "How do you mean?"

"Never mind." Ivan let go of Susan and stepped toward Alberg. "I've got no intention of getting into the sordid details of my marriage with you, Karl." He hesitated, then made a halfhearted gesture. "I'm sure you understand." He sat on an ottoman. Susan was standing behind it, glancing from time to time into the kitchen.

Alberg looked over at Eddie, who said, "Do you know a woman named O'Hara, Mr. Dyakowski?"

Ivan looked at her blankly. "O'Hara? No. I don't think so."

"She's your cleaning woman. Well—your wife's, now, I guess."

Ivan shook his head. "I know we had one. I might have encountered her once or twice, I guess. Don't remember anything about her. Why?" He turned to Susan. "Could you rub my neck, hon?" She moved closer and placed her hands on his shoulders. Ivan turned to Alberg. "I'm—I've been through a lot, these last few days."

"Yeah, you've had a whack on your head, there, I guess," said Alberg sympathetically. "What happened?"

"Oh, it was—a kind of an accident," said Ivan vaguely, his face coloring. Susan massaged his neck, expressionless. "I'm fine now. Nearly fine."

"Your wife seems to think Mrs. O'Hara has it in for you," said Eddie, referring to her notebook. "Do you have any idea why?"

He gave her a look of utter amazement. "*In* for me? What the hell does that mean?"

"Well, Ivan," said Alberg gravely, "it means that Denise thinks Mrs. O'Hara might want to kill you."

Astonishment was scrawled all over Ivan Dyakowski's face. "The cleaning woman? I don't even know her! I wouldn't know her if I bumped into her on the street!"

Susan stopped her massage and stepped back, clasping her hands in front of her.

Eddie looked uneasily at Alberg, who was studying Ivan as if he were a laboratory animal.

"It's Denise," said Susan Atkinson suddenly. "It's Denise who wants to kill him."

"Don't!" said Ivan. He took a breath. "Don't say another word, Susan."

A quiet moment happened then. Susan stood tall, with her head lifted high. Ivan was bracing himself, on the ottoman, leaning heavily on his hands. Eddie's eyes scurried back and forth between them, as if she were watching a portentous moment in a movie.

Then, "Talk to me, Ivan," said Alberg. His tone was impersonal and detached.

Ivan said miserably, "Oh Christ. It's so fucking humiliating. . . ."

They drove back to the detachment in silence. Eddie was busy trying to imagine the Dyakowski woman thwacking Ivan over the head. With a cast-iron frying pan, no less. What a cliché.

"Do you think Denise just wanted to embarrass him?" she asked Alberg, when he had parked the Oldsmobile but seemed in no hurry to get out. "I mean, do you think she came to you with the story about the cleaning lady so you'd end up talking to Ivan, and he'd have to tell you that she'd almost killed him?" She had a sudden vision of Denise laboriously maneuvering the unconscious body of her husband into the trunk of his car. "Jesus," she said. "I can't believe he doesn't want to lay charges. Are *we* going to charge her? We've got a good selection of felonies. Attempted murder's only the biggest. There's also—"

"I want you to check out who Andrew was trying to talk to that day." Alberg undid his seat belt. "And if it turns out to be Mrs. O'Hara, I want you to proceed as we discussed, look for a connection between her and Rebecca Granger. And the vanished waitress, too."

They got out of the car, and Alberg locked it.

"So you think Mrs. D. really is concerned for him?"

"Maybe it's Mrs. O'Hara she's concerned for," he said, as they walked up the steps to the detachment. "What I do think is that Denise Dyakowski is too smart to draw attention to herself. If she was planning to make another attempt on her husband's life, she sure wouldn't come to the police station first."

"I think I'll go talk to Andrew tonight," said Eddie, following Alberg through the door.

He turned, stopping her in her tracks. "Nothing's going to happen to Ivan Dyakowski tonight; he's safely tucked away in that apartment with his girlfriend. So go home, would you, please? Get some sleep." He started off toward the hall that led to his office, then stopped and turned around again. "What's the matter with you, Sergeant? You do have a home, don't you?"

"Of course I've got a home."

Behind them, phones rang and Alberg heard laughter. He had a sudden image of himself alone in an office somewhere in downtown Vancouver, a lamp pouring an even-edged pool of light onto the desk blotter in front of him. He saw himself lift his head to look into the darkness and the silence of the room. He saw himself smile.

Yet he would miss this place. These people.

He walked back to stand next to Eddie, who had remained near the door. "What is it, Sergeant?" he asked quietly.

She removed her cap and rubbed her forehead. "I've been getting some phone calls."

"What kind of phone calls? Obscene? Threatening?"

She shook her head. "It's nothing, Staff. It's not the job. It's a personal thing."

They were standing close together, speaking in tones that had become almost hushed. Alberg suddenly felt awkward. He nodded at Eddie, who he thought looked grim, but capable. "Okay." He hesitated. "You've got my home number."

"Right."

"So you call me. If you need anything."

"Right. Thank you, Staff."

TWENTY-FOUR

Saturday, April 6

———

Susan eased out of bed, slid her feet into slippers, and took her robe from its hook on the back of the door. She left the bedroom, closing the door quietly behind her so as not to awaken Ivan, and went to the kitchen to make coffee. While it brewed, she stepped out onto the balcony to take a quick look at the morning.

Her bed was far too small for the two of them, even though it was a double. Ivan was a restless sleeper, flinging his limbs recklessly about; Susan was frequently awakened by an arm thudding onto her chest, or a cold foot seeking purchase on her calf. She had thought his fitfulness might be a temporary condition, caused by the recent traumatic events in his life, but he had told her, no, this was the way he always slept. Susan thought something could probably be done to bring tranquillity to his slumber. Exercise, perhaps. A change in his diet. Pills, if absolutely necessary.

It was a soft, tender morning. There was scarcely a breeze, and the sky was the palest of blues, faded and tremulous. Susan could hardly hear the sea. The waves stirred absentmindedly back and forth upon the gravel beach, so lethargically as to create almost no sound at all.

But the sunlight was strong. Its warmth struck her firmly, fell deeply upon her. It felt so good that Susan dragged the ottoman out onto the balcony and fetched a mug of coffee when it was done, then sat down, wrapping her robe tightly around her, and watched the day come alive.

She had plans for this Saturday—shopping, mostly: she and Ivan had pretty well emptied her cupboards since his arrival on Monday. But she also wanted to get Ivan to talk about his plans. Just a little bit. She knew it was far too soon for him to be making important decisions about the future. But did he intend to stay on in Susan's apartment, for instance? Or would he be getting one of his own?

Down on the beach, the white-haired man was once again walking his corpulent, slow-moving dog. Two teenagers on bikes pedaled lazily along the sidewalk. A large, gray-haired woman sat on one of the benches, gazing out at the water.

Of course, he was perfectly welcome to stay as long as he liked. But Susan thought that once this business with Denise and the cleaning woman had been resolved, Ivan might want more room, more privacy, than was available to him in her small apartment.

A young woman wearing shorts and a sweatshirt appeared on the beach, spread a blanket on the gravel, and sat down in the middle of it. She pulled a thermos, a paperback book, a Walkman, and a bottle of what Susan decided was sunscreen from her backpack and took off her sweatshirt, revealing a halter top. It was a warm morning, Susan admitted, but she hadn't thought it warm enough for sunbathing. The young woman hooked herself up to the Walkman, rubbed lotion on her bare legs, arms, and midriff, and sank back on her elbows, offering herself to the sun.

"Hi," said Ivan, placing his hands on Susan's shoulders. "How about some breakfast?"

She loved his eyes, his thin lips, the space between his front teeth.

He leaned down to kiss her cheek, and her neck, and Susan took hold of his hands and moved them under her robe onto her breasts. She tilted her head back and watched his face come nearer and nearer. She could scarcely breathe, but opened her mouth, in invitation. This—the sex—was still so good.

Mrs. O'Hara, sitting on the bench, gazing at the quiet sea and the sky, which was the color of a robin's egg, found herself propelled back to the last springtime she had spent in the Fraser Valley. She recalled it as an endless parade of sun-drenched days with skies that were always blue, seductive breezes, and floral perfumes everywhere—and a full moon every night for weeks. At least, this was how she remembered it, the season of Tom's betrayal.

She poured another cup of tea from her thermos and glanced again at Susan Atkinson's balcony. It was empty now. They had gone inside. They might not leave the apartment at all today, of course. Or one of them might leave, but not the other.

Mrs. O'Hara admitted this possibility, but didn't take it seriously. It was too nice a day to spend indoors.

"I haven't a clue what it means," said Ivan, shoveling corn flakes into his mouth. "Denise didn't say anything about the bloody cleaning woman when she brought me the note," he said, his voice a mumble. "So I'm not taking it seriously."

"But the police, they're taking it seriously," said Susan, sitting opposite him, drinking her third mug of coffee. She never ate breakfast, but made up for this at lunch and dinner.

"Oh, I don't think so, hon," said Ivan, pushing the empty cereal bowl away from him. He put a slice of bread in the toaster. "Karl came to see me out of courtesy. He thought he had to pass on what crazy Denise had to say because we're friends, he and I. Well—acquaintances." He scooped marmalade out of a jar that sat on the table and dropped it onto his plate. "Come on, Susan, really." He laughed. The toast popped up and he grabbed it, slathered it with butter, then marmalade, and took an enormous bite. "A deranged cleaning woman?" Bits of orange peel were lodged between his teeth. He laughed again. "Denise had some kind of damn hallucination, that's all."

"Hurry up, Ivan, will you?" said Susan, with a sharpness that surprised her. She got up from the table, glancing at her watch. "Let's get going. I want to get out of here."

Mrs. O'Hara had been waiting for a long time, stirring frequently upon the hard seat of the bench, when she saw them. They slipped out the apartment door and crossed the grass to the parking lot, moving slowly, casually—undeterred, then, Mrs. O'Hara guessed, by whatever the police officers might have told them.

When she had seen them drive away, Mrs. O'Hara checked the time, then got up from the bench—awkwardly, because her joints had stiffened—and walked several blocks to the small shopping center where she had left the van. She drove it to the apartment building, unloaded her cleaning supplies into two pails, and trudged up to the door, where she buzzed the caretaker.

Crackles emitted from the intercom.

"Joey?" It's Mrs. O'Hara."

"Hiya, Miz O'Hara."

"I got me a new client. Susan Atkinson. Supposed to do her place this morning, but she forgot to get me a key."

More crackling occurred. "Doesn't surprise me a bit," said Joey.

"Can you let me in?" asked Mrs. O'Hara.

. . . .

Eddie found Alberg at Earl's, where he was having lunch: poached eggs on toast with side orders of bacon and whole wheat toast. She thought he looked slightly guilty when she slid into the chair across from him, and decided that he probably wasn't supposed to eat eggs.

"You went to see Andrew last night, didn't you?" Alberg accused, but Eddie figured he just wanted to divert her attention from his plate.

"Yeah, I did," she admitted. "It only took a half hour or so."

"And?"

"Mrs. O'Hara cleans the store." She grinned at him.

"And he told her about his wife's abortion?"

Eddie nodded. "He says she was vacuuming at the time, so he had to shout. Can you imagine?" she said, wincing. "Anyway, he says she just kind of grunted, but then she wanted to know where his wife worked, and where they lived."

"You seem to be making a connection between this woman's abortion and her homicide," said Alberg, pushing his plate aside.

"Am I?" said Eddie. "I don't know. Maybe." He'd only eaten one of the eggs, Eddie noticed, as Earl arrived, carrying a pot of coffee and a cup for Eddie.

"Top you up?" he asked, and then for some reason threw back his head and laughed.

Alberg gave him an irritated glance and didn't bother to answer. Earl swooped down with the pot and filled Alberg's cup so full that the coffee sloshed into the saucer. He laughed again and hurried away.

"What the hell's the matter with him today?" asked Alberg. "He's been giggling into his chin ever since I got here."

"I heard he sold the café," said Eddie.

"Sold it?" said Alberg incredulously. "You mean, he was serious?"

Eddie nodded. "Apparently his sister in Vancouver is pretty sick, and she wants Earl to go there and take care of her."

Alberg was gazing at her, spellbound. "How do you know these things, Sergeant? You've only been here, what, a few days? Although, I admit, it seems like longer."

Eddie frowned at him. "I hang out in the bar, Staff." She opened her notebook and flipped through its pages. "Mrs. O'Hara also cleaned for Rebecca Granger's mother," she said. "And for a while, she used to clean right here. For Earl." She let the notebook rest in her lap.

"And this was during the time that waitress, Rochelle, worked here?"

Eddie nodded. "So. What do we do now?"

Alberg got his wallet from his pocket and dropped a five dollar bill on the table. "You get a warrant," he said. "For Mrs. O'Hara's cabin, and her vehicle. Thanks to her visit to Denise Dyakowski, this shouldn't be a problem."

It was mid-afternoon when Eddie Henderson and two constables arrived on Mrs. O'Hara's doorstep. She must have heard them coming, because she opened the door before Eddie had had a chance to knock.

Mrs. O'Hara barely glanced at the warrant. "You're arresting me, then," she said calmly.

"No, Ma'am," said Eddie. "We've got a warrant to search these premises, and to perform a similar search on your vehicle, that's all."

"Will you take the van away to do this?"

"Yes, Ma'am. I'm afraid we will."

Mrs. O'Hara regarded her curiously. Such a big, strong young woman, the sergeant was. Probably blunt, if not always candid. Probably physically capable—she must have learned some kind of self-defence skills at police school. Karate, maybe? Plus she was armed, of course. What a lot of time and trouble that would save. She was returning Mrs. O'Hara's examination with a steady gaze of her own, standing there easily, her feet slightly apart, her right hand outstretched, offering the warrant, left hand resting lightly on something attached to her belt: handcuffs? a radio? And Mrs. O'Hara found her attention beguiling.

But she shook her head.

"It's all right," she said, "I don't need to see that. Please wait a minute, while I get my jacket. And maybe you'd allow me to take along a thermos of tea?"

"Take it where?" said Eddie, sounding somewhat witless.

"To the police station," said Mrs. O'Hara patiently.

"I told you, Ma'am, you aren't under arrest."

"Well I'd better be," said Mrs. O'Hara. "I'm confessing to you, Sergeant. Here and now. I'm confessing to murder."

"There's no law against it," said Alberg.

"But she ought to see a lawyer," said Eddie.

"You heard her. She doesn't want a lawyer."

"But she *has* to have a lawyer."

"Yeah. I agree. But not yet. Not if she says she doesn't want one. I'm going to give her what she's asked for, Sergeant."

They were standing in the hall outside Alberg's office, where Mrs. O'Hara was ensconced because the interview room was being painted. She sat in the black leather chair, and as they had left to consider her request she had poured herself yet another cup of tea.

"Go give her a ring, Sergeant," said Alberg. "Tell her to get over here."

Fifteen minutes later Cindi Webster burst into the detachment. She was wearing a skirt, blouse and jacket, and pumps and pantyhose. She had left her huge shoulderbag at home and carried only a brand new notebook and a pen. "Here I am," she said, breathless.

Eddie threw Alberg a look that might have been disgust, or only exasperation, but that certainly made her displeasure plain.

Alberg took Cindi into his office, and Eddie followed.

"You're still writing stories about people and their work?" said Mrs. O'Hara to the reporter, who nodded, slowly. "Can we be alone in here?" she asked Alberg.

"No, Ma'am," he said. "The sergeant's going to stay here with you. And this tape recorder, too," he said, setting it on top of his desk.

Mrs. O'Hara was looking at Cindi. "I hope you're up to this," she said.

Cindi looked at her with huge eyes and said nothing.

"Here," said Alberg, pulling a folding metal chair into the office. "Sit," he said, and Cindi sat. Alberg left, making sure the door remained ajar.

Eddie Henderson stood against the wall opposite the window and watched Mrs. O'Hara, who seemed immensely weary, all of a sudden, as if the effort of holding her head upright was soon going to be more than she could manage.

"What they're going to find in my cabin is absolutely nothing," Mrs. O'Hara said to Cindi.

Eddie walked to the desk and switched on the tape recorder.

"What they'll find in my van," said Mrs. O'Hara, "—they'll find a wrench, and a cloth that I wrapped it in, and this cloth will have traces of blood on it."

Cindi, scribbling, suffered a violent twitch to her shoulders.

"It's the blood of that waitress. I forget her name. She's

the only one that bled, thank god. And I guess they'll find other things, too, I don't know, fibers, whatever. Anyway, that doesn't matter because I've already told them I did it."

"You did . . . you . . . you—killed Rochelle," said Cindi, whose body was hunched in upon itself, and whose hair hung down on either side of her face, concealing it.

Mrs. O'Hara looked at her irritably. "Will you sit up, please?"

Cindi immediately straightened, and pushed back her hair.

"Yes," said Mrs. O'Hara. "The waitress, yes, who put her father in a home. And the woman who aborted her child. And the girl who killed her dog. Yes. Yes. Yes." Her voice had risen in volume and pitch.

Eddie shifted uneasily by the door.

"Why?" said Cindi.

Mrs. O'Hara stared at her. She planted her hands on her thighs, fingertips almost touching, and leaned forward, toward Cindi. "Because they were sinners," she said.

Cindi scribbled again, fervently, with a shaking hand. Eddie wondered if she'd be able to read her handwriting later.

"And there were others," said Mrs. O'Hara.

"Others," Cindi repeated.

Mrs. O'Hara sat back and looked up at the window, through which a swath of sunlight stretched to the floor. "It started with Tom. More than ten years ago, it was."

She talked, telling them facts, putting one fact after another like one foot followed another. She spoke haltingly at first, then with growing confidence. As she talked her voice grew hoarse, and the swath of sunlight crept closer. Mrs O'Hara made a bargain with her deity: if she finished her story, got it all rightly and properly told before that swath of sunlight had crept across the floor to her feet, that would mean that she would have succeeded. But she wasn't allowed to leave anything out, or to talk faster than was normal for her. And she would keep to this bargain, because she had an honorable soul.

Mrs. O'Hara told them about Tom and Raylene. About pushing Raylene down the basement steps and having Tom blamed for it. She told them how her life had changed—she described as best she could her reluctant commitment to winged fate, and her refining of this commitment: ten sweepings in ten years.

Cindi scribbled. The sergeant's gaze remained on Mrs. O'Hara's face, a gentle curious prodding.

Mrs. O'Hara told them about the hardware store that had burned down. Twice.

She told them about the pastor she had killed in a car crash.

She told them about the young mother she had poisoned.

And about the old woman she had smothered to death.

She stopped, occasionally, to catch her breath, to drink some more tea, and tried to see the expressions on the faces of her confessors. She squinted at them, shielding her eyes from the encroaching sun.

"I'll close the blind," said Eddie, starting to move toward the window.

"No," said Mrs. O'Hara quickly. "No." The sun was in her eyes, which accounted for her inability to read the faces of the reporter and the sergeant, but it hadn't yet reached her feet—not yet.

"The next three were different," she said, and tried to explain how they had been different.

"You changed your method," said Eddie. "Why?"

"I don't know," said Mrs. O'Hara. "I can't say." She started to shake. "I have no explanation," she said loudly. The shaking got much worse. "I wanted to see their faces," she said finally. It came out as a sigh. She waited, her head bent. "I wanted to see their faces when I struck them."

Cindi managed to get it down—"I wanted to see their faces"—before the strength left her hand, which had become numb, and the pen fell from her fingers. She looked at it lying on the floor. Finally, Eddie picked it up and handed it to her. Cindi looked up at her gratefully, and Eddie saw that her eyes were filled with tears.

"What did you do with Rochelle's body?" asked Eddie. "Rochelle—that's the waitress," she added, trying to keep her voice expressionless.

Mrs. O'Hara had hoped, perhaps, for compassion. She heard none in this woman's voice. But perhaps that was because of the sunlight, which was dreadfully bright now and certainly strong enough to distort sound. "I came across an excavation," she said. "Someone building a house, I believe. Out in the country. Away from everything. Like my cabin is. Except my cabin doesn't have a basement. I put her in the excavation and shoveled dirt on top of her, from the pile that was on the ground."

Cindi stretched her hand and massaged its fingers, then wrote again, laboriously, in her notebook.

"How long did your husband get?" asked Eddie.

"He was out in eight years," said Mrs. O'Hara. "But never saw him again. I don't know where he went, or what happened to him."

Eddie was about to ask her another question when Mrs. O'Hara said, "Ah," so regretfully, so sorrowfully, that for a moment Eddie thought this was remorse. "I didn't quite make it," said Mrs. O'Hara, looking at her feet. The metal toes of her workboots glinted in the sun.

Alberg had Ralph Mondini usher Mrs. O'Hara into a cell while he listened to the tape recording of her confession.

Then he sat back in his chair and planted his foot on an open desk drawer. "Ten," he said. "She'd set herself a goal of ten."

"Yeah," said Eddie, who was standing by the window, looking outside. She thought she was hungry, but she wasn't certain.

"So. Tom. Who got off easy. Raylene. The reverend."

Eddie turned and saw that he was referring to his notebook, where he had jotted things, from time to time, as they listened to the tape.

"The hardware store guy." He glanced up at her. "That was here—in our jurisdiction. Arson. Yeah." They had suspected the owner for a while, or tried to, because he was such a mean and nasty son of a bitch. "So she didn't always kill them." He looked at the notebook again. "That's four. Plus the one who died of food poisoning. Five. And there's the old lady she smothered—six. Plus Rebecca Granger, Rochelle Williamson, and Janet Maine." He squinted at Eddie, waiting.

"That's nine," said Eddie. "I guess she's gonna be short."

"Hmmmm," said Alberg. He lifted his foot from the drawer, closed it, and sat up. "I think I'll go have a talk with her."

He spoke to her through the bars of the cell. "You only got nine," he said.

Mrs. O'Hara, sitting on the edge of the cot, didn't reply.

"So what about Number Ten?" asked Alberg. "What about Ivan Dyakowski?"

If it hadn't been for that shaft of sunlight, Mrs. O'Hara told herself, she would have made it. If they had started talking just a few minutes earlier, she would have finished before the sunlight struck her shoes. Or if the conversation had taken place somewhere else entirely, then it never would have occurred to her to make that stupid bargain.

But make it she had.

And now she would have to be satisfied with nine.

"I'm going to die soon," she told Alberg. And as she spoke, a revelation stole quietly, cordially, across her soul. She was already dead. She had killed herself. Like a snake eating its own tail, the blows she had delivered on behalf of justice had been lashes stripping away her own flesh.

She looked at the policeman in amazement. She had never felt such pain.

She was Number Ten, she realized, thunderstruck. The accumulation of Numbers One through Nine, beginning with poor, pale Raylene, had compelled this.

How could something so manifest have been hidden from her for so long?

It was a flawless truth.

A mockery.

She told him, then, about the marmalade on Susan Atkinson's kitchen table.

TWENTY-FIVE

Sunday, April 7

———

Alberg was up early the next morning, sitting in his backyard drinking coffee and craving a cigarette, for some reason, for the first time in months and months.

After his talk with Mrs. O'Hara he had called Susan Atkinson, then sent Ralph Mondini over to her apartment to collect the jar of marmalade.

He had also arranged for Mrs. O'Hara to have a lawyer, whether she wanted one or not.

Cindi Webster had sat on the bench in the reception area while all this was going on, looking dazed. Eddie eventually took her off to Earl's for coffee and a sandwich.

"I think I'll talk to her lawyer," Cindi had said on her way out the door, "before I write anything."

"That's probably a good idea," Alberg agreed. He stretched out his hand. "Thanks for your help. I appreciate it."

Alberg picked up his mug of coffee from the white plastic table next to him and took a sip.

They had to look for Rochelle Williamson's body now. And investigate the earlier deaths for which Mrs. O'Hara had claimed responsibility.

Alberg put the coffee mug down again and stirred restlessly in the canvas chair that sat upon his small brick patio, listening to the birds and the far-off sound of a boat motoring out of the harbor at the bottom of the hill.

"Dad," said Eddie. "I'm sorry to call so early." She was standing in the middle of her living room. The blinds were yanked up as high as they would go, letting spring sunshine spill into the house, which was dusty and felt disorganized because she had not unpacked and arranged her belongings personally but had let her father do this for her.

"What is it, Eddie? There's nothing wrong, is there?" he said anxiously.

"I don't know, Dad. You tell me. Did you give Alan my phone number?"

Susan Atkinson's apartment, now—that was the kind of place Eddie could be happy in. Lots of cheerful colors. No damn dust.

"Dad? Answer me." But in his silence, he already had. "Shit. You did, didn't you?"

"Edwina, he cares so much about you—"

She hung up. "Jesus Christ." She ran her hands through her long, thick hair. She threw her head back and laughed. Planted her fists on her hips. "Jesus H. Christ."

She considered phoning Alan. But he would probably take that as encouragement.

No—she'd wait for him to call again. She knew he would. And when he did: "Alan," she would say to him. "Fuck off. Don't ever call me again. Or—or—"

Or what?

Eddie wrapped her hair around her hand and pinned it on top of her head.

The phone rang. She knew it would be her father—it was far too early for Alan—but she ignored it and looked critically around her house. Today she would organize things the way she damn well wanted them. And she would do the laundry, she thought, as the phone continued to ring. And the ironing. And buy some groceries, so that she could finally begin eating at home, as she'd planned. And tomorrow she'd find someone to come in once or twice a month to clean the house.

A cleaning lady.

Eddie sat down on the sofa, her spine ashudder. Jesus.

The phone rang and rang—she had unhooked the answering machine.

A cleaning lady.

Cassandra watched Alberg for a while from the sunporch before opening the screen door and going down the steps to join him. She sat in a lawn chair next to his and took his hand. Alberg turned his face to her, but didn't speak. Cassandra stroked his cheek, slowly, from the prominent bone at the outer edge of his eye down to the corner of his mouth, her fingertips loving, and curious. "If you start the paperwork now," she said, "how long will it take?"

He leaned into her hand, which she flattened, then, against the side of his face. "I don't know. A few months, maybe. It depends on who replaces me. How soon they can replace me."

"Oh, well then," said Cassandra, "in that case, we'll never get out of here. It's well known that you are completely and utterly irreplaceable."

Alberg grinned and took hold of her hand, placing his lips in the middle of her palm.

"Let's do it," said Cassandra softly. "What the hell."

ABOUT THE AUTHOR

L. R. WRIGHT is the author of twelve
novels, including the previous Karl Alberg
mystery, *Strangers Among Us*. She is a two-time
winner of the Arthur Ellis Award for best
crime fiction: first for *A Chill Rain in January*,
and, in 1995, for *Mother Love*, which also won
the Canadian Authors Association Award for
literary fiction. *Kidnap*, the first Edwina
Henderson mystery, will be published by
Doubleday Canada in 2000. L. R. Wright lives
in Vancouver, British Columbia.